THE WATCH & WAND

Other titles by Allie Potts:

Project Gene Assist
The Fair & Foul

Rocky Row Novel
An Uncertain Faith

THE WATCH & WAND

PROJECT GENE ASSIST
BOOK TWO

ALLIE POTTS

AXIL HAMMER PUBLISHING
2017

First edition
ISBN-13: 978-0-9968320-1-4
ISBN-10: 0-9968320-1-7

This book is a work of fiction. Any similarity between the characters and
situations within its pages and places or persons, living or dead, is
unintentional and coincidental.

Ordering information
Special discounts are available on quantity purchases by corporations,
associations, educators, and others. For details, contact the publisher.

U.S. trade bookstores and wholesalers: Please contact Allie Potts at
www.alliepottswrites.com

FOR MOM

Who taught me to follow my dreams wherever they lead
provided I leave GPS coordinates to keep her from worrying
too much.

This is all your fault and I love you the more for it.

PART ONE

ONE

"Now entering the arena," a female voice announced in Stephen's earpiece. He toggled the command to open up his inventory menu, selecting the missile launcher. A pixelated rendering of a dark cylinder appeared on his avatar's shoulder. Stephen smiled. The graphics in the program were terrible, but his chosen weapon was as unmistakable as it was deadly.

"Nice of you to show up," said another voice belonging to player Wes51d3 or, as Stephen called him, Wes.

"You could have gotten started without me. As slow as you read through the objectives, I would have caught up in no time."

Wes snorted. "What, and miss out watching you blow yourself to bits? Again." His friend's laughter relayed all too clearly through his earpiece. "Or did you forget we decided to play one of the close quarters and hostage themes today?"

Stephen scowled, returning to the inventory menu. *Killjoy.* Replacing the missile launcher with a handgun with good range and killer accuracy, he replied, "You're jealous because all you know how to use are knives." *Besides*, he told himself, *my character hadn't self-destructed that much.*

Stephen lost track of how many missions they'd gone on together. In all that time, he had never once seen Wes's avatar brandish anything resembling a gun. He muttered into the microphone, "You know what they say about bringing a knife to a gunfight."

"That even with a knife, I am still a hell of a lot more effective than you." Wes's avatar, clad in an identical uniform featuring three-dimensional geometric shapes, supposed to represent camouflage, dropped into view. There had once been better games out there, with graphics and sound effects so realistic, players forgot where the game began and reality ended, but this one had what all the others hadn't. Staying power. The game, *Colony Defenders II*, had somehow found a way to survive even after the breakdown of civilization, as they knew it.

The simple interface started with all players in a neutral zone upon login, a feature designed to give noobs a safe area to practice the game's commands and work out a basic strategy while the computer issued mission goals. Enemies weren't programmed to appear until players crossed through a flashing starting gate. Thus, it came as a surprise when the screen flashed red and Stephen's health meter dropped a point. "What the—?" Stephen shouted. Considering Wes was the only other person left in the world besides himself who still knew about the game, the hit could have only come from one source. *With friends like mine...*

"Demonstrating a point."

Stephen flipped a finger at the screen even though his machine lacked a camera. His friend's laughter played in his ear as if he saw the gesture anyway. Stephen's frown deepened as he scratched at his thin raisin-brown hair tickling his jawline. He should shave, but other priorities had a way of taking precedence. *Not that how you look matters.*

"Oh, don't be a baby." Wes's avatar threw him a virtual medic pack, restoring Stephen's health meter to full value. "So are you ready to do this thing or not?" Wes's character vanished through the start gate.

"Let's go." Stephen followed. The background dissolved into a gray corridor as soon as they passed under the gate. Large brown blocks representing crates lay scattered along its length. *Whoever designed the game must love crates,* Stephen thought for the millionth time. Fifty more than were necessary were always strewn about in every mission. A green-skinned four-armed creature popped up, and Stephen fired. The scoreboard showed a direct hit. Then the screen flashed red again as Stephen's health meter took another dip. He turned; another creature must have snuck up on him from behind. He fired another shot. "What in the… Wes, you are supposed to cover my rear."

"It's not my fault your rear is so big," Wes replied. His avatar jumped up on a crate, slashing at another would-be assailant.

The creatures froze while alien hisses continued to play in stereo over his earpiece. Stephen didn't need to see the action to know his avatar was under attack even if the screen didn't show it.

"Dude. Are you waiting for an engraved invitation? According to the map, the hostages are supposed to be in the room to your right."

A map icon flashed in the upper right-hand portion of the screen. Then the entire display became awash with purple, yellow, and blue pixels. "Damn it." Stephen slapped his monitor, even though it wouldn't do any good. "My system's going down again."

"Why do you bother with that old machine anyway?" Wes asked. The screen flashed an icon recommending immediate plugging in of his machine. Stephen scowled. His eyes followed the length of cord from the inlet connection to the electrical outlet on the wall. He jiggled the plug and the icon vanished, but the game's action remained frozen.

"You're right." He slapped his forehead. "I'll just walk over to the store and get a new one." Stephen snorted at the thought. The system was a relic—technology considered ancient fifteen years ago. The only reason Stephen could communicate with Wes at all was because someone must have decided it would cost more to recycle for parts than chuck into the back of a forgotten storage closet.

Without the benefit of store-bought components, it had taken Stephen more than two years, and a bit of luck, to get the system up and running again. He should have been praised. Instead, his grand accomplishment, the testament to his engineering genius, had to be hidden away. Stephen's scowl deepened at the difference fifteen years could make. At least, he'd been told life wasn't always this way. *Repeatedly.* Stephen wouldn't know. He'd been four when the world went mad. *Must have been nice.* Stephen ran a hand over his face in frustration. The plug-in icon reappeared.

He kicked the wall and winced when he heard the wood crack. The glorified shed they used as a barn didn't need his help accelerating its declining condition. "One of these days you are going to have to tell me why you never have any of these problems."

"I keep telling you, you need to come see me."

"You know why I can't." Something rustling in the corner caught his attention. *Please don't be another rat,* he thought. He shouldn't care, but the beasts had a way of popping up at the worst possible times. If he didn't know better, he might think they were showing up on purpose. All he had to do was sneak away to work on his computer or play games. Even worse, once spotted, they never ran away back into the shadows as Stephen thought a rat should. Instead, they would sit there, watching him with their beady eyes, until Stephen worked up the courage to chase them off with a broom or shovel. Just thinking about another rat in the room gave him the creeps.

"About that. They…you…" Wes's voice broke up.

"What about me?" Stephen scanned the room. The rustling could have come from something else, like a draft, it didn't have to be a rat. *Right. Keep telling yourself that.*

Wes sighed, the connection clear again. "Never mind. Lost my train of thought. But hey, you know the invitation is always open. So…the usual, but on time for once?"

"I wasn't that late."

Wes asked the same question week after week to the point that Stephen wondered if his friend suffered from some sort of short-term memory loss. He might have teased him about it, but with his computer acting up again, there wasn't time to give his friend a hard time. *Don't forget, you might not be alone in here.* He shuddered.

"Don't make me track you down."

"Quit complaining. I'll have the old girl working by then." *That's it. Time to find a cat.* Maybe if he started leaving scraps out, one would show up. His stomach grumbled at the thought of going without even a sliver less food. *Probably would wind up attracting more rats.* Nothing was ever easy, at least, not in Stephen's memory.

"All right. If you want to talk before then, I'm a keystroke away. Later, man."

"Wes51d3 has left the arena," announced the female voice, more garbled than before. The screen flashed again. An empty battery symbol replaced the plug-in icon.

"I get it. I get it." He toggled the keys to initiate the shutdown sequence. Nothing happened.

Stephen removed his headset and held the power button until the whirl of the computer's fan confirmed complete system shutdown. Why he bothered escaped him. The machine would have powered itself down in another two minutes. It was just one of those things he had gotten into the habit of doing. Once off, he closed the screen and hid the device beneath a loose board in the barn floor.

He rustled the crease in his hair from the headset before stepping out of the barn. The windmill a few yards away caught his gaze. Its propellers remained stationary even though a gust of a fall wind caused Stephen to shiver. He zipped up his cotton jacket. *Well, that explains the power.*

"Generator's out again, Ed," Stephen announced, entering the farmhouse on the other side of a dirt and gravel path connecting the two buildings. A slew of screws, nuts, and metal plates littered the kitchen table. "But it looks like you already knew that."

Ed Thomas appeared from the other room. A cream and brown cloth wrapped around his left hand highlighted the swath of dark freckles running up the rest of his arm.

"What happened?" Stephen asked.

"I think squirrels must have gotten into it. Again."

"No. I meant to your hand." Stephen said, pointing.

"Oh. That. Driver slipped." Ed gestured at the offending tool on the table. As he did so, Stephen noticed a red circular stain on the cloth. Stephen didn't need to see the wound underneath to know that it would be ugly. They always were. No doubt in the coming weeks he would have yet another pale line to add to the collection of scars along his hands, arms, and legs—assuming, of course, he'd manage to sew himself up without infection. They'd been lucky so far, but Ed had always been more than a little clumsy and seemed to be growing even more accident-prone every year. A serious injury was no longer an *if*, but a *when*.

"How bad?"

"Needs a new solenoid."

"Once again, not what I meant," Stephen asked, nodding in the direction of the bandage.

"I should live. But I may need you to pick up a little more around here for the next few days."

Stephen glanced back toward the kitchen door and the barn across the way. Sneaking in thirty minutes between his chores already created a stiff challenge. If he had to pick up Ed's too, it was going to be difficult if not impossible to get the machine rebuilt in time for the next virtual meet-up with Wes.

"Yeah. Not how I intended to spend my golden years either." Ed grinned at his joke, but Stephen failed to see the humor in his comment. It wasn't right. Ed was far from what should have been considered old. He wouldn't have even been called middle-aged, but now… Stephen glanced again out the window to avoid looking at the white-laced hair where fiery red should be or at the spots of age that now dotted his skin in between the freckles.

"You see something?" Ed asked, on guard.

Stephen sighed, rubbing his face as he pulled his gaze from the barn. It didn't take much to spook the man. Edward's paranoia made Stephen's feelings about rats seem downright sensible. "Just checking to see how much sunlight we have left. If I leave now, I can get to Earthaven by nightfall."

"You aren't going to Earthaven." Ed arranged the tools and fasteners on the table using an indecipherable, system-bucking sort of logic.

"Someone has to." Stephen pointed at the components scattered on the table.

"And where would you go then? You know it's too dangerous to be out at night."

"It's only Earthaven." Stephen imagined walking over to the table and switching out one bolt for another just to see how long it would take the older man to notice.

"Yes, and there are reasons we're here and not there." Components clinked together as Ed moved the piles around.

"But…Earthaven…" Stephen turned his face before Ed could see him roll his eyes.

"Just because nothing has ever happened in the town doesn't mean nothing ever will." Ed gestured with his bandaged hand as he spoke, scattering the contents of one of the piles.

"And we're still talking about Earthaven," repeated Stephen as he bent down, picked up a screw from the ground, and placed it back on the table with the others. Ed picked it up and placed it in another pile.

"Not this again." Helen Thomas entered the farmhouse holding a bowl of vegetables. Dirt smeared her otherwise reddened cheeks. Strands of her hair, also more white and gray than the brown it should be, rebelled against the plaited braid.

"Let me help you with that" Ed reached for the vegetables, sending more metal parts to the floor.

"Oh no, you don't. I harvested them. I can wash them." As she batted his arm away, Edward winced. "Operating on yourself again, I see? I swear, Stephen, I turn my back on him for one second…"

Stephen grinned. "Sorry. Didn't realize it was my turn to watch him."

"So what were you two arguing about?" Helen asked as she turned the dial on the faucet, allowing water from the rain barrel to flow for a few seconds into the sink basin. The contents of the barrel could fill the basin with more to spare, but the summer had been dry, and a little conservation now could make a huge difference in the days or weeks ahead unless the weather turned.

Then again, Stephen thought, *it could rain for a month and Helen would still act as if they were in a drought.* "My ability to walk five miles." Stephen reached down and handed her a small potato that had rolled away from the others.

"After dark," grumbled Ed as he rearranged the contents of the piles, making their composition even less consistent.

"I'm nineteen now. Weren't you both considered adults at this point?"

Helen's shoulders slumped. "Honey, we know you aren't a kid anymore, but the world is nothing like it was when we were your age. There were millions of more people for starters." She looked at Ed's piles of components. "Not to mention reliable power." She paused. Her lips twisted. "And if we got into trouble, we had phones."

"Yeah, and yet you somehow have managed to live all this time without those things. All I am asking is the chance to do the same. To actually live."

Helen scrubbed the potato with a stiff brush before transferring it to a cardboard box near the sink.

Ed broke the silence first. "This isn't the life either of us wanted for you, but—"

"No, he's right." Helen put the brush down. "Good or bad. It's time we give him the opportunity to make the occasional decision." Helen moved to the table and picked up the component that had thus far eluded Ed's notice. She placed it in his good hand. "Goodness knows you could have used a little more practice back then." The two shared a grin over some secret joke before Helen turned back to the basket of vegetables. She turned the root over in her hand as she cleaned it, inspecting its skin and eyes before placing it to the side of the basin rather than in the box with the others.

"Besides, as he said, it is only Earthaven. Jim will keep an eye on him."

"My point exactly." Stephen raced over to kiss Helen on the cheek, grabbing a washed sweet pepper harvested along with the potatoes.

"But what if...?" Ed gestured again. A piece of fabric from the bandage caught on one of the components, sending the piles tumbling once again to the floor.

Helen came over to Ed's side and helped him gather his supplies. "Who's left to remember, let alone care about—?" Helen started. She glanced in Stephen's direction and dropped the sentence. Returning to the sink, she continued as if the words had never been spoken. "Besides, you clearly aren't fit to go."

Stephen didn't want to risk Helen changing her mind by asking either of the two to go into more details about whatever it was. *More of Ed's paranoia, I bet.* Stephen bit into the pepper, tasting dirt as much as vegetable as he raced to the door. He wiped the pepper's skin on the side of his jacket as he threw open the door and jumped down the stairs. "I'll be back in the morning," he shouted without looking back.

"Keep your eyes open," Ed called out as Stephen ran into the woodlands hiding the farm from casual view. Stephen's ears barely caught Ed's last words. "And don't trust anyone."

Two

The sky was a deep purple, the color of one of Helen's favorite eggplants, when Stephen reached the edge of Earthaven. A handful of stars freckled the horizon. *What would it be like if you just kept going?* he wondered, looking out to where the land met sky before returning his attention to the buildings up ahead making up Main Street. Earthaven was little more than a village, designed as an experimental community more than seventy years ago. In the years leading up to the economic crash to end all crashes, it had become almost a theme park, providing visitors with a glimpse of the distant pre-industrialized past. The fact that the residents were already used to off-grid and self-sufficient living was the main reason it survived when so many much larger communities failed.

As he walked down Main Street toward Piper's Tavern, the lamplighters were already hard at work, illuminating towers filled with chopped wood rather than electric bulbs. According to Ed, Piper's Tavern used to be a restaurant and still was if anyone asked, but it had since morphed into a place where goods and services of all kinds were exchanged. It was also one of the few places in town Ed and Helen ever went, though they never stayed long. The rest of the town might as well have been on the other side of the world.

The door squealed on its hinges as Stephen opened it, alerting its proprietor, a lean individual, more bone than man, to his presence. "Stephen," Jim called out. "Is that you? Gosh, it must be a year since your folks stopped by. People were beginning to think you all had moved on." He placed a rag on the back of a chair and grabbed Stephen's hand, giving it a quick shake. "I'm afraid that it's close to closing," said Jim, gesturing to the room behind him. A single table remained occupied by a trio all wearing bands of tied red cloth on their left arms.

Jim frowned, lowering his voice to a near whisper. "I know your folks don't like to travel much at night, but it's best they turn back. The folks around today haven't been the kind they'd be interested in trading with." Glancing over Stephen's head at the torches and the evening sky, he added, "Where are your folks anyway? Are they taking the scenic route?"

Stephen buried his disappointment. He'd hoped to make it in time to track down the part tonight so that he would have more time to be on his own in the morning before heading back to the farm. "Don't worry. They aren't coming. Do you know where I can stay for the night?"

"Jim, the way you've chased patrons out this afternoon it is amazing you are still in business. The kid looks like he's exhausted. Why don't you offer the boy a drink?" a woman at the table asked, leaning in her chair.

Jim pursed his lips. "Can I get you some water before you go?"

"Thanks, but a room would be even better." Stephen glanced at the woman whose attention had turned back to the pair of men beside her.

Jim shook his head at Stephen's quick response. "I still can't believe the old man finally let you off the leash." Jim let go of the door and walked toward the bar area to pour Stephen a drink. "That's something I never thought would happen."

Stephen's smile faded as he took the offered glass. "I'm not on anyone's leash."

He held up his hands in surrender. "I didn't mean anything by it." Jim began wiping down the bar with a second rag. "Would it be too much to hope that your folks gave you something for a room?" As Jim continued his work, Stephen grimaced. He hadn't thought that far ahead, so eager to get away from the farm before Ed changed his mind. Perhaps he shouldn't have been so quick to eat the pepper. Food in hand always went a long way at the bargaining table.

Jim sighed having read Stephen's expression. "Yeah, it's just as well. I don't think most places would be willing to take in a stranger nowadays, even a paying stranger. At least not any of the places I'd be comfortable recommending."

"Please. I can't go back tonight, and I don't know any place else to go."

Jim rubbed his hand over his forehead. "Hmm. I guess I could put you in the back office, but you'd have to work for it."

"The back room would be fine." Stephen eyeballed the rest of the room's empty chairs, calculating that three of four of them put together might prevent him from having to sleep on the floor. "What do you need me to do?"

As if Jim read his mind, he added, "I keep a cot back there—for emergencies." He walked over to a small closet and pulled out a broom. Handing the broom to Stephen, he said, "And you can start by finishing the sweeping up."

"So, what brings you into Earthaven?" the woman asked, rising from her chair along with the pair of men who flanked her sides.

"He's passing through, Dr. Lambda," Jim answered from the other side of the bar.

"Is he?" Dr. Lambda's eyebrow arched. "From what I overheard, it sounded like you were old family friends." The woman's eyes narrowed. "Your face looks familiar. You're what? Somewhere between eighteen and twenty-one?" Her companions nodded with her assessment. "Have you ever visited the Watchtower?"

"Nineteen, and no. I've been lucky. Never had worse than a cold."

"Well, that is lucky, indeed. I've seen plenty of patients who would love to know your secret."

"Good genes, I guess."

The corner of Dr. Lambda's lips crept up. "I guess."

The slap of the rag on the counter behind him startled Stephen. "Well, I hate to break up the conversation, but if I don't close up now, I will have one angry missus to deal with. She likes being walked home." Jim stretched his unburdened hands above his head with a yawn and then rolled his shoulders as his joints made an audible popping sound.

"There you go kicking out customers again." Dr. Lambda chuckled, dropping a handful of coins on the bar.

"I'd rather take my chances with the Watch than an angry wife," Jim answered. Dr. Lambda's smile slipped as Jim's face flushed bright red. "Oh, that didn't come out right. I mean…I mean… Have you met my wife? No, of course you wouldn't have. Why would you?" Jim winced.

Dr. Lambda's smile returned, but it seemed different to Stephen's eyes than the one flashed before. More knowing than welcoming. "That's all right, Jim. I'm sure no one on the Watch would find being compared to your wife offensive."

Jim whispered to Stephen, "If you need anything, I'll be across the street, but don't tell anyone. Most people think I live here."

Gripping the broom, Stephen got to work as the doctor and her escorts made their way outside and didn't stop even after he heard Jim turn the latch on the tavern door. The entire exchange had been the most excitement Stephen had seen in months and all it would cost him was a few extra hours of hard labor. Maybe after tonight, he'd convince Ed and Helen to allow him to make more solo runs in the future.

The air smelled of smoke from all but one of the extinguished candles as Stephen made his final sweep across the room. As Stephen placed the broom in its closet, he heard a *scratch-tap-tap* at the glass window nearest the door.

"Psst," a female voice whispered. "Psst," the voice said again, this time more insistent. "They'll be here any second."

Stephen picked up the remaining candle and began walking toward the back office.

"I know you are in there." While still a whisper, the voice now took on tones of panic. "I can see light under the door. Let me in."

Stephen hesitated.

"Fine. Be like that. Just know that when I get questioned, I will be sure to tell them what is also on the Piper's menu."

Stephen had no idea what Jim was involved in, but without Jim and Piper's, he'd never have an excuse to leave the farm again. The bolt was a hair's width out of the locked position when the door opened and the girl entered the room.

The girl might have come up to his shoulder if they were to stand next to each other and was as slight in frame as Jim. She wore a thin charcoal sweater that had seen better days and a brimmed dark knit hat, which covered all but a few stray ends of white blonde hair. He tried to get a better look at her in the dim candlelight, but before he could make out more of her features, she kicked the door with her heel and spun to refasten its bolt. Grabbing Stephen by the arm, she pulled him down the hall toward the back office.

"Hey!" Stephen shouted as she closed the office door. "Just who do you think—?"

The girl placed a hand on his mouth, muffling his words. Satisfied that he would not utter another word, she dropped to the ground and placing her ear next to the floor.

"I don't think…" Stephen started. He'd made a huge mistake letting the girl in. Ed's parting words not to trust anyone mocked him in his mind. *Jim is never going to trust me again.*

The girl twisted, glaring up at him, cutting off the rest of his statement with an expression that said, *no, you don't,* as clearly as if the words had been spoken aloud.

The silence broke with the sound of glass shattering. Several voices shouted out from the street, although their words were indistinct. Stephen made a move back toward the door to investigate. The girl placed her hand on his leg. She crouched in a ready-to-run stance, as if waiting for the door to the back office to burst at any moment.

Minutes passed as the voices faded into the night.

Stephen offered his hand to the girl. She batted it away and rose unassisted. The shadows danced across her face, making her scowl even fiercer. *What got into her breakfast*, he thought.

"Where's Jim?" she demanded, crossing her arms over her chest as if he was the inconvenience rather the other way around.

"Gone." If she wanted to hand out attitude, he was happy enough to return the favor.

She tapped her toe. "You are sure?"

Stephen rolled his eyes. The girl was cute under that hat, he'd give her that, but her appearance did not make up for her lack of people skills. He shrugged. "Do you see him here?" He glanced in the direction of the main entrance. "Look. I was told to sweep and keep the door locked. That's it. A job I now realize I should have done better." He pointed at the door. "If finding Jim is such an emergency, I suggest you head back out there."

The girl's scowl deepened. Crossing her arms over her chest, her fingers tapped on her arms just as her toes had a moment before. Glaring at Stephen as if he had the power to rematerialize Jim and was holding out on her, she asked, "Is he coming back?"

"I'm not his keeper, but my guess? Not until morning." *You just had to go and try to do the nice thing. That'll teach you.*

The girl rubbed her hand across her face, shielding him from what Stephen was sure had to be a dagger-like expression. "Then I guess we are roommates tonight."

The room was the size of a glorified closet with a folded cot wedged in one corner. Though small, it would have served Stephen's needs for the night considering what he had available to trade for the privilege, but there was no way it could sleep two, especially if one of those two prickled more than a cactus. He glanced at the girl again. She glared back. *Nope, her staying here with me was not a good option.*

He cleared his throat. "I think you'd better find someplace else."

Stephen heard the girl mutter to herself, "So much for that plan."

He'd taken a step back when the back of his foot met a bucket by the wall. *What are you doing, man? You gotta step it up.* He puffed out his chest and returned to his original stance. "I don't know you." His claim to be able to take care of himself replayed in his mind. He couldn't even make it a day without finding trouble. "And I don't want to."

"Do you not understand what is happening out there right now? Who I just protected you from?" She threw her hands up in the air.

Stephen paused, wondering at her words for a split second. *Nothing to do with you*, he told himself. *Don't back down now. She's the one with the problem. Not you. You were just fine until she started banging on the door.* "I let you in, remember? From where I am standing, I protected you," said Stephen as he gestured at the door, "from whatever or whoever has gotten you so worried."

Her body seemed to deflate as she absorbed his words. Stephen heard her mutter to herself, "New plan."

The way she talked to herself made him wonder if she had spent much time around other people. *Perhaps she doesn't realize other people can hear her.* He started to comment, but decided he was safer not saying anything.

She looked up at him, her face once again hard and resolved. "The Watch is conducting a raid." The candle flickered, causing their shadows to dance upon the walls. "If you were smart, you'd be worried, too."

"A raid? The Watch?" Helen called them thugs. Ed seemed to make it a point not to mention them at all, but they were all that stood between civilization and complete anarchy in this part of the world. *Weren't they?* The doctor lady from earlier was one of them and she didn't seem so bad.

"Yes. Them."

Stephen shrugged. "I've got nothing to fear from that group." He thought of the barn with his hidden stash of electronics and fought any guilt from showing on his face.

"Oh really? What about your family? I assume you have one. Can they say the same?"

Ed and Helen weren't technically his parents, but they were the closest thing to family he had. While it was true the couple hadn't adopted him through the traditional legal channels, he was sure what they'd done would no longer be considered a crime. Stephen doubted an official process existed anymore. Why would there be? So many people had fallen victim to either the riots after the initial crash or the plague that followed. Who would care about who anyone lived with? *No, they'd done nothing wrong.* If anything, by opening their home to some random kid, his guardians had done something right. He nodded to himself. Besides, that was years ago. If pressed now, he wasn't sure he could even tell anyone what his old last name started with. At least not with any certainty.

But, doubt gnawed at him. Whether it was the fall of civilization or their natural-born inclination, Stephen's guardians had always seemed cautious to a fault, at least in Stephen's opinion. The three of them kept to themselves unless they had no other choice than to make a trade for other supplies, and those they traded within the tavern had already been grayed around their edges with skin marked with age spots as early as he could remember. There were never any new faces. *Were they hiding bigger secrets?*

No, they couldn't be. Not from him. They might be holed up in the middle of nowhere, but Ed couldn't keep a secret from the family if he tried. Stephen remembered the time Ed caught him sneaking a treat one evening. Rather than scolding him, Ed had joined in, telling him it would be their little secret only to turn around and confess everything to Helen the next morning. All Helen had done was frown at the tray. Well, he almost confessed everything. Ed had taken the majority of the blame, making Stephen out to be his accomplice and him the mastermind. No, the thought of Ed keeping a secret was ridiculous.

Still…

"Fine. You can stay. But I get the cot." He looked at the folded piece of fabric on its wooden frame. *It is too tight in here,* he thought. Stephen opened the door to better maneuver around his roommate, but swung it too far, knocking into a bookcase in the process. Pots and other goods staged for trade the following morning came tumbling down.

From the front of the tavern, Stephen heard a pounding on the door. "Guess the jig is up." He reached for the knob.

The girl clenched her teeth, but it didn't prevent her from saying, "Idiot."

"As I said. I have nothing to hide. What's the worst that can happen?"

The sound of an explosion answered him. Stephen fell to the floor as the ground shook and a flaming piece of roofing broke through the tavern's front window. He watched in disbelief as the fire spread onto a pair of thick curtains. The smell of smoke filled his nostrils. "What should we do?"

"Now," the girl grimaced, "we run."

THREE

The girl latched onto Stephen's arm, pulling him back through the tavern's kitchen as the flames from the great room continued to spread up the wall. "Jim would have had an escape plan. There should be another door," she said, feeling the wall. The fire in the other room caused shadows to stretch and dance. Edges became difficult to judge as the red-orange glow of the destructive light reflected on the metallic appliances in the room.

Stephen took a breath and regretted it as the smoke filled his lungs. "There's nothing there." He pulled her back before succumbing to a coughing fit.

"It's got to be here." Her voice rose in pitch as she continued to scratch at the wall. "Look for a panel. A secret knot. Something."

Her refusal to accept the obvious would get them both killed. He pulled her again toward the main room door. They could still make it through the front door, but that would mean facing the Watch. Still, it was better than getting burnt alive. "All I see is a wall. Come on, we have to go."

"No!" A combination of confusion and terror reflected in the girl's eyes. He pulled again, but the girl refused to budge. It was as if she thought being consumed by the growing fire was the better option. "You don't understand. I can't."

Leave her. A voice whispered in his mind. *You don't owe her anything. Save yourself.* The light from the other room was now bright enough for Stephen to see scratches along the wall where the girl had dug in. *She'll die if you leave her. Could you really live with yourself after that?* Desperate for another option, Stephen's eye caught on a grid-like shadow a few feet away. "There." He ran over to what he had assumed was another shelving unit in the kitchen. "It's a ladder! Maybe it leads to a roof access."

Stephen began to ascend. His head came into contact with a metal plate, causing his grip to slip. "Shit," he exclaimed as his vision blurred.

"What?" asked the girl from the base of the ladder.

"The panel, it's stuck."

"Fix it." Gone was the panic from her voice and in its place was the bully from the other room.

Oh, did I miss that this is my fault? Large beads of sweat had begun to drip down his face. Visibility at the top of the ladder was already nonexistent with more smoke filling the room. This was it. If he couldn't get the access panel open, they'd go back out the front whether she liked it or not. Stephen traced his fingers across the plate's edge until he discovered a square box hanging from one end. "It's locked," he shouted down to the girl.

"Maybe there's a key," she answered. He heard her open cabinets and pull drawers out, sending their contents to the ground.

Stephen's thumb passed along the base of the box and each of its sides. He couldn't detect a keyhole anywhere on it. Only a ridge made of narrow buttons and concave surface. "Not that kind. It's electronic." He could hear the crackle of fire now. He didn't have to look to know the main room no longer contained it. *Too late.* Going out the front wasn't an option now even if he knocked the girl out and dragged her by the hair.

The heat from the fire warmed the metal ladder where he gripped it. The image of Ed and his injured hand sprang into Stephen's mind. *I guess I don't have to worry about picking up Ed's chores.* He wanted to laugh. He coughed instead. He was going to die in this room. And for what? All because he took pity on some paranoid girl.

"I found a crowbar," announced the girl. "Can we break it open?"

"Cracking the case is the last thing we want to do. Whole thing will permanently fuse together."

Metal clattered to the ground. "I'm open to ideas."

Stephen guessed they had maybe five to ten minutes before the whole building became nothing more than a smoldering heap and even less time to breathe. "Grab me a knife."

"I thought you said we don't want to break it."

"Just do it."

She climbed up and handed him a steak knife. Stephen located a tiny hole at the base of the lock and jammed the knifepoint into it. A red LED flashed while Stephen pressed and held the buttons in a particular combination. The heat from below tempted him to use more speed, but the timing was just as important as the sequence. The LED flashed again and turned yellow. Stephen placed his thumb on the pad.

The box twisted in Stephen's hand causing him to drop the knife. "Look out below," he said. Stephen pulled himself as high as he could go without choking on smoke or hitting the metal plate with his head again. He pressed the pad one more time. A gap between the box and the plate opened. "Got it," he shouted downward as he yanked the lock free from the latch.

Stephen pushed on the metal plate and his vision cleared, showing the star-filled night sky. He gasped for breath as he pulled himself through the square opening.

The surface of the rooftop was cool against his cheek as he crawled further away from the opening. In the dark night, he heard the girl as she followed suit. Once Stephen regained his breath, he rose to a crouch, scanning the rooftop. The fire's light, escaping through the access hatch, illuminated a slight wall running along the perimeter. The building shuddered as the flames consumed more of the building's interior. "Great. Now what?" he wondered aloud.

The girl jumped up and ran in the other direction, hurling her body over the side of the wall. Stephen raced over to that edge and saw a large dark shape several feet below. The girl stood on the ground next to it, unharmed. She glanced in the direction of the tavern's entrance and then back at him. Gesturing to the dark shape, she waved her hand, for him to jump.

She's crazy, Stephen thought as he scanned the wall for a ladder or other exit point. Looking down, he saw the girl raise her hand again, making the okay sign. He shook his head.

The building groaned as the sounds of glass shattering punctuated the night. The girl glanced in the direction of the tavern's entrance and back at Stephen. She gestured for him to follow again with more urgency. Stephen hesitated. The girl took a step backward as the building shuddered again followed by a crashing sound below. It wouldn't be much longer before the tavern's roof collapsed.

"If she can do it," he grumbled to himself, "I can do it." Taking a few steps backward to allow him to gain some extra speed, but also to keep him from chickening out, Stephen ran and jumped over the wall. Then he was falling.

Idiot, he thought to himself, echoing the girl's words from before as his body made contact with an unyielding metal surface. *Dumpster*. Stephen tasted blood in his mouth. He must have bitten his tongue upon impact. It had been everything he could do not to scream while he descended.

A pale white hand touched his leg. Uncertain about the condition of his body after his fall, Stephen rolled to the dumpster's edge. The feeling of solid ground beneath his feet almost sent tears to his eyes. Stephen spit the blood out of his mouth as if it was the physical manifestation of the terror he had experienced.

"You should go," the girl whispered in his ear. "Run as far as you can."

"But why?" Stephen leaned against the wall while he regained his sense of equilibrium. The brick was as warm as if it were noon during the peak of summer. "I mean, I get you're involved in something, but why should I have to run away like some sort of criminal when I'm not? And what about Jim?"

Stephen didn't need to see the whites of her eyes to know she'd rolled them. "What about him?"

"You were desperate to find him before. Why aren't you worried about him now?"

"I didn't find him in time."

"What do you mean?" The wall was even hotter now than seconds before.

"Do you think the building across the street blew up by accident? Jim's dead."

More glass shattered. She cocked her head and pushed Stephen behind the dumpster.

"Hey—"

She covered his mouth.

Voices echoed from the front of the alleyway. "Boss isn't going to be happy."

"No shit. There goes our lead."

Another voice joined the mix. "Neighbors say they saw a girl sneaking around. Description fit. Kid let her in right before."

"You think he's part of it?"

"You'd have thought he'd come out by now if he wasn't."

"Well, guess they're toast then."

"I don't believe that for a second. No, they are still here somewhere. I can feel it."

"So what do we do?"

"We find them." A groan like a threatened beast filled the night and brickwork toppled to the ground. Stephen heard shouts and more footfalls as the men scattered.

"Well, that's that. How far is your place from here?" she whispered as she pulled him back up.

"My place?" Stephen's throat begged him to cough and for cleaner air. "Don't you know another place we can go, like another safe house or something?"

"Do you think I would still be standing here with you if I did?"

The plot of land that made up their farm was only a few miles away, but it would be near impossible to find now that evening had fallen. Ash filled the air, choking out what remaining light the moon and stars offered.

Stephen suppressed a wince as he stepped away from the burning building and into the dark night. He must have damaged his leg in the fall. Gritting his teeth, Stephen increased his pace to a run as they made their way through the town's network of back alleys. No matter what twists or turns they took, the girl matched his pace stride for stride, never pulling ahead of him nor slowing unless he did, too. "So, are you going to tell me now why they are after you?"

"Are you going to tell me how you knew how to hack that lock? I'm pretty sure that's on someone's no-no list."

How could he explain it was one of those things he'd just known, like rebuilding the computer or connecting it online. Once he'd stopped thinking about the fire, the locks had become another puzzle demanding a solution. Electronics spoke to him. He hardened his jaw and looked straight ahead. It was not a skill that was healthy to admit.

"How about telling me your name then," said Stephen as the town receded in the distance. His lungs burned from the effort and his right ankle now throbbed in time with the beating of his heart. *It's going to be purple in the morning. Ed's never going to let me leave home again.*

The girl answered him as if they were taking a casual stroll in a park. "You can call me Bean."

"Bean? Like the vegetable?" Stephen asked in a winded voice, slowing their pace to a walk. He looked back. The road behind them lay empty and there was no sound of sound of pursuit. Maybe the Watch had given up.

"You have a problem with that?" Her shoulders tensed, and one hand balled up into a fist.

I'm guessing I'm not the first to ask that question. "No. It's just…unique."

Bean laughed. Her fist relaxed and her fingers wiggled. "Well, so am I."

Stephen turned from the road without warning and walked down a grassy slope and into the woods off to the side.

"Wait?" Bean asked, pausing in mid-step. "We're not going through there."

Maybe she's not as tough as she lets on. "You said you want to go to my place. This is the way." *I wonder how Helen will react to me bringing a girl home*. Stephen's smile slipped. Not well, considering the strict anti-visitor policy in place as long as he could remember. Ed's reaction would be even worse. *Maybe it would be for the best if she stays in the barn.*

"Aren't there roads where you live?" she replied. She touched the ground off the side of the road with a toe in the same way Stephen might test the water in the nearby creek in springtime.

Stephen snorted. "Scared of the big bad woods?" he asked. It was hard not to be nervous, seeing the dark mass of trees in front of them, and for good reason. The ferocious way his guardians had hammered into him how easy it was to get lost in the woods in the dark had always come across like a lesson they'd learned through hard experience. A stick cracked under his feet and an owl hooted.

"Woods, no." Bean frowned. "Things that live in the woods, yes."

There used to be a road connecting the farm to Earthaven, but even if they could find it, it wound around the woods for miles more than necessary. It would take days to get there by foot, which is why they never used it. Going through the woods was a more direct option. "We'll be fine." He took another step off the road.

The forest encircled them as they ventured further away from the main road. Doubts began to eat at his mind. *This is a terrible idea.* While smoke no longer filled the air, the trees blocked much of the light from the moon to the point that Stephen lost his confidence they were still moving in the right direction. *Go back to town. They aren't looking for you.* Bean remained close based on the sound of crunching leaves. Maybe going by the road wasn't such a bad idea, even if it would take all night. *But what if they are?* Bean froze, and he strained his ear for sounds of pursuit. He had to acknowledge that Bean knew more about the Watch than he did, and that was enough to send her diving over the side of a building without a second thought. If the Watch was still looking for them, the road was the last place they wanted to be.

Another owl hooted. *Or was that the same one? Have we gone in a circle?* Stephen heard a large thwack to his left as a large piece of wood broke in two. "What was that?" he asked. He'd grown up surrounded by these woods, which never stopped looking menacing at night. He could only imagine the terror that must've been going through his companion's mind by now.

"You scared? Big stick," answered Bean. "I figured I could use it as a club."

Or not, Stephen thought. *Yeah, Ed's not going to like this one bit. She's definitely sleeping in the barn tonight,* thought Stephen as they continued into the forest. *Assuming we ever find it.*

Four

Stephen cursed the night as they stumbled through the woods. In the darkness, familiar landmarks such as a large rock or fallen tree looked much like any other shadow. His nostrils flared as they took in an unmistakable odor. Stephen held out an arm to stop Bean in her tracks.

"Why are we stopping?" she asked.

He heard a whoosh as she brought the club-like branch up, ready to swing.

Stephen reached over until he touched the limb and pushed it down. "Do you smell that?" he asked, cringing at the thought of how loud their voices must sound compared to the forest's usual nocturnal inhabitants.

Stephen heard Bean's intake of breath followed by a coughing fit. "Ugh. What is that? Smells like something rotten."

Who'd made it this long without ever smelling a skunk before? he thought. "Skunk." He shook his head. *She must be from a bigger city, but what city is still around and bigger than Earthaven?*

"Is it nearby?" He sensed her inch closer.

"Near enough." He took a breath to calm his racing heart, regretting it almost at once. "But that's not what I'm worried about."

"No? Getting sprayed seems pretty bad to me."

Stephen fought the urge to laugh at her remark, although to be fair he wasn't thrilled with the idea of smelling like a skunk for the next week either. *Yeah, that would go over swell at home.* "I'm more worried about whatever threatened the skunk. Think about it."

"Oh." He heard a twig snap as she took a step closer, but couldn't tell if the step had been intentional or not. "So we're not alone."

"Smells that way." *Could be a bear,* he thought without saying aloud. Humanity's population was a fraction of what it once was. The local wildlife had been more than happy to make up the difference.

She huffed. His hand brushed hers. It was shaking. *She is afraid. Jim probably told her about that time he thought he saw a werewolf in the woods.* The story shared over a trade had given him a nightmare for a week. Helen hadn't been amused. "I know it's scary out here, but it's too late and too dark to go back. It's hard for me to tell if we are going in the right direction as it is. I hate to say it, but we might be better off stopping and staying here until I can see landmarks in the morning."

"What about our company?" She shrugged off his hold.

Stephen was clueless, but she didn't need to know that he'd never spent a night away from the farmhouse, at least he hadn't as long as he could remember. Stephen made a mental note to look up wilderness survival techniques the next time he got online. He'd need them if supply runs became his regular thing. "I can take care of it. Give me the club."

"I don't think so," Bean replied. "I'm the one who found it."

Animals can sense fear. They'll smell it on her. "Will you just give it to me? I've got this."

A fiery pain flared across his arm. A jagged wooden edge dragged across his skin. "What the...?"

"You asked for it," she answered. "I was just trying to hand it to you. Not my fault you weren't paying attention."

I was better off taking my chances with the Watch. Once in hand, he hit trees next to him and stomped his feet while growling.

"Are you sure you know what you are doing?" Bean asked. "Won't that attract more attention?"

So asks the girl who up until now had been treating the forest like her own personal piñata. "With any luck, whatever it is will think we are a bigger than them and will move along." Stephen plastered a smile on his face, injecting his voice with a confidence he didn't feel.

"But what we if aren't bigger than whatever it is?"

"Then we can either run, which, by the way, is a terrible idea when you can't see anything, or we climb," he said while slapping a nearby tree trunk. "Now try to be as still as possible and listen." A chattering sound caught his attention. "Wait, are you cold?" The woods were always several degrees cooler during the day thanks to the shade of the canopy, and the temperature had started to fluctuate wildly at night, but even so, it was far from what Stephen would consider cold. Then again, she was wearing a knit hat in September. Maybe she hadn't been afraid, after all, but was more sensitive to the cold than he was.

"I'm okay." The chattering continued.

Stephen reached out and found her hand in the dim light. It was like touching an icicle. "You're freezing," he announced.

"I'll be fine." Her words were clipped. Her teeth sounded more like a woodpecker with each passing second.

"No, you aren't." He unzipped his jacket. "Here, you can borrow this."

She took a step back. "Really, don't worry about me."

"You need it more than I do." He closed the distance between them with the intent of spinning her around and forcing the jacket on her whether she wanted it or not but stopped when his hand found wetness near her shoulder. *What is that?* He pulled his hand back and examined his fingers. Something dark and smelling of metal covered them. "Are you bleeding?" He touched her sweater again. The fabric was torn and half of the back was soaked. "Why didn't you say something?"

"I might have gotten a little scrape at the tavern when you dropped the knife. No big deal." It took Stephen a heartbeat to make sense of her words.

"No big deal? A little scrape wouldn't do something like this." Spending the night outdoors in the woods was no longer an option. Not if she was bleeding. The smell would be irresistible for a predator. They might as well turn on an 'Open for Dinner' sign. As if summoned by the thought, Stephen heard rustling leaves. He swung around at the sound, grasping the makeshift club in both hands.

"Bean," he whispered. "We need to go."

"I thought you said that was a terrible idea."

"Well, now I am saying it's a great idea. Best I've had all night."

"Can't we stay here? I'm so tired."

Her teeth were no longer chattering. *That's not good.* "Yeah. Well, get over it."

Bean yawned, sinking to the ground. "Just a quick nap."

Not good. Not good. Not good. "No nap. We gotta go, Bean. Now."

Stephen let go of the club. He reached out and around in the darkness until he found her forehead. Her skin was still icy cold but damp with sweat. The leaves rustled again. This time closer, and whatever it was, it was large. Stephen braced himself for an attack, placing his body between the girl and the sound. The girl had survived a blind jump from a burning building. She was tough, he'd give her that, but she would be no match for something like a bear. *Neither are you*, the voice in his mind whispered.

The urge to flee whatever threatened in the woods grew stronger. The voice grew more demanding. *And why haven't you yet?* She'd made it clear she wasn't a friend and he'd already helped her more than enough. Hell, he might not even be in this situation if it wasn't for her. *Leave her and save yourself.* More leaves crunched. Louder this time. A branch scraped his forehead, startling him out of his thoughts. The source of the sound was his own footsteps. He hadn't even realized he'd stood up. *Don't be an idiot.*

Stephen returned and pulled Bean up from the forest floor. The sweater was a weight they didn't need and its scent would attract more danger. She whimpered as he removed it, letting the garment drop to the ground while replacing it with his own. He left the jacket unzipped so that her skin might be warmed by contact with his own as he held her close. She wavered and her body sagged further onto his until only his chest was keeping her upright. She wouldn't be walking further tonight. A wave of exhaustion threatened to undo him, too, but he scooped her up into his arms. His injured leg protested as he carried her away in what remained of the pale mottled light. Bean made no sign to suggest she was aware they were moving.

"For the record, I'm the one protecting you," he whispered.

Bean's body became like an anchor as the last of the adrenaline left Stephen's system. He wanted nothing more than to shake her awake and force her to carry her own weight, but that would require stopping. *If I stop now and she doesn't wake, I'll never be able to pick her up again.* Stephen once again fought the temptation to drop her under a tree and come back in the morning. *Your problem would be solved,* the voice in his head whispered, *one way or another.*

Stephen grimaced, focused on placing one foot in front of the other until each step became a victory. *We have to be almost there by now. Just another mile or so.* His toe found a root and he adjusted his stride in time to avoid a fall. *I am so fucking lost.* Stephen looked around. The trees had begun to thin, allowing more of the moon's light to pass, but he didn't recognize any of his surroundings. The farmhouse could be around the corner or ten miles away for all he could tell.

Stephen's back began to spasm as his knees trembled. Deep down he knew that leaving Bean to fend for herself while he sought help wouldn't be a choice he could delay much longer. *That's assuming you don't collapse beside her,* nagged the voice in his head.

He closed his eyes as if he could deafen his doubts as easily as his vision. *Just another puzzle. Focus,* he told himself. No solution came. The light appeared dimmer than it had before when he opened his eyes. He couldn't be sure, as the tree cover did prevent a clear view of the sky, but Stephen guessed that clouds had begun to roll in. Rain. *Yeah, because this night couldn't get any more perfect.*

Bean groaned as he shifted her weight. Her skin remained cool to the touch and clammy. He didn't need formal medical training to know she was running out of time. Stephen picked up his foot. His ankle throbbed. He took a step. His side complained. Then the ground before him seemed to lighten as if it glowed. He glanced backward, but there was only more darkness. *Stay ahead of the rain.* His thoughts took on the beat of a guiding mantra as he pushed them forward. Without any noticeable landmarks to guide him home, Stephen chased the light and hoped that they both might just survive the storm.

FIVE

The first blush of dawn bloomed across the sky when Stephen broke through the tree line. Hours must have passed, but as far as Stephen was concerned, it could have been years. His entire body was covered in a sheen of moisture from sweat, not rain. He had no idea how they'd managed to avoid the downpour, but they'd done it. The threat of rain was the only thing that had kept him from giving up. There had been so many times he'd wanted to rest, to catch his breath, if for a minute, but the sound of the drops of rain hitting the leaves behind him as the storm broke had become like a whip, urging him forward.

Well, maybe the rain hadn't been the only thing. He shifted Bean. During all that time, she hadn't stirred. *You better not have died on me.* He hadn't wanted to risk stopping to check. *We're here. We made it.* He wanted to laugh but was too exhausted to even lift his lips into a smile. Somehow, against all the odds, and against all his guardian's warnings, he had found his home even in the darkness. *That's me. Stephen Thomas, friendly neighborhood homing pigeon.* He shook his head at the thought of comparing himself to a comic book superhero. If he had superpowers, he'd have been home hours ago. He gritted his teeth as he entered a field of tall grass. At least he was almost there now. The sea of grass was all that stood between him and the barn. *Only a few more yards to go.*

Midway through the field, he saw the windmill. Its fins were still as frozen in place as when he'd left. Stephen groaned. *The parts.* He'd forgotten all about them. He'd have to go back into town, sooner rather than later. That was assuming anyone was still willing to trade after last night. *And where would they go?* Bean shivered in his arms, reminding him of the immediate issue. *First things first.* Ed wasn't a doctor, but considering how often he'd operated on himself, he had to know what to do. Stephen just hoped he wasn't already too late.

"Ed," he shouted. "Ed. Helen. Anyone. Help."

He staggered through the grass no longer able to feel his arms. Bean tumbled to the ground in front of him as he attempted to correct his balance. Released of her weight, his body seemed to spring forward of its own volition. In one second, his vision changed from a view of the farmhouse to the view of an approaching rock. He twisted his body by instinct, avoiding the imminent collision by an inch. Then everything went black.

Stephen woke at the touch of a rough wet cloth as it dabbed his forehead. A sapphire blue sky arched over him, indicating it was now well past morning. All trace of rain from the night before was gone. The sky was the only clear thing in his vision. His other surroundings were blurred shapes and colors. He blinked to clear his vision. A blotch of tan and brown overhead sharpened, and the edges refined until he saw Helen staring down at him, her concern all too clear.

"Don't sit up too fast, honey," Helen said while placing a hand on his shoulder. "You're okay. I'm here." She leaned down to kiss his forehead.

"I got lost," he replied while groaning at how weak he sounded. *So much for finally being treated like an adult.* His head throbbed.

Helen shook her finger as she pulled back. "Which is exactly why you were supposed to stay in town for the night. I thought we'd taught you better."

Stephen's vision blurred as he attempted to follow the movement. "It kind of wasn't an option." An insect landed on his nose.

Helen waved the bug away. "I'm listening."

"The Piper is gone."

"Gone? What do you mean *gone*? What about Jim? He couldn't have given up on the place. Not after all this time. Did he get sick? Is he okay?"

"I don't know. I didn't see him after the explosion. But I don't think so."

"Explosion?" Helen covered her mouth. Her nostrils flared. "I knew I smelled smoke in the air last night." Stephen coughed. Her fingers were cool on his skin as they stroked his forehead. "Did you see it?" she asked, clearing a few loose strands of hair away from his eyes.

"See it? I was there when it happened." Her eyes grew wide as he spoke and glistened with unshed tears. "One minute I was helping Jim tidy up and then, boom." Stephen's voice rose in a disbelief. "A piece of debris came crashing into the tavern, and the next thing I know, the whole place on fire. I barely got out in time." His fingers curled in the grass. "The Watch was there. They must have done it."

Her mouth tightened, blinking away the moisture before tears could fall. "Well, it's over now. You are here and they are not. But if you ever frighten me like that again—"

"Where is she?" Stephen asked, remembering Bean. He swiveled his head from side to side but didn't see her. "There was a girl with me."

Helen's frown deepened. "With Ed, in the house. What were you thinking? Bringing a stranger here?"

"Is she… Will she be okay?"

"Honey, I am more worried about you right now."

"But she's okay?" Stephen's stomach turned. "I didn't carry her across half the forest last night for her to die on me the minute we got here."

Helen pursed her lips. "Whatever did you do that for? Her legs seemed to work well enough. Has she never been outside a city before?" Helen snorted at the thought, expressing without words what she thought of a person who would ask to be carried through the woods, let alone at night.

"She was hurt."

Helen frowned. "From what I could see, there's not more than a scratch on her. You, on the other hand." She tapped at his shirt, though her fingers were gentle. "You want to tell more about this stain?"

Stephen sat up, resting the bulk of his weight on his elbows. As he did so, he touched the dark spot on his shirt. It had dried hard and the fabric clumped together. *No amount of scrubbing is going to get that out*, he thought. Stephen sighed. It had been his favorite shirt, one of the few that wasn't a shade of brown. *Doesn't matter*, he told himself. *It's not like I am out to impress anyone.*

"That's what I was telling you. The blood's hers."

"But that doesn't make any sense." Helen's forehead knit in confusion. She reached out to touch Stephen's clothing again as if the color might fall off in clumps like his usual covering of dirt did. "Are you sure you aren't hurt? Maybe you hit a tree branch or something?" She pulled at his collar, examining the skin underneath as her brow wrinkled further. Her eyes widened. She held up three fingers. "There was a rock next to your head. Did you hit it when you fell? How many fingers am I holding up?" She stopped and looked into his eyes.

"I would remember. And three." Stephen closed his eyes for a moment and lost himself in the memory of the fire as it claimed the walls all around. His heart raced as he recalled their frantic escape from the rooftop.

He opened them again at the touch of Helen's hand upon his cheek. There was a weariness in her eyes, though her jaw was clenched. "It's Jim's, isn't it?"

"No, I told you. I didn't see him again. I didn't see anything." Stephen thought about the voices in the alley. *Technically, that's not a lie.* Helen was already worried enough. *I got away.* He didn't need to add more to her troubles than he had to. "I'm telling you, it's hers," said Stephen. "She was hurt. Bad. I know." He grimaced. "I may have stabbed her with a knife."

"You did *what*?"

"It was an accident. See, there was this lock blocking the roof access and a ladder, and yeah, I might have, sort of dropped it on her." Helen sat back on her heels as Stephen continued, "I couldn't see how bad it was in the dark, but I think it sliced her back on the way down. Then there was the skunk and maybe a bear and she got all cold and clammy." *So much for not adding to her worries.* The words continued to spill out. "It's why we couldn't wait to travel in the daylight. And why I carried her. She would have died out there if it hadn't been for me. I'm actually a little surprised she didn't."

Helen's lips twisted as if there was something she wanted to say, but was interrupted by the rusty metal pull and thwacking sound of the farmhouse door spring as it opened and shut.

"He's awake," Helen shouted over her shoulder to what Stephen assumed had to be Ed. Stephen closed his eyes. *Nope, Ed's never going to let me leave the farm again.* He took a breath as he reminded himself that after last night, never leaving might not be the worst thing that could happen to him.

"Why is he upright?" Ed asked. "Did you find the source of the blood?"

"It isn't his. Claims it is the girl's."

"But there's so much," said Ed. "Did you see his jacket?"

Helen didn't answer as she stood. Ed arrived by Stephen's side. He bent down and lifted Stephen's shirt with his good hand. Stephen batted Ed's hand away. "I'm fine. Tired, but I'll live." Stephen looked to the farmhouse. There was no sign of anyone other than Ed or Helen. "Where's Bean? Is she inside? Is she really okay?"

"Bean?" Ed asked as he helped Stephen stand. "The girl's name is Bean? What kind of name is that? Bean, like in the garden?"

"Be careful saying that to her. I think she is sensitive about it." Stephen started to chuckle. His laughter turned into a fit of coughing.

Ed and Helen's eyes narrowed in sync. "A bit banged up here and there, but she's fit enough to continue on her way as soon as she finishes eating," said Ed. He lowered his voice. "I shouldn't have to tell you I think it would be better if you make your goodbyes quick."

"But she was hurt. I know she was. Shouldn't she stick around," Stephen asked. "I mean, at least for today, just to be sure she will be able to make it on her own?"

"No," said Ed. Helen placed a hand on his shoulder and nodded her head in the direction of the farmhouse as the sound of the door opening and closing echoed through the yard. Ed muttered under his breath, "I don't trust her."

"You don't trust anyone," Stephen muttered back.

Ed arched a single eyebrow.

"Well, it's true," grumbled Stephen. Ed took a deep breath. He opened his mouth, only to cover it with his hand. Stephen's stomach took that opportunity to growl, reminding him that Ed mentioned Bean eating. Suddenly, all he wanted was to go inside and eat a pig or ten.

Helen and Ed turned and began making their way to the farmhouse where Bean waited by the stairs. Stephen started to follow. His leg responded like a wet noodle. *So maybe you aren't as fine you think you are*. He took another step. His leg was steadier now. *That's better. Now walk it off*. He continued, trying to look as unaffected as possible. Working windmill or not, if Helen saw a limp, he might as well forget about going on another supply run any time soon. He'd be lucky if she let him leave his room.

Bean leaned against the building just outside the door as they approached, holding his jacket. As he grew closer, she looked down at his ankle for a moment, before her eyes met his. At the tavern, he'd thought they were the color of slate before, but by the light of day, they appeared more like jade. The corners of her lips inched up in a soft smile. The expression made her look like a different person. The candlelight had made her features sharp and as dangerous as a raptor's, but now, she looked like... his mind trailed off as he tried to come up with a word to describe her. *Girl*, his mind grunted. She looked like a girl, and his mind didn't mean the child kind. Thoughts of food evaporated as he found himself very reluctant to see the last of her.

Six

"Glad to see you decided to wake up," said Bean as he reached the farmhouse. "Here," she said, handing him his jacket back. "Though I don't know how useful it will still be." The jacket was covered in mud and grass and smelled like a bonfire. "What a night," she commented, as if the near-death girl he had carried the night before never existed.

"I've had better," answered Stephen. Helen and Ed were no longer by his side. A quick glance around told him they must have gone back inside, though he hadn't heard the door close. Then again, knowing how paranoid Ed could be, he guessed they hadn't gone too far out of earshot. "How are you acting like you are perfectly normal?"

She glared at him. "I am perfectly normal."

"I don't mean it like that. I mean, how are you not dead?"

"And how is that better?"

"Gah." He pinched the fabric at the jacket's shoulder. The bits of fabric not covered in dirt were pockmarked with burn marks, rips, and charred edges, but he didn't see a bloodstain where he thought one should be. *Weird.* "The knife. Me carrying you all night? Any of that ring a bell?" He dropped the ruined garment. Helen might be able to salvage a rag or something similar out of it later.

"Not really. I mean, I remember you saying we should stay in the woods last night. Then I fell asleep, and when I woke up, we were here and I was wearing that." She shrugged. "I'm not even going to ask what you did with my sweater. You're just lucky I had something on underneath." Her expression softened. "Your parents were pretty worried about you, especially when you didn't wake up right away. Your mom wanted to move you inside, but your dad was afraid you'd hit your head or something. I told them your skull was too thick to be damaged, but maybe he was right."

Had he fallen asleep in the woods, too? Was the entire race ahead of the storm the result of a bad dream?

"They aren't my parents," Stephen replied without thinking. *Why did you have to go and say that?* He scanned her face for a reaction. She chewed the bottom of her lip but didn't ask for clarification. *Great. Now it's awkward. Don't be a freak. Say something. Get back on topic.* "You look tanner today." *You look tan? What the heck? You sound like an idiot. Maybe she's right about that thick skull, after all.* Stephen grimaced, thinking of how much time had continued to pass. *Ugh. She hasn't answered. Say something. Do something.* His stomach took that moment to rumble loud enough he was sure the sound could be heard by the barn. *Way to go. She thinks you are an idiot and a freak.*

Bean's smile returned in force. "Hungry much?"

Great. Now she's laughing at me, Stephen thought. His cheeks began to burn.

"I know the feeling. You should eat." She gestured at the farmhouse door as the smell of food emanating from inside tempted his nose. "It is amazing what a little food will do."

Stephen remained frozen in place.

"Well, I guess it's time for me to head out then." Bean glanced out to the forest. He saw her swallow.

"You don't need to go yet," he heard himself say. *Wasn't this the same girl you couldn't wait to get rid of the night before?* He waited to hear Ed object from the inside of the house, but the objection never came. *Maybe they aren't eavesdropping after all.* "You should rest. Besides, you'll need a guide to get back to the main road."

The corner of her lip turned up. "I've survived worse. Really, I'll be fine. Now, go and grab something to eat before whatever was in the woods with us last night misinterprets that growl as a mating call."

"I'm not that hungry." His stomach grumbled. *Liar.* Unwilling to make eye contact after, he followed her gaze to the forest. "And what if the Watch is still looking for us?" *When did 'us' happen?* Stephen found himself wondering.

Bean's lips tightened. "All the more reason for me to go. You've done enough."

"What about the Watch?" Helen asked from the doorway. Stephen jumped. His guardians had been listening, after all. She made a *tsking* sound. "When you didn't come inside, I started to worry you collapsed again." She crossed her arms over her chest once more and looked at him like he was ten years old again. "I also came back to tell you that your food is ready, but that can wait."

"Wait for what?"

"Don't even try to pretend you don't know what I am talking about. Why would the Watch be looking for you? They shouldn't even know you exist."

"I told you. There was an explosion." Stephen caught himself looking over Helen's shoulder for Ed.

"So you did, but you didn't tell me why the Watch—who you said may have been responsible for it—would be interested in you." Her fingers began tapping her arm, signaling the countdown before the end of her patience. The same gesture would send Ed scurrying to make amends in seconds. Faced with all its implications, Stephen now understood why Ed ran.

Helen's face transformed as he related the events from the night before. By the time he finished the story, her face was pale but as hard as granite. Helen turned to Bean. The icy chill of her gaze sent a shiver down Stephen's spine. Gone was the face of the kind woman who had kissed his injuries growing up; in her place stood a woman capable of gutting Bean like a lion might a gazelle.

"Your turn." Helen's tone commanded an answer.

"My turn for what?"

"To tell why they were really chasing you."

"He told you what happened. The Watch came. They'd found out about the illegal trading going on in the tavern. I knew that they were on their way and was there to warn Jim."

"Right. And it so happens that they picked last night of all nights to stop turning a blind eye to what has been going on there for years." Helen clucked her tongue. "I don't buy it. Everyone knows about Piper's. And no one, not even those in charge, wants to see it shut down. What goes on in there may be against the rules, but it is all that keeps the people from rioting out of hunger some months. If they were there, it meant that there was something—or more likely *someone*— worth their attention." Bean's lips twisted as Helen continued, "And I know that someone wasn't Stephen, not until you dragged him into whatever mess you're in. I hate repeating myself, but I'll ask again. Why is the Watch interested in *you*?"

Bean's hand reached back and touched the farmhouse wall. Her lips tightened. She pushed away from the wall. Spinning on her heel with the forest to her back, she met Helen's gaze full on. "You're better off not knowing."

Helen's frown deepened as Stephen winced. He had seen her mad enough over the years to be able to anticipate how she would respond to such a blatant challenge, and it didn't bode well for Bean. His body tensed in anticipation of the imminent fireworks. Instead, Helen turned to him. "When the Watch comes, I expect you to turn her in."

"Oh, you don't have to worry about that. I'll be long gone before they arrive."

"Is that so?" Helen replied, placing her body between Bean and the forest beyond.

"Trust me. If you would move to the side, I'd leave now."

Helen's arm shot out, grabbing Bean before she could take another step.

"Hey. What's the big deal?" She twisted in Helen's grip to no avail. "Let me go."

Muscle developed from years of farm labor had given Helen an unbreakable grip. Stephen winced. She'd used it on him a time or two as a kid when he'd tried to skip out on chores.

"Seriously? What's your problem?" Bean continued to struggle against Helen's hold. "I'll leave now, and you'll never have to worry about me ever again. All you have to do is let me go."

"Unfortunately, I can't do that. Now that the Watch knows about us, we need to give them a reason to believe we aren't a threat." She turned to Stephen. "I'm sorry, but this is the only way."

The ground below his feet seemed to shake as a sound like thunder rumbled in the distance. The field of grass parted as the tops of heavy-duty vehicles came into view.

"Let her go." Stephen pulled at Helen's arm. "I didn't carry her all this way just to hand her over to people who might kill her."

Helen shot him a pointed glance. "You made a mistake."

Stephen blinked as Helen's words registered. The question echoed his guilty thoughts from the night before. *Had it really been a mistake? Should I have left her in the woods? At the tavern?* He remembered the voices in the alley and the rustling in the woods. He might have dreamt the knife wound, but there had still been a real danger. *No,* he told himself. *You made the right call.* "I was just trying to do the right thing—to protect her."

"And now I'm trying to protect you. To protect us." Helen's shoulders slumped as the fight left her. "We've always known you were a good boy." Her body sagged as if it had aged another decade. "It's just unfortunate you couldn't prove us wrong this once."

Taking advantage of the distraction, Bean slipped from her grip and bolted behind the farmhouse. Helen looked in the direction where she had run, but the girl had vanished into the countryside. Helen's lips tightened, but she made no move to pursue. "There goes our bargaining chip."

"It's better this way."

Helen patted his arm. "Oh, sweetie, if only that were true." She leaned away from Stephen and shouted toward the door. "Ed, we are about to have more company."

The spring screamed in protest as Ed flung the door open and joined them outside. "Go to the barn, Stephen," he ordered, throwing a backpack at Stephen. "And take this with you. In case you need to run."

"But what about you?" Stephen struggled to pull the pack on. It was strange. He'd never seen it before. Where had Ed had gotten it from?

"We can handle this. Now go before they see you."

"Ed…" began Helen.

"I said go."

A car door squealed on rusted hinges, but Stephen did as instructed. He raced toward the barn. *This is a big misunderstanding*, he thought as he came to a stop across from the windmill. *I did nothing wrong. I should just go back there and explain myself.*

From behind him, Stephen heard the sound of a second door opening and the same woman's voice from the night before carried over the worn path between house and barn. Though he'd convinced himself he didn't have any reason to fear, he stayed in the shadows as he continued his approach.

"I apologize for bothering you folks, but you didn't happen to see a pair of young people pass by, did you? A boy and a girl, between eighteen and twenty years old?" she asked. "I'm Dr. Lambda, with the Watch."

Ed answered, "We don't see very many people out here. Prefer it that way."

"We don't want any trouble," Helen spoke up.

"Nor do we, but you should know there was an incident in town last night, and we have reason to believe they witnessed it. People died. Property was destroyed. We're looking for answers."

"I saw a girl, but I sent her on her way. That way," Helen added.

Stephen scowled at the speed in which Helen had given Bean up until he realized that she gestured in the opposite direction from where he'd seen her flee.

Dr. Lambda nodded to someone in one of the other trucks who fired their engine back up and began backing out of the field. "Thank you. I can't tell you how refreshing it is to know there are still honest people in this world."

"We're good people. We just want to stay here and grow our crops in peace."

"And no wonder. It is such a lovely place. Now that I know about it, I'd love to visit more often."

"Ah, well…please don't take this the wrong way, but we'd prefer to be left alone."

"I understand your position, but I'm a doctor. Perhaps one of the only ones left in fifty miles. I would feel it is my duty to check in on you from time to time. You might think I am exaggerating, but I've seen whole families wiped out by a sneeze. Families who might have been saved if they'd been less quick to turn me away. You wouldn't want that to happen to you or your husband." She craned her head to the side. "Or your son."

Stephen stepped out of the shadows.

"It's nice to see you again."

"He's a good boy," Helen interrupted, throwing her arm out as if to stop Stephen's approach. "He's never even been to town on his own before last night."

"I'm sure he is, which is why you should have nothing to worry about. We just need him to come with us so we might get to know him a little better. He'll be back with you in no time." She paused and tapped her temple. "In fact, now that I think about it, perhaps it would be best for your nerves if you came with us, too. Both of you."

The truck's doors opened again as several men exited.

"I don't suppose we have any choice," Ed commented.

"You always have a choice," the woman replied. "I just am hoping you make the right one."

SEVEN

A medicinal scent picked at Stephen's senses. It was like the rubbing alcohol Ed used to treat his constant wounds but several times stronger. The smell grew more intense as Dr. Lambda gestured for Stephen to climb into the closest vehicle while she followed inches behind. *She must bathe in the stuff*, thought Stephen as he watched the other pair of men similarly escorted Ed and Helen into the other truck.

"I didn't catch your name before," said Dr. Lambda while closing the door. She followed Stephen's gaze. "I'm sorry I had to separate you from them, but it would have been a little too cramped on the way back to the Watchtower." When Stephen didn't reply, she added, "We were expecting to bring back two."

"Stephen," he grunted as he swung the backpack around and positioned it on his waist.

"Stephen?" she repeated.

"Yeah, you asked me my name. That's it. See, I'm willing to answer your questions. Why can't you ask them here?"

The corner of Dr. Lambda's lip curled up as her gaze met that of the truck's driver. "Ah. Well, you see, as I mentioned before, we're not used to people being honest with us, and find it best when we ask our questions in a more…controlled environment. You know. Where we can be sure to check everything off all at once? For example, I noticed you haven't given me your full name."

"So what?" replied Stephen, ignoring her implied question. "Are you going to torture me for it?"

"Torture you?" Dr. Lambda laughed. "Why ever would you think we'd do something like that?"

"Oh, I don't know. Maybe it has something to do with the fact that everyone in town is terrified of you."

Dr. Lambda's smile slipped. "Earthaven is full of bored individuals who would do well to spend less time making up stories and more time contributing to the greater good." She sighed. "I recognize our methods might seem intrusive to some, but it is for the best. How else can you be sure that the neighbor who keeps to themselves down the road isn't stockpiling weapons that could be used against you when food grows short, or carrying the next strain of virus that can take out the rest of us?" Her voice softened as she looked at him. "You are too young to understand."

Stephen snorted and rolled his eyes.

Dr. Lambda shook her head. "You think you do, but you don't. You have no idea what it was like. When the economy collapsed and the children began dying." She closed her eyes. "And for what? So people had an excuse to wait in line for the next big gadget?" Her chest rose with a deep breath, and when her eyes opened, they were clear and bright. "Well, we sure aren't waiting in line now." Her back straightened. "I vowed we'd never be so irresponsible again. Not if I could help it. Not on my watch."

The driver slapped his palms on the steering wheel in his support.

The gravel drive that once served to connect the house with the main road hadn't been maintained in years and was now more ditch and grass than drive. The vehicle carrying Ed and Helen dipped and stopped. Its driver exited and gestured for their driver to roll down his window. "Sorry. I must have hit a pothole or something. I think we blew a tire," said the first driver to the second. "Damn post-apocalyptic infrastructure. Can't anyone bother to fix a road?" Their driver grunted in agreement. "Can I get some help changing a tire?"

Dr. Lambda motioned for their driver to assist the other vehicle. He switched the engine off and rolled the window back up. Dr. Lambda reached over and locked the door before Stephen could react. "Now that we are alone, there is another reason I wanted to talk to you. My men found blood in an alley next to the tavern."

"I don't know anything about that."

"But I think you do because I think it's yours."

Stephen remembered landing in the dumpster and spitting blood from his bruised tongue. "So? Is that a crime? You try jumping from a burning building and not getting a little banged up."

"You could have gone out the front door. That's what a normal person would have done."

"Oh yeah? A piece of the building across the street just came flying through the front window. Forgive me if it didn't seem like the safest place to be."

Dr. Lambda's lips narrowed. "I can see I've upset you."

"Oh, I'm not upset. I just don't know anything and would prefer to be able to eat some breakfast and maybe sleep in my own bed right now." His stomach growled as his faked yawn became a real one.

She reached into a cooler by their feet and pulled out a small apple. Handing it to him, she said, "I'm sorry, but you won't be sleeping in your bed for quite some time."

"Because you are taking me to your headquarters to torture me." Unable to resist, he bit into its side. It was more delicious than any of the shrunken fruit they were able to grow and harvest. *It must be nice to be allowed to use machines.* It was gone all too soon.

"Again with the torture. No, because you are going to do a job for me."

"Yeah, thanks for the offer, but you see, I'm all booked up with the harvest coming up." He handed her the core and eyeballed the contents of the cooler.

"Agree to do this job for me and, not only will I take care of your parents, but I'll also make sure it is clear your family is under the Watch's protection. We could locate a working tractor for you or help you rebuild that windmill of yours. We have the best mechanics. Moreover, you wouldn't have to worry about trading in secret anymore either. Being a friend of the Watch has a number of advantages."

Stephen thought of Ed's wounded hand. He thought of the chores that could go so much faster with equipment that worked. He channeled his best Helen impersonation. "I'm listening."

"There is a tower east from here. I want access to it."

"Why don't you go there and do it yourself?"

Dr. Lambda's lips tightened before answering. "If it was that simple, I would. But I am afraid the residents have been less than accommodating."

"So why do you think they'll put out the welcome mat for me?"

"Because I believe you share a version of the same affliction they do."

"Affliction?" Stephen blinked. "As in, you think I am sick?"

She placed a hand on his knee. "Not sick; at least not yet. There is something wrong with your DNA. Think of it as a genetic disorder. One if not both of your parents were seduced into thinking they could somehow alter their DNA without consequences. They were wrong. Delusions. Insanity. Homicidal tendencies. Those are just the start. You've been fortunate to have managed to hold it back for this long, but it is only a matter of time before the negative side effects come out of their dormancy."

Had Bean's knife wound and the glowing forest floor been early symptoms?

"What kind of delusions?"

"The people who live in that tower have come to believe they have magical powers." Dr. Lambda leaned back and sighed. "That they can do things with their bodies. Shapeshift. Become invisible. Some probably think they can fly. Those are the claims we've heard about." She shook her head. "Unfortunately, few are seen outside. We don't know how many there are or what goes on on the inside, but we do know it's a cult, and like any cult, each day it goes unchecked will make it more dangerous. Not just for its members, but for the rest of us as well. I need access to the building and its residents so I can study the cause and determine a treatment before people like them cause further harm."

"And you think these crazy people will let me in?"

"Not crazy. Deluded, but yes."

"And if they don't?"

"You have to make sure they do."

"And what if I say no?"

"Then I'm afraid your parents might be staying with me for quite some time."

Stephen looked into the rearview mirror. The top of the motionless windmill poked out over the top of the tall grass. The rest of the farmstead was out of view.

"I'm sorry, but I do need to hear you say yes."

The doctor's words came back to him. You always have a choice. *Yeah, easy for her to say.* "Okay. I'll do it."

"Excellent." She handed him a slip of paper. "Here are directions. You'll know you are almost there when you get to the bridge."

Stephen stared at the directions. He wouldn't need them. He took a breath. He'd seen them before.

"Now don't tell anyone you are working for me, even those you meet on the street. The people who live in the tower don't leave, but they might still have friends. I'll make sure my people are following you. Run from them. Hide. Tell the people at the tower we are after you. That you are being persecuted. It will make your story seem more believable and make them less likely to kill you on the spot."

"Wait, what?"

The vehicle in front of them lurched forward as the man who had been driving their truck turned and began walking back. The first vehicle was well underway when a rock streaked across their view, hitting the returning driver who crumpled to the ground.

"Where did that come from?" Stephen asked. Dr. Lambda remained in her seat. "Aren't you going to go help him?"

Dr. Lambda smiled. "No. This simplifies matters."

"Simplifies? How? What?"

"You have two weeks to find me a way in, or we will be forced to find another way. You should know, not everyone's methods in the Watch are as peaceful as mine. Lives are now in your hands."

Another large rock flew into the windshield, producing a hairline fracture in the glass.

"Roy?" Dr. Lambda opened her door and leaned out, her face a mask of concern. "Everything okay out there?" Her body went limp as she tumbled out the vehicle, taking the antiseptic smell with her. Stephen clenched his fists, preparing himself to fight this latest threat.

"You coming?" Bean asked, grinning from the tall grass by the driver's side as she waved for him to follow her outside. "Or do I need to send you an invitation by carrier pigeon?"

"What the...? That was you? How? Why? Are they dead?"

Her eyes twinkled in the light. "A, I'm a fast runner. B, I'm rescuing you; feel free to thank me later, by the way. And C, not even close. Not that I didn't consider it. Now I'd suggest you come with me, because I really don't think you want to be around when they wake back up. Trust me."

Stephen's hopes lifted. "What about my folks?"

Bean's smile slipped. "What about them?"

"The Watch put them in the other truck."

Bean chewed her lip as she glanced down the road. "Yeah, they are long gone by now," she replied with a small shake of her head.

"Right, but if the doctor is here"—Stephen gestured toward the unconscious figure laying on the ground—"wouldn't they come back when they noticed she's not behind them? We can rescue them, too." It was perfect. All they needed was to hide and wait for the truck to come back. Then they'd free Ed and Helen and then disappear together. There was no need to go to some tower to the east and risk his life over some crazies. *Except you heard the doctor. Without a treatment, you might be going crazy, too.* Running away would also mean abandoning the people in the tower to the mercy of the Watch—everyone in the tower, including the one person in this world he considered a friend.

She frowned. "Yeah, that's not a good idea. Their guard was down and I got in a lucky hit, but they will be on alert now, especially if they see either sleeping beauty. Don't forget there's still more of them than there are of us. We only saw three trucks, but there could be more waiting at the end of the road. No, we need be far away from here before anyone thinks to come back. You know these woods. Any ideas where we can hide?"

The doctor's comment about things simplifying now made sense. Bean's rescue provided the cover he would need, but she would have to come with him if it were to work. "Well, we can't hide in the barn."

She groaned in exasperation. "Then we go someplace else. There's got to be another place you can think of. Somewhere no one else would think to look. Not even your parents-but-not-parents."

Stephen grimaced at the way she threw the words he'd used to describe Ed and Helen back at him but did not argue. "There's a guy I know. But I should warn you, it's a bit of a hike."

Bean's grin returned. "I don't mind walking. Which way?"

"Northeast." *Wes, that invitation better still be open.*

"You haven't had many dealings with the Watch, have you?" Bean said.

"Never had any reason to." He strained his ears to hear any sound of pursuit. Dr. Lambda had said her people would chase after them, but seeing how she'd slumped when hit, there was a good chance their pursuers wouldn't know it was supposed to be for show.

"Must be nice." Bean looked straight ahead. "I've had more than enough for the both of us."

"You never did tell me why they were after you in the first place."

"No, I never did."

Stephen swatted at a group of gnats. "Well, will you?"

"Knowing doesn't make it any better." Bean started walking away again. "Trust me."

Between the buzzing of the gnats, the headache that refused to go away, and his growling stomach, he lost his hold on his patience. "And what's that gotten me? If I hadn't trusted you enough to let you inside, I might not be in this mess."

Bean spun on her heel and marched back to him until their chests were a hand span apart. "Right. It's all my fault. The Watch treating people like animals. The explosion. Almost getting burned alive. All of it. It's my fault. Yeah, I totally wanted the one person who was more of a dad to me than my own father to—" She clenched her fists. "So yeah, go on thinking that." She turned. "Jerk." She walked ahead, leaving Stephen with his mouth agape. "I could have left you with them, but I didn't."

She could have. Stephen paused. *She still could. Idiot. You need her. Remember?* Stephen glanced back in the direction of the farmhouse. He could hear the sound of shouting in the distance. The Watch must have found their fallen comrades. Thunder rolled in the distance, and the light dimmed as gray clouds began to fill the sky. *Great. Guess the drought is over.* Somehow, it seemed appropriate. He picked up his pace until he was once again beside her. When she didn't pull away, he said, "Look, I'm sorry. I know none of that is your fault. I'm just worried about my folks, so I said something stupid. I'm afraid something is going to happen to them, and I can't do anything about it. You know?"

A squirrel darted in front of them in search of shelter from the coming deluge. Bean muttered something under her breath. Louder, she said, "Look. I know the Watch is capable of doing any number of terrible things, but your parents—or whoever they are—made it this long without catching the Watch's attention. I'm sure they can manage a few nights on their own while you figure something out."

She's right. Stephen told himself. *Even if Dr. Lambda doesn't wake up right away, there is still no reason to think either of them is in immediate danger. They haven't done anything.* He thought of Ed's bandaged hands and scars on his arms. *It might even do Ed some good, forced to get some rest. There are worse places he could be than with a medical doctor.* Wes, however, remained in danger. "So does that mean you can forget I said what I said?"

"I guess." She shrugged. "I mean your parents, or whatever you want to call them, love you, so you can't be all bad. I mean, I personally don't get it, but there must be a reason." Raindrops began to fall. "Now are you going to stand there getting soaked, or are you planning to lead the way?"

PART TWO

EIGHT

Towers, rising up in the horizon like pillars holding up the sky, caught Stephen's eye as he shook the canteen. He'd found it in Ed's backpack along with other survival gear. A sheet of thin silver material folded into a square the size of Stephen's palm had provided a surprising amount of warmth. There were also a handful of freeze-dried meals and a water filtration system, but if Ed had saved an extra supply of water for an emergency, he must have stored it in another bag. Stephen shook the metal canteen again as if that might change their remaining level of water. They had gotten lucky on the second day, discovering a creek thanks to the reflected light of the rising sun. Their luck, so early on, had made them careless. Now, even after rationing their remaining supply, they were going to have to find another source for fresh water, and they needed to find it soon.

Stephen glanced toward the horizon again. The sun, unhindered by any cloud, cast a golden hue on their surroundings as it dipped lower in the sky. *Because of course it doesn't rain when you actually need water.* As long as they kept their pace up, they might even still make it to the towers before dark. A breeze tickled his hair with icy fingers. It hit him then, exactly what the towers in the distance were. Stephen doubled his stride.

They had already passed by a number of buildings where civilization once thrived. Several windows were boarded up. More were blackened. Those that had once been stocked with goods such as food or bottled water were long since raided, but what was just as troubling to Stephen's senses was the complete lack of other souls on the roadway. Even members of the Watch had yet to make their appearance. Had the recent storms kept all the people indoors, or were the streets that abandoned? The emptiness made Earthaven feel like a metropolis by comparison.

"And you're sure you know where we are going?" Bean asked.

Stephen had gotten so used to hearing the question asked at least three times a day, he had stopped answering, but as he looked into the blacked windows of yet another warehouse that might as well serve as a tomb now, he found his confidence wavering.

"You see those towers?" He pointed ahead. "They hold up this huge bridge." He didn't know if he'd answered her again for her benefit or his own. Bean didn't appear as wide-eyed as he felt. He also didn't know if he envied her worldliness or pitied her for it either. "That's where we're going."

"Oh?" Bean asked with a smile. "Have you come this way often?"

"I've looked at maps, okay?" he grumbled, thinking about the images online he'd poured over the first time he'd received Wes's invitation. "But considering we're going to an island, it's a pretty good guess." As if in confirmation, the scent of brackish water filled his nostrils. *Water.* His thirst grew at the thought. *Would it be drinkable though, this close the ocean?* he wondered. His bad mood evaporated as it occurred to him that he was going to see the ocean. Seeing it for the first time with his own eyes would almost be worth putting up with Bean's never-ending quips. *Almost.* He shook his head. If they spent much more time together, he'd be in danger of enjoying them.

"…we're coming." Her voice cut through the clutter that was his thoughts.

"What?"

Bean sighed. "I asked you a question. You said you know someone there. Do you have any way of letting him know we are coming?"

Stephen shook his head as he focused on the road ahead—anything other than looking in her direction. He heard her mutter, "Well, this is going to be interesting." Her foot connected with a rusted can littering the roadway. The noise sent a nearby gull back into the air in fright.

He looked at the sky again. They could make it to the bridge before sunset, but they would need to press on at full speed. Another breeze sent a shiver down Stephen's spine. He took several steps before realizing that Bean had fallen back. "Come on, we're almost there." He saw her wobble and noticed then that while her cheeks still showed dots of color, the rest of her skin had taken on a pale waxy sheen. *Way to hog the water; now she's dehydrated.* "Here," he said, walking back. He handed her the canteen.

Their fingers touched and a spark passed between them. "Must have built up some static," she said, shifting and breaking contact. Her fingers lingered on the canteen's surface instead, but she didn't take the vessel from his hands.

"Go on, you need this more than I do."

Her lips twisted as she pushed the canteen back at him without taking a sip. "Save it until we get to the other side."

She was maddening. *Maybe there is a faster way to the bridge than the main road.* Stephen glanced up at a rusted street sign. The words meant nothing to him, but Bean wouldn't know that. *Would it have killed the people who'd once lived here to post better signage?* Tall grass grew out of a broken window across the street. Hundreds of thousands, if not millions once lived here. The majority died here, too. Living in isolation, it had been easy to think of those deaths in terms of numbers rather than people. He wouldn't be able to do that any longer.

Bean turned and her face broke out into a smile so brilliant it seemed to banish any evidence of her earlier exhaustion. "We can go by boat," she announced.

He forced a smile on his face. She didn't need to know the depressing nature of his thoughts. "Which would be a great, except for the fact that we don't have a boat."

"It's worth a look." Bean pointed to a sign alongside the roadway. "Don't you think?" Most of the text had long since been weathered away, but a mold- and dirt-covered outline of the word 'marina' could still be seen.

The rest of the signage hadn't fared much better, and Stephen's hope that they might yet reach the island before the last of the sunlight departed diminished with each step they took further away from the highway. The red sheen of twilight replaced the golden hour. Stephen found himself tiring, though Bean now walked with a bounce in her step. It was Stephen's turn to struggle to keep up. His side had begun to develop a cramp as they reached land's edge. *Yep, maddening.*

A sign painted on a faded arch announced that they had arrived, but a rusty metal gate, dotted with the remains of chipped white paint, blocked the pier itself. The long empty pier stretched out behind it. The closest thing to a sign of life was a small reddish-brown bird picking at the ground. For some reason, the shade of its feathers reminded Stephen of Ed, even though his hair hadn't been that color for years.

Marina. It might as well be a graveyard, Stephen thought, growing angry.

Cities weren't supposed to be like this. He looked at the towers across the water. The windows on the island appeared just as empty as the ones on this side of the river. Dr. Lambda said there were people there, but all he could see were broken buildings and more failed dreams. *What was the point of coming here?* There was no one left to save. He thought of Ed and Helen boarding the truck to the Watch's headquarters. *I should never have agreed to this.* Stephen's knees began to buckle under the weight of the mental refrain as he fought the urge to collapse. *I've made a huge mistake.*

Bean turned just as he reached for the back of one of the benches encircling the place. "Are you okay?"

The earth seemed to move under his feet. Stephen clenched his teeth, preventing the words that had taken over his thoughts from passing through his lips; however, it didn't prevent him from calling out in his mind. To whom, he wasn't certain, but he found he didn't care at the moment who answered.

"Stephen?"

He glanced at his hand. His knuckles were white. So white, in fact, that they didn't look like his. *When had that happened?* They looked like they would have better fit on a mannequin. Stephen's body shook as humorless laughter from the pit of his stomach began to bubble to the surface.

"Steve? Steve-o? Hey, it's going to be okay. We'll take the bridge."

His vision blurred as wet droplets streaked across his face. Last he checked, the sky was still clear. *Where is the rain coming from?* His lungs burned as he struggled to fit a breath in between the mix of sobs and laughter. A hand touched his back. *Bean. Her fault,* the small voice whispered, repeating his accusation from before. The intensity of the thought almost undid what little control remained. He gripped the bench tighter to keep from lashing out.

Her other hand covered one of his and began prying his fingers away from the metal.

"You don't want to do that," Stephen growled as his body continued to shudder.

Her hand froze for a moment overtop his. "Yes, I do," Stephen heard her whisper, and it was as if her voice was a key in a lock. His grip loosened, and then his hand was in hers once more, and her body became the only thing holding his up.

She reached up, cupping his cheek with her hand after wiping a tear off his face. He closed his eyes before she could search them. He feared what she might find. Behind closed eyes, he saw the girl on the road bathed in moonlight and the woman fierce enough to face down an approaching doom. She had ruined his life, part of him remained sure of it, and yet, and yet? Did she even feel half as conflicted about him? He realized he didn't want to know as a warmth spread from where they touched as blood began circulating in his hands once more.

Stephen lost track of how long they stood frozen by the beach near the entrance of the marina. Then, Bean pulled her hand away, causing Stephen's body to sag where Bean's palm once lay. "We're not alone," she whispered.

His eyes, dry and clear once again, snapped open at her words. Stephen turned. The water was dark like ink under the now violet evening sky. The towers on the island across the way were nothing more than black outlines.

"There," whispered Bean as she pointed to where land and water met.

Stephen followed her line of sight. "I don't see anything."

"Look again."

A light flickered midway across the water; a small, round, and white light.

"I think that's just the moon's reflection."

"Too full."

Stephen looked up into the sky. Bean was right. The moon in the sky looked like a bite had been taken out of it, but the light on the water's surface appeared to be a full circle. If it wasn't the moon's reflection, what could it be? The light's color proved it wasn't an insect. Could it be a reflection from a torch or nearby campsite? Stephen glanced around, on edge. The light from a fire would be warm and dancing, and the air lacked a hint of smoke.

Then the light blinked off, as if it knew it had been spotted. Had the Watch caught up with them again?

Stephen dropped to the ground, pulling Bean with him. In the silence, Stephen noticed now what he hadn't a few minutes earlier. A slapping sound came from the direction where the light once shone. Bean lifted her body into a crouch.

"Get back down here." He grabbed at her shirt in an attempt to pull her back down.

"It's a rowboat." Bean stood the rest of the way.

"What are you trying to do? Get their attention?" Dr. Lambda's warning that they might be killed on sight popped into Stephen's mind. *Make it look like you are being pursued.* "What if it's the Watch?"

Bean walked over to what remained of the rusted gate protecting the pier. "I think the Watch would send more than a single person in a rowboat, don't you?" Stephen, still prone on the ground, watched as Bean examined the metal bars before grasping the railing. "Besides, I thought the whole reason we are here was because you were friends with these people." She vaulted over the top of the gate as Stephen scrambled to pull himself off the ground and follow suit.

"A guy. Emphasis on *a*. Not people. That could be anyone." A jagged piece of the metal rail caught on his shirt as he attempted to mimic the jump, causing him to stumble on landing. By the time he'd caught up, Bean sat at the end of the pier with her feet dangling over the side. He grabbed her shoulder. "We have no idea whether or not whoever that is, is friendly."

"Maybe they are, maybe they're not. But I, for one, want that boat."

Stephen's hand dropped from her shoulder as he noticed the short length of metal she had pulled from the gate as she made her way over the side. It was positioned within arm's reach of her body, but still out of view from the waterfront.

The slap sound of oars on water grew louder. Whoever it was would be arriving in short order. Realizing what Bean was suggesting, Stephen grabbed the piece of the bar from her hands. If it was a member of the Watch, they might hurt Ed or Helen in retaliation. If it was one of the tower cultists, they might not let him inside and Wes might die when the Watch arrived. He looked at the bridge in the distance. Going back wasn't an option either. The bridge was too far. Bean might act invincible, but she needed water. They needed more water. He turned the metal fragment over in his fingers. *You always have a choice.*

He looked at Bean. She stuck with him this far and he'd no idea why. He had been afraid to ask for fear that she might realize he needed her more than she needed him. She was just as much a victim of the last few days as he was. He had to stop blaming her for everything that had happened. *Time to make another decision—good or bad.* Stephen nodded to himself. He'd brought them this far. He'd take them the rest of the way. "Go hide. I've got this."

NINE

Stephen clutched at the metal spike as he readied himself to do whatever it took to capture the vessel. *You got this. You got this.* The pier creaked as Bean moved around behind him, though her footsteps were silent. The metal pressed into his hand. If he gripped it any tighter, it might break through the skin. He took a deep breath. *Here we go.*

"Yo, can you help me tie up?" shouted a voice from the boat as a figure rose to a half stand.

At first, all Stephen noticed was the length of rope in the figure's arms. Another idea crossed Stephen's mind. Perhaps it wouldn't come to extreme violence. All they had to do was scare him, then tie him up and go on their way. No one had to get hurt. Given another option, Stephen's heart began to slow its pounding refrain.

"Yeah, you. On the pier. Little help, man?" The figure came closer. The person holding the rope had to be similar to Stephen's age, if not a year or two younger.

Without the sound of his pulse rushing around his eardrums, Stephen caught the figure's voice. Its tone and cadence cut through his consciousness like a bullet. *Or a knife.* Stephen jumped up, releasing the metal spike into the water where his feet dangled a moment before.

"No way."

"Mont?"

"Wes?"

"Dude!"

"I take it it's safe to come out now?" Bean returned to Stephen's side from wherever she had hidden.

Stephen pointed to the boat and gestured that he was ready to catch the rope as soon as it was tossed. "It's him. I can't believe it." Stephen pointed again. "The guy. Seriously, what are the chances?" His eyes threatened to fill once more with tears. At the same time, Stephen wanted to laugh but feared that if he started, he might never stop. It was perfect. Wes would take him inside. He'd leave the door open. The Watch would come, do their inspection, create a treatment, and then Wes could come back to the farm with him if he wanted. He squashed the urge just as he had done with the tears. *Get a hold of yourself*, he thought, while tying the rope to a worn bracket on the end of the pier. "Wes, this is Bean. Bean, Wes."

Satisfied that the boat was secured, he grasped Wes's extended hand. "Nice to finally meet you." Wes tripped as Stephen pulled him onto the pier, sending a pair of glasses tumbling to the ground.

"It's nice to meet you, too," Bean replied, although her tone had an edge to it.

"Meet?" Wes's brow knit. An awkward silence passed. Then his eyes widened. Wes slapped his forehead and then extended his hand out to Bean. "Sorry. I meant that for Mont, but, er, I mean, yeah, it is nice to meet you, too. What did he say your name was? Bean? Like the—"

Stephen coughed and shook his head.

"I'm confused. If you and *Mont*…" She raised her eyebrow at the name but didn't correct him. "If you have never met, how do you two know each other?"

Stephen answered, "Through a gaming site."

"A gaming site," Bean repeated. "Right."

"I know what you must be thinking," said Stephen with a grin. "The network's been down for years."

The corner of Wes's lip turned up. "Not everywhere."

Stephen laughed. "Right. Not everywhere. As I... As *we* found out."

Bean turned to Stephen. "Are you telling me that all this time that house in the middle of nowhere has had network access?"

Stephen's cheeks burned, glad that the crimson blush he knew coloring them would be hidden in the darkness. "Just because we lived away from town, doesn't mean we're hicks."

"I didn't mean it in a bad way." Bean's shoulders slumped as she shook her head. A grin spread wide across her face, which she covered with her palm. "It's just I figured being so close to Earthaven it was one of those off-grid places, too. How did you keep it from the Watch for so long?"

"Yeah, well, don't tell my folks, okay? They didn't know about it either," muttered Stephen.

Wes took a step backward. "Right. Well, we should get going if we want to make it back to my place before midnight."

The amazement left Bean's voice. "Not that we're not grateful for the ride and all, but why are you here?"

This time it was Wes's turn to point at Stephen. "For him. Er. Um. Yeah."

"And you just happened to show up here. Now." She gestured at the rest of the marina behind them. "Doesn't that seem a little odd to you?" She looked at Stephen. "I thought you said you had no way to contact him."

Stephen glanced at Bean and then at Wes. His smile slipped. Bean was right. It was an impossible coincidence.

Something was off about the situation. He took a step closer to Bean, regretting dropping the metal bar in the water.

Wes pursed his lips as he resettled his glasses on his nose. "Lucky. Not odd. Mont's never missed a week. When he didn't show up for game time, I thought either something was wrong, or he was finally on his way here. Either way, I thought I would go and find out. As this is the one and only marina left with a functional pier, it was either come here or go by the bridge. This way's easier, as you must have also realized." He turned to Stephen. "I told you not to make me track you down."

Bean caught Stephen's eye. He shrugged with relief. As impossible as it might be, Wes's story made a certain amount of sense. Bean raised her eyebrows in response, but didn't argue beyond saying, "Whatever."

Wes's held up his hands. "I get it. It's hard to know who you can trust. If I didn't know it to be true, I might not believe it either."

She looked over Wes's shoulder at the towers on the other side of the river. "So now that you've found him, do you think you can manage to get us to the other side?"

"Do you have any water?" Stephen took another look at his friend. His arms and legs were thin. By the look of him, his muscles had gotten more of a workout in the last hour than they had in the last month. Growing up on the farm had given Stephen a much stronger build. "You just need to tell me where to go and I can row, but we need a drink first if you have one."

Wes threw him a plastic bottle, which Stephen handed to Bean. Only after he'd seen her drink did he take a gulp of his own. Then they grabbed oars and were underway, but the difference in their upper body strength caused the boat to turn, and after the fourth course correction, Stephen took Bean's oar as well as his own. Soon, she was slumped on the seat and her breathing had slowed to a rhythm matching the slap of the wooden oar upon the water. Stephen wanted nothing more than to sleep as well, but there was still another half of the waterway to cross.

"I haven't been entirely honest with you. Who I am," Wes said. "I know why you didn't feel like you could leave home, but you've never asked me why I've not offered to come see you before."

Stephen clenched his teeth together to keep from responding right away. *You can't tell him you know about the cult.* "It's cool. You used a screen name. I get it. I did, too, and my folks aren't exactly the welcoming type."

"What do you know about your parents?"

Wes's question caught Stephen off guard. "Ed and Helen? Well, I know they aren't my birth parents, but they might as well be. I've been with them since I was four. But I've told you that before."

Wes's lips tightened into a fine line. "But why you?"

"Why me what?"

"It was the end of the world as they knew it. People were going mad, kids were dying, and the power grid collapsed. Why would anyone take on some stranger's kid back then?"

"They are just caring people." His eyes tightened at the thought that the people who had sacrificed so much for him his entire life could be suffering now all because of him.

"So caring that they hid you away all your life?"

Stephen frowned. "It wasn't like that at all."

"Tell me then. What was it like?"

"Ed and Helen knew my mom before she died. When the world first went crazy, Helen had gone to check on me and my dad." He shrugged as he rowed, sending the boat off course.

He took another rapid stroke against a current, eager to return them to the mainland.

"So she just decided to walk into your house and take you from your dad because the news reported a few buildings came down?"

"Rioting broke out just down the street. When no one answered the door, she found a way into my house. The streets were too dangerous. She needed a place to wait it out. She didn't expect to find anyone inside. Instead, she found me there. Alone. She didn't have a choice."

"And you're sure about that?"

"Yes."

For a while, the silence was broken by the sound of the oars as they hit the water. Then Wes spoke again. "I know I must sound like a dick, but I wouldn't be if I were you. Sure, I mean. If Helen was telling you the truth, then your dad left you, a four-year-old, home alone." The oar slapped the water. "Who does that?"

"Apparently, my biological father." Water sprayed into Stephen's face as the boat cut through the river.

"And have you ever wondered why?"

Stephen tightened his grip on the oar, as he slammed the wood into the water once more. "Of course I have, but he never came back, and Helen gave up waiting. So, yeah, I guess you can say she took me, but I'm glad she did."

"Steady there. It took me weeks to get this rig seaworthy again. I'd rather you didn't ram it into the pier."

Stephen stabbed the water with the oars in an effort to break the forward momentum. He would have to take Wes's word that they had reached their destination. To his eyes, all that lay ahead of them were more shadows. He cringed as he heard a thud coming from the direction where Wes sat.

"Whoops. Just me getting the flashlight out. Hit the seat."

"You still have a working flashlight?" *That would explain the bright light on the water from before.* Stephen remembered goofing off with one when he was a kid. He had found it in a drawer and had spent several minutes flicking it on and off, but he had gotten a little too noisy with his play, drawing the attention of Helen. She took it away, declaring that it was for emergencies only. Then one day, years later, as he was helping pull together supplies for Ed's upcoming trading run, he found it hidden in the back of a cabinet. He pulled it out with the intention of giving it to Ed, but it hadn't functioned. The batteries inside had corroded the electrical contacts, and he had never seen another. He'd just figured there were none left. Now, seeing Wes's, he suspected it was a device people weren't willing to part with.

Wes pointed the light forward and in its beam, Stephen could now see the pier. He adjusted their trajectory and speed until they were alongside the platform. Wes handed him the flashlight as if it was just another tool and not a family heirloom. "Hold it steady while I tie us up."

Bean sat up, turning her face with a pained squint away from Stephen and over to Wes. "Ugh. Too bright."

"Have a nice nap?" Stephen's shoulders protested as he continued to hold the flashlight up so Wes could see. *The morning is going to be rough. At least I won't have to carry anyone the rest of the way.* He noticed Bean's lips curl into a smile as if she was aware of his thoughts.

"Any nicer and I might think I was sleeping in a bed again."

"All ashore who's coming ashore," called Wes.

Stephen attempted to stand as his hindquarters protested. "How far do we still have to go tonight?"

"A few blocks, but don't worry, we won't have to go much past the barricade."

"Barricade?" Stephen strained his eyes as if he could somehow increase the projection of the flashlight's beam through sheer will alone, but he saw nothing. Dr. Lambda hadn't said anything about a barricade.

"Don't worry, it's not far from here."

"It's not the distance. I am curious as to why there is one."

Stephen heard Bean snort and suspected that wasn't because her nostrils were stopped up, although the air did smell like a combination of mildew and refuse. His own nose wrinkled in disgust.

"You'll find out soon enough," was all Wes offered as an answer.

TEN

A gust of wind took Stephen's breath away as they began their way down the darkened city street. Every step seemed to echo, and Stephen's shoulders tensed.

"What are your views on magic?" asked Wes.

Stephen had almost forgotten about the mass delusions. *Should I be honest, or should I play along?* How should a person respond to a question like that in a situation like this? He chose honesty. "That it doesn't exist."

Wes chuckled. "I'm not surprised you'd say that, but I like to think of it another way. Take technology for example," said Wes as he adjusted his grip on the cylinder in his hand so that his fingerprints fell into series of well-worn grooves. The bulb flared to life. "Imagine if you didn't know what a flashlight was." He swung the beam around until it came to a stop on a wall made of rusted car doors, cracked glass, and broken chairs at least twenty feet high. "I could call myself a wizard right now and, as far as you'd know, I'd be telling the truth." Wes opened his grip, and the barricade of debris was illuminated by the light of the night sky. Crickets resumed their chirping. "I would also be telling the truth when I say you should be careful with things you don't understand." He placed his empty hand on Stephen's shoulder. "And there is a lot here you don't understand. At least not yet anyway."

He gestured for Stephen and Bean to follow as he turned and walked toward the wall, coming to a stop where the collection of garbage appeared darker than the rest. The starlight cast shadows across his face, but not enough to hide his knowing smile. "I'd ask you if you were ready, but I suppose it's already too late for that to matter now. Here we are."

Stephen shut his mouth, which had fallen open at the sight of the barricade. In his mind, he'd expected maybe some boarded-up doors or a car or two in the way. Nothing like the monstrous wall in front of them. It was no wonder the Watch hadn't gotten through yet. He glanced around. Bean stood next to Wes. The light from the flashlight allowed him to see her lips curl in a grin. He couldn't blame her. She didn't know about the affliction or the people inside. As far as she knew, that wall represented safety, but it sent him a different message. *You are so screwed.*

"I kept saying you needed to visit sooner." Wes slapped him on his back.

Stephen sucked in his breath. *Now what?*

Wes led them one by one through a narrow path cutting through the wall. Stephen couldn't get a good sense of the wall's depth due to the labyrinth of twists and turns. He'd never find his way back to the entrance unguided. When they first entered the barricade, the stars overhead could still be seen in the clear night sky, but little by little, their light was obstructed as they continued deeper inside.

The path stopped. Wes leaned against the wall and turned off the flashlight, making the darkness around them absolute. "Home sweet home." A series of six mechanical pops broke the silence. Then a green glow blossomed, illuminating Wes's hand on a wall-mounted keypad. Wes reached out and twisted a doorknob Stephen hadn't noticed before. A yellow light shining through the crack was Stephen's only warning before Wes pushed open the door. Stephen squinted as his eyes adjusted.

"Wow, that's bright," whispered Stephen, as if his subconscious was afraid he might scare the light away. "Where is it all coming from? How?"

"See? Magic. It exists." Wes's grin came close to splitting his face in two as he stretched his arms out as if he could touch all the fixtures. "It's amazing what you can power when all the windows in a building are made of solar panels."

"But it's so dark on the outside." Stephen frowned.

"Another trick also known as privacy glass. We found that leaving the lights on for the entire world to see attracted the wrong sort of people. When the lights come on, the glass goes dark," Wes answered. His arms dropped to his side, and the smile left his face. Wes nodded at the door. "It's also why the doors are locked and alarmed at all times."

Seeing him under the steady glow of artificial light, it occurred to Stephen that Wes looked nothing like the person he'd imagined playing the video game. He hadn't thought about it when they first met on the pier. Then again, it was dark out. *And you were getting ready to kill him; don't forget that part.* Stephen crushed that last thought. Even if it hadn't been Wes, he still would have figured out another way to take the boat. *Of course, you would have,* the small voice whispered.

"Unfortunately," continued Wes, oblivious to the darkness of Stephen's thoughts, "the panels power the lights, water filtration, and circulation systems, but little else, meaning no elevators." Wes turned down another hallway on the right where another door stood marked with a figure descending a flight of stairs and away from an icon shaped like a flame. "Just be glad I live on the third floor and not the thirteenth like some people."

Bean arched an eyebrow. "I suspect the people who live up there would say the view is better."

"You have water? As in running water?"

Wes laughed as he gestured for them to follow. "Mont, my friend. Prepare to have your mind blown."

Stephen's lower back and sides ached as they made their way through the lobby, mirroring the pain across his shoulders. He might have more muscle mass than Wes, but it was clear his build wasn't that of a regular rower. "So, how many people live here?" he asked as he massaged his side.

"Eh." Wes shrugged as he pulled open a door marked as a stairwell entrance. "Most everyone keeps to themselves. I think the only ones who might know everyone are Finn and maybe my dad."

"Who's Finn?" asked Bean before Stephen could say anything.

It was almost as if Bean could read his mind. He wanted to smile or joke about how they were now finishing each other's sentences, but even the muscles in his cheeks were exhausted. At this point, he wasn't quite sure he would have the energy to make it up the stairs.

"You'll get the grand tour tomorrow. For now, follow me."

The muscles in Stephen's side and calves burned as they climbed the last flight. When Wes stopped at the first door in the adjacent hallway, Stephen's vision blurred in relief. Wes touched the handle. There was a series of clicking sounds and another green light blazed. Inside, more lights dawned in a warm yellow glow, illuminating a large couch along one wall framed by a number of thriving houseplants. A large pane of black glass filled another wall.

Wes continued through the apartment to an open-style kitchenette where he placed the flashlight onto a stone counter. He then pulled out a pair of drinking glasses from one of the cabinets. Stephen's eyes nearly bulged out of their sockets as Wes filled each with clear water from a polished steel faucet. When Wes handed a Stephen one of the glasses, he stared at it, as if it might disappear if he blinked. Then he took a sip. He almost spit it out in surprise. Not only did it not have a mineral taste, the clear water was also cold.

Wes gave the other glass to Bean, who drank as eagerly as Stephen had. If she was as surprised, she covered it well. *Oh come on, even you have to be a little impressed.*

"Scott? Is that you?" a voice called out from down the hall.

"Right." Wes blushed. "I got sidetracked before. About my real name—"

"You were supposed to be back at sunset." A man emerged from one of the back rooms. White tufts of hair ringed his otherwise bald head. A matching white mustache covered his top lip. "You know better. If you were missing after curfew—"

"I know, Dad. I meant to leave a note."

"What have I told you about lying, son?"

"That practice makes perfect?" Wes laughed.

The man patted his pocket and took out a pair of glasses as thick as the ones Wes wore. Placing them on his nose, he directed his attention to Stephen. "Now, who is this?"

Wes slapped Stephen on his back again, almost causing Stephen to drop his glass. "This is the friend I told you about. Mont. Mont, this is my dad." Wes paused as if debating whether to say more.

His father filled in the rest, "Dr. Edward Thomas." He extended his hand in greeting.

Stephen stood in shock at hearing the man's name. His hand stayed by his side. *First, Wes shows up on the riverbank as if summoned out of thin air, and then his dad is also named Ed Thomas?* The coincidences were getting more unbelievable by the second.

The corner of Bean's mouth quirked up as she offered her hand in his place. "I'm Bean. Thanks for the water. If I didn't come across as grateful to meet your son on the road earlier tonight, I want to correct that impression now."

The pain between Stephen's shoulders and back refused to be ignored any longer. He gave into a yawn and grimaced. Even his jaw hurt.

A wave of scarlet cascaded under Wes's skin from the top of his head down into the collar of his shirt. "Oh, man, I am so sorry. I completely forgot you'd be exhausted." He glanced at Bean, then at the couch, then at a room through another doorway that likely contained a bed. His lips compressed into a thin line. "Like I said before though, I didn't expect you to bring company." Wes's words trailed off.

"Don't worry about me," said Bean. "I can sleep on the floor."

"No," both Wes and Stephen replied in unison, causing Wes to throw his head back in laughter before muttering something that sounded like "great minds." Wes's attention snapped back on Stephen. "There's a thought." Wes's forehead knit as his eyes took on a vacant appearance.

"What is?" Stephen asked while looking longingly at the couch.

Then the dazed look was gone and Wes was once again smiling. "Finn will let me stay in his spare room. I'll need to go there and tell him about you two anyway." Wes sheepishly looked at his father. "I mean, that is, if you don't mind letting them stay here without me?"

"I suppose." His father looked at Stephen and Bean. His lips twisted, sending his mustache up like a furry cloud. "Unless you two would prefer to share a room."

Bean laughed. "We're not like that."

Stephen's cheeks burned, but that was due more to Bean's quick denial than Wes's father's implication. Wes also looked stricken. "I didn't even think of that," he said. He flared crimson from neck to forehead. "I mean, sure. That would work, too. If that's what you both want."

Bean caught Stephen's eye. "I'd settle for sleeping any place where I don't have to listen to anyone's snoring."

"I don't snore."

"Well, I guess that is settled then." Wes's father turned to his son. "We'll discuss this more in the morning." Then he disappeared back down the hall the way he came.

Stephen closed his eyes and gulped down the rest of his water, enjoying the cool sensation that followed as the liquid flowed down his throat while he regained equilibrium. When he opened them, Wes was gone, leaving only he and Bean in the kitchenette.

"I hope you know I meant it," said Bean.

"Meant what?" His thoughts went to her quick dismissal of their relationship.

"Meant you can take the bed."

"Don't be ridiculous. Of course you can have it." He tried to laugh, but it became another yawn.

"Why is offering you the bedroom ridiculous when even a blind person could see you need the sleep more than I do?"

Stephen sputtered. "Because...because you're a—"

"A *what*? Bean scowled. "A girl?" She closed the distance between them until she was so close he thought he could almost hear her heartbeat. "You think I can't handle a night on a couch after a week in the woods? What do you think I am?

Some delicate flower? Well, I am sorry if your whole sense of masculinity is feeling a little threatened right now, but it just needs to get over itself. I am just as strong as you, if not stronger, especially when you are this tired. If I say I can get by sleeping on the couch, then I damn well mean it."

The heat of her eyes locked on his and pulled at him like gravity. He was struck by how beautiful she looked when angry, yet at the same time, he wanted nothing more than to replace that scowl on her face with a smile. *Not a girl*, he thought. *A woman*. He closed his eyes as his body leaned in toward hers. And then he was falling backward.

"Hey. You shoved me" he shouted, incredulous.

She reached out a hand and helped pull him back upright. "You fell asleep on your feet."

"I wasn't asleep."

"Could have fooled me. You were practically snoring. And yes, you do." Without releasing his hand, she led him through the open doorway into Wes's bedroom. Then the warmth of her hand vanished as she disappeared back the way they'd come.

As Stephen collapsed onto the mattress, he thought he heard the apartment door open and shut again, but couldn't summon the energy to open his eyes or care. Instead, his last thought before sleep claimed him was, *What just happened?*

ELEVEN

Dozens of travel posters covering gray walls filled Stephen's vision. Disoriented, he sat up on the bed and placed his feet on the floor. As he attempted to banish the last of sleep from his head, memories of events that had led him to this place trickled in. While it came as some relief to know where he was, Stephen had no idea how much time had passed while he slept. Aside from the posters, there were no windows or clocks on the wall.

He stretched against the protests of his muscles. However long he'd slept, it hadn't been long enough. A sound of doors closing and water running caught his ear. At least one other person was awake and moving around in the apartment. He padded over to the bedroom door, opening it a crack.

"Good morning, sunshine," Wes called out from the direction of the kitchenette. Stephen heard the faucet turn off as he returned to the main room. "We were beginning to wonder if we were going to need to go to more extreme methods to wake you." Wes jiggled a raised glass and pretended to toss its contents at Stephen.

"If you'd spent much time off this island, you might not find wasting water quite so funny," said Bean taking the water from Wes and draining it in a single movement. "Ah." Her face radiated pure pleasure. "Then again, why would you ever want to leave?" The knit hat she'd worn even while she slept over the past few days no longer covered her head. Her hair was short, falling an inch or so below her ears, with a streak of pure white cutting through the balance of pale yellow. She touched her hair as if embarrassed by its condition. Stephen's gaze followed Bean's finger as it pushed a strand of hair away. "Running water also means showers." She took her cap out of a back pocket and pulled it over her head, hiding her hair from view once more. "You should try one."

The hat brought his attention back to her face. Her green eyes twinkled. Wes poured another glass, handing it to Stephen when full. "Here. Saw your supplies—or should I say, I didn't see them. You were lucky to make it to the pier when you did."

That's an understatement. Stephen winced at the thought of how empty the pack had become. *If Wes hadn't found them when he had...* He let the thought trail off unanswered.

"My dad would not approve. He's always going on about how everyone needs to stay hydrated," said Wes as he moved about in the kitchenette. Stephen's stomach growled in appreciation as a large slice of bread and a piece of fruit appeared on a plate in front of him. It was all Stephen could do not to dig into it like a beast. "Food is well and good," Wes mimicked his father's tone from the night before, "but water can make the difference between life and death." The door to the other bedroom opened as Stephen licked the last crumbs off his fingers, revealing Wes's father. "Speaking of which"— Wes didn't look up—"Finn says Gavin needs you."

Wes's father frowned. "Gavin can wait his turn, the same as everyone else."

Wes glanced at his father. "Do you want to be the one to tell him that?"

Wes's father's arm fell back to his side. "Fine," he muttered as he shuffled back to the door. He picked up a black bag and removed a ball cap from where it hung on the wall. "I tell them not to overextend, but what do I know? I'm only a licensed doctor. *The* licensed doctor, I should add."

Wes rolled his eyes in the direction of the apartment door where his father had exited. The gesture should have put Stephen at ease. Instead, Stephen's shoulders tightened. A sensation much like an itch danced across his skin. He had forgotten that other people lived in the building. Last evening, he had been too tired to care, but now that he was more awake, he found the idea of so many strangers in close proximity unnerving. "Why does he want to meet with us again?"

Wes shrugged. "He likes to talk to newcomers. You know, to make sure they will fit in, but it's no big deal."

Yeah, no big deal. It's not as if I have the lives of my parents and an entire tower resting on my first impression or anything. "And what happens if I don't make the cut?" Stephen joked.

Wes sent a pointed glance at Bean. *Had they talked while I was asleep? And if so, about what?* The hairs along Stephen's arms prickled, as if a winter wind had stirred them. Wes wasn't telling him something. He caught Bean's eye and she turned away. *And Bean knows it.* Stephen's stomach turned. *You are overreacting. Your stomach's probably just not used to having real food in it again.* Another troubling thought occurred to him. *Did Dr. Lambda say paranoia was another symptom?*

"You don't look so good. I can ask for more time."

He'd lost too much time already. "Nah, I'll be fine. Lead the way."

Finn lived on the sixth floor of the building, but unlike the other floors they'd passed, a black panel fit into the wall beside the stairwell's exit door. As they approached, the panel transitioned from black to a glowing pale blue.

Wes paused. "We don't have to go in. We can go back to my apartment if you want to rest more."

"Now is fine."

"Are sure? You still have bags under your eyes."

"I don't think this Finn person will care how I look."

"What about you, Bean?"

"Do you not want us to meet Finn?" She tucked a stray hair back under her cap.

Wes blanched. "No, no, that's not what I am getting at. It's just—"

"It's just *what*?" Bean teased out. "Oh, I get it. Are you afraid we'll embarrass you? After seeing how this guy makes a first impression, I can't say I blame you."

The color returned to his face. "That's not it. Forget about it. I was trying to be considerate." Wes squared his shoulders and stood in front. The panel's glow pulsed and returned to black. Another green light illuminated on the door handle. As Wes swung the door open, he commented, "Finn can be a little old school. You'll get used to it."

They passed several doors before coming to a stop behind one that looked identical to all the others. Wes glanced back but did not reach out to open the door. "Aren't you going to knock?" Stephen asked.

Wes shook his head. "No need." The door opened. "We wouldn't have gotten this far unless he knew we were here."

A dark-haired man stood waiting on the other side in the center of a near-featureless room. He looked to be in his early thirties, although Stephen hadn't been around enough other people to gauge a person's age with confidence, especially younger people. The plague had been hard on their generation. There was something about his eyes, however, that made him seem much older. *Being a teenager during the end of the world would do that to you.*

His hair, which was neither short nor long, swept back behind his earlobes, but the most striking part about him was the clothes he wore. His shirt was brilliant white and moved with him like a second skin as he crossed the room. Stephen stared in envy. White was impractical, and even if you found something in that color, it almost never fit and it didn't stay that way long.

"Mont, is it?" The man reached out with a hand that lacked dirt under the nails, sun-hardened skin, or other scars.

Stephen glanced down at it, unsure whether to take it. *Were delusions contagious?* The man seemed sane enough to him. *Sane enough to live the easy life.* "And I take it you are Finn," Stephen replied, grasping the man's hand in his own.

Finn released Stephen's hand with a quick nod and turned, extending it to Bean. "And you are? Bean, is it? That's a unique name."

Bean looked at Finn's hand but didn't take it. "So I've been told." She glanced Stephen's way. Her lips twitched as if daring him to laugh at a shared secret. It was a look that gave him hope that in spite of her protest the night before, she wasn't as opposed to the idea there might be more between them than she'd let on.

Finn's eyebrows rose for a moment before he dropped his hand back to his side. "Now why don't you both come in the rest of the way and make yourselves comfortable." Finn gestured for the others to follow him into his suite of rooms. "Can I get you anything to drink?"

"I don't suppose you have anything to eat?" Stephen asked as his stomach rumbled loud enough for the others in the room to notice.

Finn pointed to Wes. "Of course. Scott here will take care of getting us all some food while I get to know you both a little better; won't you, Scott?" Wes hesitated before nodding and disappearing out the way they had come.

"Normally, I prefer to meet one-on-one with our new arrivals unless they're…" Finn's words trailed off suggestively. Stephen's shoulders tightened. Together or not, he had no intention of leaving Bean alone with a stranger, let alone a potential deranged cult leader. Bean made no motion to suggest she was willing to go to another room either. Finn sighed. "So, not a couple, but you don't keep secrets from each other?"

Stephen fought the urge to laugh. *All we have is secrets.* "We've been through a lot."

Finn lowered himself into a velvet couch and motioned for the two of them to take a seat on the opposite sofa. "You know my name. What else do you know about our group?"

"To be honest, not much," said Stephen. *You need to earn his trust.* "You have a nice setup. I've never seen any place like it."

Finn leaned back in his chair and grinned. "Life here has its advantages. Are you interested in staying?"

Careful now. Don't seem too eager. If he so much as suspects you have another motive for being here, it will be game over.

"It seems nice enough, but I don't know."

"Let me guess. You've heard rumors."

"Maybe." Stephen glanced toward the door. How much should he say? He suspected most people wouldn't appreciate being told they were considered delusional cult leaders. *Don't forget the part about the affliction causing homicidal tendencies*, the small voice whispered.

"I assure you the truth about us is even more unbelievable. At least it can be for the average person, but you're not average, are you?"

Stephen's brow knit. *It's a trick question. Abort. Abort.* "I wouldn't know. I didn't grow up around a lot of people to compare, to." *Well done.*

Finn nodded his head. "Would you like to find out?"

Bean's pinkie grazed his.

"I suppose." *What's the worst that could happen?*

TWELVE

"Close your eyes and think of a wall." Finn paused. "Both of you."

Stephen cocked his head to the side at Finn's instruction.

"It will make sense soon."

Stephen glanced at Bean, who shrugged and closed her eyes. *Anything you can do…* A soft noise like waves crashing filled the room. Stephen had no idea where the sound came from. He squeezed his eyes shut tighter in an attempt to isolate and ignore the noise. The noise became more distracting. A sound like someone striking a metal plate joined the mix. Stephen grit his teeth. He couldn't afford to mess this up.

All he could imagine was a large black rectangle. "Try to relax," said Finn. Stephen took a breath and let the muscles around his eyelids go limp. "Good. Now try again. This time, relax your whole body." The waves continued to crash. "Focus on the wall. Only the wall." The noise grew muffled. The couch's softness was far too welcoming. He felt himself drifting off.

"Now imagine there is a door in the wall. Visualize it down to the grain." Finn's voice brought Stephen out of his half-dream state.

He kept his eyes closed as he imagined a brick wall and a small blue door. As he concentrated, the door became clearer. In his mind's eye, he visualized it made of the type of wood he'd seen in the barn, with streaks of chipped paint. Oil rubbed bronze hinges and handles decorated its surface.

"Now open it."

The door opened with ease, but there was nothing but blackness on the other side.

"You find a river." Stephen heard Finn's muffled voice command.

The blackness surged at him like a torrent of water. Stephen's eyelids remained shut, though not by his choice now. He was frozen, as if the deluge assaulted his mind. He tried to call out, but no words would come.

"Let yourself bathe in it."

Bathe? I'll be lucky not to drown, Stephen thought as he fought against the surge of darkness. His imagination was trying to kill him. *Right. It's your imagination.* Stephen focused his thoughts and imagined his arms. He visualized picking them up and moving them, forcing the darkness to part.

Still, for every inch he swam, the unseen force pulled him back. It seemed as if he would never break the dark water's surface. Without a frame of reference, Stephen couldn't tell if he was swimming up or making his problem worse. His heart raced as pressure continued to build around him. *Help!* He wanted to cry out, though that would be pointless. *If only there was some light in here.*

A faint mote of light, like the furthermost star, bloomed into existence, as if summoned by his command. As mysterious as the light's source was, it was as familiar as a mother's touch.

"Take control of the flow," commanded a new voice. It was deeper than Bean's and cooler, almost robotic, and yet feminine. It reminded him of the announcer from his video game.

Is this what it's like to lose your mind? Stephen's lungs screamed in need as he fought to take a breath. He was drowning in the inky water. *Wake up. Wake up. Wake up.* He wanted to scream. He locked his focus on the pinprick of light. The sense of direction it offered kept him from losing himself to panic. *If only it was brighter.*

A second light bloomed into existence. "You have to take control, Stephen. Now!" Bean's voice joined the other woman's, echoing her command. *Was she experiencing something like this, too?* The second light was closer, but still out of reach. Stephen's imagined arms ached as he swum to reach it.

The body that he'd visualized began to shake, and he could feel his temperature drop. Muscles that should have been a figment of his imagination cramped. Still, the light remained always a fingertip away. *You aren't going to make it.* His focus fractured as the lights had begun to fade. *Let there be light*, he wanted to shout, but no new lights appeared. *Please. Don't go.*

Thoughts became harder to form until he was left with one thought as much instinct as a word. *Help.* The lights pulsated once as he reached toward them one last time. Then both were gone, and darkness surrounded him again. Only this time, a warmth wove its way around and through the nothingness where he'd once imagined his hand. His consciousness clung to the sensation like a lifeline. Focusing on the warmth, he willed himself to rise out of the depths.

After so much darkness, the color of the painted door threatened to blind him as he emerged from the dark waters. Hovering above its torrent, he imagined a valve in the wall until he could see it as detailed as he had seen the door. He twisted it, and the flow below him slowed from a river to a more manageable flow.

Curious, he dipped one re-imagined finger into the stream. The water this time was warm to the touch. Like the door and the valve, the stream became more detailed as he focused his attention on it. As the image sharpened, he began to notice subtle differences in its makeup. The stream wasn't black at all, but instead, made up of thousands of colors and layers upon layers of images.

This time when Stephen attempted to open his eyes, his lids complied. Bean's face filled his vision. He glanced down and saw her hand grasping his own. The warmth must have been from her. *She saved me.* Her lips curved up into a sly smile. Stephen's eyes widened as blood rushed to his face. *She did not just read your mind.* He thought in a panic. *Because that would be impossible.* He blinked several times. *Yeah, because everything that's happened today is just so possible.*

"I was beginning to worry," Finn said.

Stephen snapped out of his thoughts. He had almost forgotten he and Bean weren't alone. He looked to the source of his irritation. "You could have warned me," he stated in accusation.

"I'm sorry, Stephen. I thought based on what you'd accomplished on your own, I expected it to be easier for you."

Even though he no longer saw the stream, Stephen was still aware of its presence, like smelling seawater or hearing gulls miles from the shore. Only, he detected this stream with a sense he'd never known before. He corrected himself. "What did you do to me?"

"I helped you remove a block, opening your mind to the data stream." Finn waved his hand as if almost dying from a very real case of information overload was a non-event. "It is a funny thing, the mind. It erects barriers, protecting itself from what it isn't able to process unassisted. You aren't the first to have such a barrier, though I will admit yours was more difficult to get around than most, almost as if someone else had erected it. Now I'm curious. Many of my people report experiencing something like dipping their toes into a stream or babbling brook the first time they accessed the data stream with intention. What was it like for you? A river?"

"River?" Stephen's jaw gaped. "More like I was under the bloody ocean."

Finn's eyebrows rose even further. More to himself he said, "I knew you'd be strong, but I'd never suspected..." He sniffed. "Well done." Louder, he added, "Look around the room, what do you see?"

THIRTEEN

He hypnotized you. That's all, Stephen repeated over and over in his head. *The river. The voices. None of it was real. It could also be the affliction,* the small voice added. *Next stop, crazy town; population: you.* He rubbed his face. *You aren't helping.* He blinked. Subtle colors twisted and flowed like clouds passing through the sky over the walls Stephen would have sworn were only gray when they'd arrived. *You are the one arguing with yourself.*

"Yes." Finn stood. "It was real, but at the same time, no it wasn't."

"I don't understand." Stephen looked to Bean, only realizing after a heartbeat that Finn's answer was to an unspoken question. Her brow wrinkled.

"Let's start with your parents. What do you know about them?"

"Only that they are gone and I was raised by friends of theirs."

"Their names are Ed and Helen Thomas."

It was a statement, not a question. Was the man reading his mind? Stephen tensed. What if Finn was reading it now? What if he knew of the deal with Dr. Lambda? He wet his upper lip and tasted a bead of sweat. The tower's defenses were no joke. The Watch might not succeed, but Ed and Helen would be as good as dead. *I've failed.*

"Before you ask, I'm not reading your mind."

Stephen's shoulders sagged. *Because that's impossible. Isn't it?*

"I don't have to. Your expression gives you away." He pointed at Stephen's face and made a circling gesture. "About your name, Scott told me. In fact, he's told me a lot about you."

"I see." Stephen's lips tightened. He buried his thoughts of Dr. Lambda and the Watch, in case Finn was lying. "He's never mentioned anything about you."

"Well, I like to consider myself a bit of an enigma, but we were talking about your story. Scott calls you Mont."

Pull yourself together. Stephen bit his lip. *Pretend you aren't losing your mind and this is a normal conversation.* "Yeah."

"But that's not your real name. Is it?"

Stephen shook his head.

"Don't be embarrassed. We're all survivors here. Many of us have used aliases at one point in time or another. Take Scott, for example. Has he told you his real name is Prescott yet?" Finn's gaze bore into his own, daring him to look away. "No, I'm not surprised he hasn't. After all, everything you two have been doing could have gotten you both into a bit of trouble out there, were the wrong sort of people to find out first." Finn looked toward the wall as if it contained a window. "Lucky for you, the Watch is no friend of ours, as you no doubt have already guessed, or you wouldn't have come." His attention returned to Stephen. "But back to names and why I've been looking forward this meeting for a while now. Your real name is Stephen Dronigh."

Stephen froze. He might have mentioned Ed and Helen's name to Wes, but he was sure he'd never told him his real name and he knew he hadn't told him his birth last name. "How?"

"How do I know your name?" Finn leaned back. "Well, that took a little more detective work. I've known your friend, Scott—or Wes if you prefer—for years, from almost birth really. When Wes told me about your little game, at first I didn't believe him. I dismissed it as a joke. It wouldn't be the first. When your world consists of twenty floors and a handful of miles, boredom can be your worst enemy. There is always some prank going on."

Finn smiled, as if savoring some memory. "But then he kept talking about you and that there were people living away from our island who were able to not only access but maintain a network. With all the challenges on the outside, I found it strange that someone would set one up for something as silly as a game."

"It's not that silly," grumbled Stephen.

"Oh, I am sure it has taught you all valuable sorts of things, like trash-talking. Scott shows off those particular skills daily."

"It teaches things like tactics—and weaponry, too."

Finn smiled. "And have you had to put these skills of yours to regular use outside the game?"

Stephen didn't need to see a mirror to know that his cheeks were now as red as Wes's hair. "I live in the middle of nowhere. I thought it would be good to be prepared."

Finn's smile faded. "My apologies, I forgot what it is like out there." He stood up and walked behind his couch. "So then one day, months later, Scott—I mean, Wes—mentioned something even more remarkable than an online friend." Finn glanced at Bean. "Are you still sure you want her to hear the next part?"

Stephen nodded. *It's not like she wouldn't simply ask me about it the minute we left the room.*

"He and his friend shared more than the enjoyment of a video game." Finn's fingers tapped the back of the couch twice before stepping away. "Your guardians and his parents just happened to have the same name. You see, his mother's name was Helen, too."

"Their names aren't that unique." Stephen shrugged, though if he wasn't trying to school his features, his eyebrows might have launched into the ceiling at Finn's revelation. *Yeah, it's totally normal. Helen, Ed, Thomas. All common names. I wouldn't be surprised if there once were tens of thousands of them. There is no reason to freak out. No reason at all.*

Finn began strolling around the room until he came to a stop by the color-shifting wall where the undulating lines blended together until Stephen could almost make out a shape. "You might not see it as anything more than a simple coincidence, but I have always prided myself in my ability to recognize a bigger picture, and that was one coincidence too many." The colors shifted, and the phantom image was no more. "It made me start to wonder about your story. And you."

It was one too many coincidences for Stephen as well, though he tried to hide it from showing on his face. "Me? Sorry to break it to you, but there isn't all that much there. I live in the middle of nowhere and like to go online and play a game from time to time. End of story."

Finn stepped away from the wall and turned to Stephen. The corner of his lips quirked up. "But that's just it. How has a person in the middle of nowhere, as you put it, managed to get a game back up and running well enough to be able to connect with the systems we have in place here?"

"It wasn't hard," Stephen muttered. He groaned inward. *Once again, way to win friends and influence people.*

Finn's half-smile evaporated once more. His jawline hardened. "Yes, it is. I designed it that way." Stephen sensed more, then saw Bean tense by his side. "So, when I found out some random unknown person from hundreds of miles away had somehow managed to hack his way past our defenses, I had to learn all about him. After a little digging, I learned who and, even more importantly, *what* you are." Finn eyes locked on Stephen's and burned with excitement.

"I'm not a hacker." The argument sounded weak, even to his own ears.

"You are. But you are so much more than that, too." Finn shrugged as the humor returned once more to his expression. "As you should be, considering who your parents are."

"I told you. I don't know them."

Finn shook his head. "But that's my point." Finn returned to his couch, but did not sit down. "I do." Meeting his eyes, he said, "Wes isn't the only one here I've known almost since birth. I knew your father. His name was Alan, and you should know his original discovery is what made all of this possible. Which reminds me, you didn't answer my earlier question. When I stood over there, against the wall, what did you see?"

Fourteen

The colors continued to flow across the wall; some grew while others shrunk, creating more shapes. *The test isn't over.* "It was a raven."

"A raven? How interesting. Why a raven?"

Was that the wrong answer? "I thought I saw wings and a beak."

Finn shook his head. "I meant why did you call it a raven and not an eagle or crow?"

"I don't know. Because that's what popped into my head?"

"How about you, Bean? I've been going on and on about Stephen here, but that was rude, and I apologize. What did you see?"

The room fell silent. Stephen swallowed his guilt as he waited for Bean to answer. He'd forgotten Finn was testing both of them. *What if she saw something else?* Another thought occurred to Stephen. *What if she hadn't seen anything at all? Did she now think he was crazy?*

Bean's face was that of a statue, hard and as pale as marble. Her eyes tightened, and she glared at Finn. "A doll. I saw my sister's doll."

Did that mean she had the genetic marker, too? Stephen didn't know whether to sigh in relief or in concern.

Finn's eyes softened. "For what it is worth, you both—" Finn's eyes took on a vacant expression similar to how Wes's looked earlier. "Ah, your food has arrived."

The door opened, and a man carrying a pair of small loaves entered. He threw the loaves Stephen's way as he crossed the room, stopping next to Finn. "Sorry, I know you hate interruptions, but we've got company."

"How many this time?" Gone was his cordial tone, replaced by that of a military commander.

"Two that we've spotted," the newcomer replied.

"So there could be at least one or two more," Finn muttered. "Let everyone know to meet in the lobby. I'm on my way down."

The newcomer nodded and returned the way he came.

"What's going on?" asked Stephen, passing one loaf to Bean as he tore into his. He'd always had an appetite and never enough food, but his constant hunger was beginning to be ridiculous. *Man, is this bread good.*

"Some uninvited guests," answered Finn. He smiled. "We'll send them on their way. Nothing to worry about." Finn flung the door open and marched out into the hallway. He glanced over his shoulder at Stephen. "However, you will want to see this."

Bean shrugged her shoulders. "Why not?"

Finn smiled, but the expression showed no joy. He stormed down the stairs without turning to verify that they'd done as instructed.

They met a group of the tower's residents in the lobby at the base of the stairwell, including the man who'd brought the loaves. Stephen searched for Wes and was struck by how young they all looked, but his friend was not among them. The others parted as Finn made his way into the center of the group. Stephen's heart began to race. It took him more than a few beats to realize that the lack of wrinkles was putting him on edge. *Nothing weird about that. This used to be a big city,* he reminded himself. *There are bound to be more young people than Earthaven.* Stephen remembered that Wes's father was working somewhere in the building. *He's not your age.* Which meant, there had to be other adults around. *Just not in this room.*

"Report," Finn barked.

A girl with a face smeared with dirt stepped forward. Some of her hair had slipped out of a tie at the back of her neck, but she didn't seem to notice. Her clothes were more in line with Bean and Stephen's own, making the cleanliness of Finn's white shirt even more striking. "It's the Watch again. Spotted the gaudy armband a mile away."

Finn's lips turned down, but the frown did not reach his eyes. "I'd hoped they'd learned their lesson the last time."

"He appears to be armed."

Finn waved the comment away. "I suppose that's to be expected."

Another voice spoke up. "I spotted a second one coming in from the North, fifteen to thirty minutes behind. Stephen did a double take as he located the voice's owner. Somehow, Stephen hadn't noticed him in the small group. The others shifted, providing Stephen with a better view. It didn't help. It was as if the speaker, another twenty-something, was a floating talking head. It took a second or two before Stephen realized that it was an optical illusion. The guy's shirt had some sort of patterning on it that made it seem as if the design was blending into the background all on its own. It wasn't the sort of camouflage featured in Stephen's video game, but that was exactly what it was.

"I thought that route was closed."

"It was last time I patrolled," said the floating head, "but it's wide open now. A train could pass through it."

"What do you think they want?" asked another girl, even younger in appearance than the first. She held the fabric in her hands, which she handed to Finn as she spoke. Finn's hands moved at a near inhuman speed, covering his brilliant white shirt with her offering. He touched a spot near his neck, and his torso also seemed to blend into the background no matter how he moved. He touched his waist, and the color of his trousers shifted, mixing with the shadows. The effect made Stephen sick to his stomach.

They could be here to help with your story like Dr. Lambda said. This is your chance to win their trust. "Um, they might have followed us," answered Stephen. More of the group swapped out their regular garb for the pattern-shifting garments. It was an act of supreme will not to turn away. "I had some trouble a few days ago, and well…"

The girl laughed. "I guess that's unlucky for them." A couple of the others in the group also joined in.

"I thought Wes reported finding you by the river," said the man who had brought them the bread.

"Gavin," said Finn "there will be time for our guest to tell us the rest of his story later." Finn placed his hand on the pad by the door. The green light blinked twice. "Gavin, Baron, you take point. The rest of you, you know what to do." The group nodded before they disappeared into several different directions. "Stick to the shadows," cautioned Finn as he held the door open so that Stephen and Bean could pass. A narrow cord appeared in Stephen's hand. "Make sure you don't drop that. You don't want to be stuck out here." The door shut on silent hinges as Finn pulled a hood over his head and climbed a ladder that had gone unnoticed the day before.

Then, they were in the maze of the barricade but several levels higher than the one they'd taken before. Stephen couldn't afford to focus on anything other than each step as they made their way through a path of twists and turns. A single misstep off the narrow ledge would send him tumbling to the ground. Higher they climbed, until they reached the barricade's top edge. Bean poked his shoulder and then gestured out to the street below. Stephen didn't see anything moving, but Bean dropped into a crouch. Finn glanced down and grinned as he followed suit.

Stephen noticed the movement that must have caught Bean's eye. A figure crept along the base of the building across the street wearing the armband of the Watch as reported. The figure stood, frozen for a moment, like an animal testing the wind. Then it raced across the final feet to the base of the barricade's wall.

"I thought we made it clear your people weren't welcome here the last time," a voice boomed from below. Stephen thought it was Gavin's, but it sounded deeper and more intimidating than it had before, so he couldn't be sure.

"You are harboring a fugitive," the man with the armband replied. "Perhaps more than one." Broken glass scattered around the base of the wall, reflecting the yellow rays of the late morning sun. It blinded Stephen as he sought a better view of the figure below.

"Fugitive from the Watch?" Gavin called out. "And why should we care? You have no authority here."

"I am within my legal rights." A cloud passed across the sun dimming the glare from below. It was enough for Stephen to see the newcomer pull open the side of his jacket. Stephen made out an emblem of some kind on his chest, but then the cloud passed, blinding him again.

"Legal? Under what law?" Gavin's voice echoed across the otherwise empty street. "Not any laws we recognize." Stephen was struck by how old and formal he sounded and wondered if this particular speech was coached.

"If you do not willingly turn over the fugitives, you will give me no choice but to take them and you by force."

Disembodied laughter echoed through the square in all directions. Stephen thought he saw the Watchman pat his pocket. "You won't be so cocky once that tower of yours comes down."

The Watchman is taking things too far, thought Stephen. With or without magical powers, the people in the tower were not messing around. *You've made my case. Now walk away and let me do my job*, he urged. *No one has to get hurt.*

"Is that a fact?" said the voice Stephen recognized as belonging to the floating head, who he assumed must be Baron.

The man puffed out his chest as he scanned the barricade, searching for the source of the other voice. Another cloud, larger than before, floated across the sun's light. Stephen took advantage of the temporary extra shadow it offered. He shifted his body for a better look.

"We know about your plan."

Do they? Stephen looked around the barricade wall in a panic. There was no place for him to go but down if he needed to get away, and no chance either Ed or Helen would be freed from the Watch.

The contempt in Baron's voice was palpable and sounded much closer to the man on the street than it had a minute before. Stephen wondered if the newcomer also sensed it. "That's right. We know about your friend up the road. You think you brought reinforcements." Baron's voice now sounded like it originated directly in front of the Watchman, but still, no one else could be seen on the street. The teen might as well be a ghost. "You didn't bring enough."

No camouflage is that good, thought Stephen. *Or is it?* He looked again for a shadow or motion. Anything that might give away the teen's location to a careful eye, but the teen remained undetectable.

"Good. Then you know there are even more behind that one." The Watchman stepped back and looked around the empty city street. "This is your last chance. This goes for your other creepy friends, too. Don't think I don't know they are watching." Louder, he shouted, "You are all guilty of obstructing justice. Give up now or else."

The Watchman opened his jacket the rest of the way and pulled out a gun, but the movement also exposed a belt lined with explosives. He turned so that everyone bearing witness to the scene might see the implicit threat, and then he took another step back so that there was no part of him hidden in shadow.

Out in the open, Stephen could see the Watchman had to be in his sixties if not seventies. His thin gray hair lay in strings upon his head, and his face had a pasty yellow pallor. Deep grooves like drooping whiskers ran the length of his face from eye to chin, making him look like a man who had seen too much, and yet a fire remained in his eyes. The Watchman's gaze panned the barricade. He smiled. Stephen should have been concerned. If not for the gun or explosives, then because of the face wielding them. Instead, Stephen was relieved seeing the man's face. It could have been the face of anyone Stephen had ever seen or met in Earthaven. Then Stephen squinted as he got a better look. It *was* a face he'd seen in Earthaven.

FIFTEEN

Bean's body tensed beside Stephen like a cat readying to pounce. She recognized the man, too, but based on her body language, Stephen suspected there was no love between them.

Finn's voice whispered in Stephen's ear. "You have a choice to make."

Stephen's eyes widened. "What do you mean?" he heard himself asking, though his gut told him he knew the answer.

"Choose to go with him and nothing more will happen, to him anyway. What your fate will be once off this island, however, would not be mine to say. Or join us and become the person I know your father would have wanted you to be."

Your father left a four-year-old home alone during a riot. Who cares what he wants?

"It is up to you, but I hope you understand there will be a price to pay either way you decide. Consider your friend as well, as either you both agree to stay or neither of you does. I'm treating you as a matched set."

Stephen looked at Bean who hadn't stopped scowling at the man below.

"I believe I know what she would decide."

Finn removed his hood as he stood and touched his collar, halting the camouflage effect. He removed the garment, dropping it on Stephen while revealing his brilliant white shirt. Stephen and Bean pulled back, but there was no way the man on the street below could miss Finn's figure on the top of the wall. "So you're the man in charge here then?" the man below shouted. "The doctor will be glad to finally put a face to the stories."

"I am sorry for what must happen next, but I just can't allow my children to be threatened." Finn's voice sounded as if it carried the weight of decades. "You were warned." He raised a fist.

Stephen looked back at Bean. She looked eager. His heart sank. She would never agree to sacrifice a chance for food or water for someone from the Watch. *Don't blame her. She doesn't know about the side effects of the genetic disorder or Ed or Helen.*

When he looked back, the Watchman was no longer alone. Several of the teens and twenty-somethings he'd seen in the tower lobby now surrounded the older man as he spun, brandishing his gun.

"Stay back. I'll shoot"

"Is that one of those smart guns?" One of the girls, whose neon pink hair shone so bright it was hard to believe she could ever stay hidden, laughed as she closed the distance and placed a finger on the weapon. "That's a little bit hypocritical, don't you think? Considering the whole technology is evil incarnate thingy."

The Watchman flicked his wrist holding the gun, knocking her hand away before aiming the weapon at the girl's forehead. Stephen pulled back as he watched the man's finger tighten on the trigger. The gun produced a clicking sound, but nothing more.

The girl smiled. "Not what you were expecting, was it?"

The gun clicked again as the man pulled the trigger again; however, nothing fired. The weapon was as effective as the sticks Stephen used to pretend with as an eight-year-old in the woods around the farm.

The time to speak up and diffuse the situation had come and gone. Stephen's shoulders sagged. His silence through the exchange had spoken volumes. Now he could only hope that Dr. Lambda would not risk sending someone else before he learned the tower's access code.

Finn looked at him. Stephen nodded, and Finn lowered his fist.

"My turn," said the pink-haired girl as she raised her hand once more and placed it on the man's extended arm. A light flashed where their skin touched, and the man dropped to the ground. The perimeter made up of others closed their ranks, surrounding the fallen trespasser until he was no longer in view.

"Is he dead?" Stephen whispered to himself.

"Laura stunned him. It's kinder than what he deserved."

Stephen shuddered at Finn's cold matter-of-fact tone. *Weren't you working yourself up to be a killer just yesterday? And that was over a boat.* Finn had a point. The man brought a gun and explosives. *He'd even pointed it at a girl's head and pulled the trigger. More than once.* He lowered his gaze from the scene. *Just because you understand, doesn't mean you have to agree with it.* "So now what?" Seeing the old man helpless on the ground, he couldn't help but picture Ed lying in a similar position, surrounded by the Watch. The Watch didn't strike him as a group who would be content to stop at 'kind.'

"As I said, I can't allow my children to be threatened." Finn stood on the wall with his chest out and his shoulders proud. The only thing missing from his profile as he looked out over his domain was a crown.

"What about the other one?" asked Bean. "His friend." She gestured at the group below. Stephen suspected his companion wasn't suffering any of the same pangs of guilt as he was. "Aren't you going to stick around and welcome him or her, too?"

Stephen turned and blinked. The group at the base of the wall was gone, including the Watchman. "Where did they go?"

"I've made my point, and they've taken him to a place where he and I might have a more private, conversation."

Stephen's eyebrow raised at the comment. "So you are going to torture him."

"Torture?" Finn chuckled. "Aren't you the imaginative one?" He sighed. "No, we aren't monsters, despite what the rumors say. I only want a chat with him. One on one. Then he'll be free to go. Although, if I were him, I might not want to leave. I would expect the reception he receives back at home after failing his mission will be quite painful." The corner of Finn's eye twitched. "But that chat can wait. I'd like to finish ours, and I don't know about you, but I could use lunch first. What do you say?"

"She wore a stunner, didn't she?" Stephen asked. The events of the past few minutes played over in his mind. He hadn't recalled anyone in the lobby taking weapons with them, but that wasn't to say there wasn't a cache nearby. He'd need to know where such a supply was just in case he needed to make a quick getaway after the Watch came back.

"A stunner?" Finn's eyebrows shot up.

"An electronic personal protection device," said Bean.

Finn's brows returned to their resting position. "Oh, I am well aware of what a stunner is, but I can't remember the last time I saw a functioning one." He cocked his head to the side. "I'm rather surprised a young person like yourself even knows what one is."

Bean snorted. "They still exist. You just have to have the right connections."

"And I'd love to meet some of your friends someday, if you'd be willing make the introductions." Finn dropped from the ladder and waited for Stephen and Bean to join him on the landing before blocking their view of the access panel with his body.

"Funny you should mention that." Stephen pursed his lips, unsure whether to ask the other question that had plagued him earlier.

"Mention what, Ms. Bean's connections?"

"No, your age. You said that like you are so much older than us, but you are, what, maybe ten years older? Fifteen tops."

Finn grinned. "I was wondering when you'd notice. Would you believe I am old enough to be your father? Older actually."

Stephen did a double take on Finn's face. Where were the wrinkles and the silver hair? If he was that much older, why didn't he look more like Ed? Was life in the tower that much easier? His jaw tightened. "So if it wasn't a stunner, what did she do? Some sort of martial art?" asked Stephen when the silence continued. He hadn't seen the girl do more than touch the man, but maybe she knew of some secret pressure point on the human body.

"Laura does have a number of skills, but how would that explain the gun not firing?"

"It jammed and she got lucky?" Stephen suggested. "I've seen it a million times." He hadn't, outside of games and old videos he'd dug up online, but Finn didn't need to know that.

Stephen's comment, however, must have caught Finn off guard. Creases appeared his brow. "The gun was functional."

"But you can't know that. We were way up there. It could have been a dummy." Stephen pointed up.

"They always have been both real and in good working order in the past." Finn waved toward the lobby door. "Why else do you think we built a wall?"

Because you guys have been stuck on this island too long and have run out of other things to do other than drag out answers to questions for an hour, Stephen thought. Aloud, he said, "Fine then, I give up. If it wasn't a stunner, martial arts, or a misfire, how did she do it?"

"Follow me, you'll want to sit down for this." He walked over to a couch lining the far side of the lobby wall where the lighting wasn't quite as bright. The cushions were worn and the fabric faded, but after traveling through the woods by foot for so many days and resting on the ground or the occasional fallen tree, it was like sinking into a cloud.

"Comfortable? Good. Now to answer your question, we call ourselves Sorcerers."

Just when you were starting to believe they weren't as nuts as Dr. Lambda said. Stephen snorted before he remembered that he wanted them to trust him enough to give him their access code. "Sorcerers? As in wizards?" *They would have to expect some disbelief at hearing a claim like that for the first time, wouldn't they?* He stood and tapped Bean on the shoulder. "Maybe the rumors were right, after all."

Finn raised his hand, and Stephen halted. "It's only a play on words. As in those who manipulate source code. One of my people mentioned it one night and the name stuck."

Stephen caught Bean rolling her eyes.

"Ahem" Finn coughed, and Stephen noticed that Finn's palm began to glow as the lights dimmed further. "Have I gotten your attention?" Finn asked. The remaining light reflected off Finn's gleaming white teeth as he grinned. "It may not be magic, in the traditional sense, but what we can do is pretty close. A few years before you were born, your father was one of a small team who found a way to merge the human mind with the Internet. But what the team didn't then realize was they had gifted humanity with so much more than a new way to access data." Finn cocked his head as if enjoying some secret joke. "At least, the rest of the team didn't immediately grasp the larger magnitude of what they'd unlocked: instant knowledge, communication at a thought, total control of one's body at a cellular level, and more. Your father…" Finn's eyes twinkled as he shook his head. "Well, I'm reasonably sure the results of that first experiment surprised even him."

"This…Alan Dronigh. He's not my father. If anyone has that title, it is Ed." An image of Ed lying in a makeshift cell filtered across Stephen's mind's eye. Stephen immediately banished the thought. *They are going to be okay*, he told himself. "And while that's a neat trick, it doesn't explain what happened outside or whatever the heck you did to us upstairs." Bean tensed beside him. *You went too far.*

"But it does." Finn sighed as if he could see the thoughts torturing Stephen playing out on the other side of the room. "I thought you were one of us. Now I see I misjudged you and wasted all of our time. Your mind will never be open enough."

Idiot. Now what?

"He's worried about his parents. His Ed and Helen," said Bean. "It makes him say things without thinking." She aimed a pointed glance at Stephen. "Doesn't it?"

Stephen closed his eyes and let out a breath. *Thank you, Bean.* But would Finn be as forgiving as she was?

"It's true. The Watch took them days ago. It's why we came here. We were hoping to hide out and figure out a plan to rescue them." Another thought dawned on him. He didn't need to worry about the Watch's deadline or an access code. "I know it sounded bad the way I said it, but that's only because I was still trying to get my head around it. What your people did out there was amazing." He stood up and paced around the room "With your help, we could go to the Watch using your super-stealth mode, then zap"—he placed his hand on Bean's shoulder—"we knock them out, rescue my parents, and come back here to live happily ever after. Mission accomplished. End of story." Stephen meant every word that spilled out of his mouth. If the only way to save his parents was to join a cult who believed they were magicians, then so be it. At least they could be crazy be together. "You can help me, right?"

Sadness clouded Finn's features. "No."

Sixteen

The single word snapped Stephen's excitement like so many twigs he'd crunched underfoot on his way to this place. "No?" he repeated back. "I see." Stephen glowered at Finn before turning back to Bean. "Then I guess we will be on our way." *So much for that plan.* He rubbed his fingers. The trip to the tower wasn't a complete waste. If what Finn said they could do was true, maybe they could rescue Ed and Helen without the help of the so-called Sorcerers. But what if all of this had been a delusion? The Watchman didn't look healthy. What if he dropped on his own and it is all another big coincidence? *Don't be a fool, you know what you saw. That's too many coincidences.* The small voice sounded different than he was used to, startling him out of his thoughts.

The corner of Finn's mouth twitched. "I didn't say no, as in we aren't willing. We would like nothing more than to put an end to the Watch, but it isn't so simple. We can't."

"Seems pretty simple to me," Stephen grumbled.

Finn raised his palm. "My people don't leave the city. At least, not the majority. A few of the more gifted ones—like the ones you saw outside—can spend two, maybe three, days off the island, but most can only last a few hours."

Stephen cocked his head. "What?"

"That's why I was so eager to find you. There is something we need. Something only you can get for us." Finn's grin bloomed once more across his face. "It's a wand. Maybe as thick as your finger and as long as Ms. Bean's hand."

"A wand." Stephen blinked. *Right. Of course it is. Sorcerers have to have their wands.* "So, what's this wand supposed to do? We wave it around and presto! Problem solved?"

Finn's eyes glinted. "I understand what you must be thinking, but I am deadly serious about this. I call it a wand for simplicity's sake, as that is what it looks like, but in reality, it is a piece of advanced technology created by a former associate years ago."

"Well, if it is so advanced, why don't you have it already?"

"It is protected."

Let me guess, by a magic spell. The conversation was getting him nowhere.

Finn shook his head. He muttered, "I told them we would never be taken seriously with that name." Louder, he added, "By biometrics. Which, I might add, is another reason I was so interested in finding you."

"Me? I've never seen your magic wand, and I don't know the first thing about hacking some biometric security system. I'm not even sure I know what biometrics are."

Biometrics: a form of computer authentication designed around individualized human characteristics such as fingerprint or iris profile.

Stephen shot a look at Bean. *Where did that come from?*

Finn leaned forward once more. "But that's just it. If my theory is correct, you wouldn't have to hack anything, as I believe you, Stephen, are the key." Finn's jaw clenched before he spoke again. "The wand would be here already if the access metrics hadn't been tampered with."

"I had nothing to do with it." Stephen took a step back with his hands raised.

Finn blinked twice, and the scowl disappeared. "That wasn't an accusation. I know you didn't. It was someone who I once quite admired. I believe she changed the access metrics so that you are the only person with permission to open the cabinet where it is stored."

"Why would she do that? Ignoring for a second the fact I don't know who you are talking about, why me?"

"Who knows what was going through her head at that time. Bombs were going off in the street set by people dressed as serpents. Everyone acted a little nutty. Maybe she wanted to take revenge on people like us by keeping us on this island, or maybe she wanted to make sure no one else could claim it until you were ready."

"If you know who this hacker is, why aren't you asking her to fix it and retrieve your wand?"

Finn clicked his tongue. "Well, that's complicated."

"Oh, I get it. She's dead." Stephen crossed his arms. "Not all that complicated."

"Perhaps. Perhaps not. But in either case, she's not around to ask, while you, Stephen, were gracious enough to show up on my doorstep. So, will you try to find the wand?"

"And if I find this wand and bring it back, you'll help me rescue Ed and Helen."

Finn nodded. "Once the wand is in my hands, rescuing your guardians will be one of the first things we do." He cocked his head and scratched his chin. "I will even forget your initial outburst and allow all of you to live here afterward."

Bean placed her hand on Stephen's shoulder. "Seems like a rather generous offer for a retrieval mission."

"Well, the locals in the area can be a tad territorial," said Finn. "But as long as you stay out of the center of town, you shouldn't have any problem."

"And once his parents are free? What do you intend to do about the Watch?"

"Then we'll follow Stephen's wishes, whatever they might be."

Stephen grit his teeth as he weighed Finn's request. *If the wand was as valuable as Finn said, then it was likely long gone regardless of whatever security system had been put in place.* Finn's request was a wild goose chase waiting to happen. Even worse, it would cost him even more time. What if the Watch came back before he returned? *But what other choice do I have?*

Finn smiled. "There's one more thing."

Stephen's eyes narrowed.

"Don't worry, it's not another condition." Finn paused and looked at Bean. "I want to teach both of you how to do what you saw us do out there. It will be useful out there." Finn gestured toward the tower door. "But also, because it is your birthright." Finn extended his hand to Stephen before looking back at Bean.

Stephen couldn't help but feel a little disquiet. There was something about the offer. Something he couldn't place his finger on. *You are being paranoid again*, thought Stephen. Still, he hesitated. Time spent training meant more time away from home.

"Don't worry. It will be quick." Stephen's lips twisted at Finn's remark. It was too close to his thoughts for comfort. "And it is in your best interest. You saw the gun. You heard his threats. Imagine meeting someone like that on the road. Now imagine what you could do with abilities like ours. You would be crazy not to take me up on my offer."

Finn had a point. He and Bean made it to the island because they'd been lucky not to have met anyone on the road. There was nothing to say their next journey would be the same. As much as he thought there had to be a catch, Stephen couldn't think of what it might be. He uncrossed his arms and let them fall limp by his sides. "Fine. A quick lesson first. But, to be clear, if I find this wand, I'm not handing it over until my folks are safe."

Finn's teeth sparkled white as he gestured for them to lean back into the couch as he took his own seat. "I'll begin with the basics." Information flooded Stephen's mind.

SEVENTEEN

Bean's eyes became glassy and unfocused. She raised her hand with her palm facing the ceiling. Stephen watched in wonder as her palm began to emit a pale blue glow like he'd seen Finn do. She blinked as her clear gaze returned to meet Stephen's. The light on her palm grew brighter. She cupped her hand. White-purple sparks jumped between her fingertips.

Stephen opened his palms and turned them toward the ceiling, much as he had seen Bean do. His fingers, however, remained skin toned. No glow or sparks of light danced across their surface.

A corner of Bean's lips turned up in a smile at his effort as she rose from the couch with her hand still aglow. Biting her lip, she took several steps out of the alcove, without turning her back on their host.

Finn's eyebrows and a corner of his lips rose as his gaze locked on the movement. "Before you go too far, I should warn you…"

I knew it, thought Stephen. "Let me guess. There's a catch."

"Not a catch, per se." Finn's lips twisted. "The data stream and what we can do is easier here. We still have the infrastructure. But out there… Well, it's like old phone technology."

Bean waved her hand, dismissing the ball of lightning. Stephen cocked his head as he attempted to follow Finn's warning.

"You see, when the signal is strong, the battery lasts longer because it isn't trying to find a better connection, but once a phone starts roaming…" Finn shrugged.

"I don't understand," Stephen admitted.

"I forget you kids wouldn't have the first idea what I am talking about. That lightning, it doesn't come out of thin air. It takes energy. Energy you won't have access to, at least not to the extent we have here thanks to this tower's self-sufficient power supply. It will exhaust you."

Stephen blinked, still not following Finn's explanation.

"Think about it this way. Imagine all you have to eat is a single apple. Eat it and stay inside all day reading a book, you might not realize how hungry you are until around dinnertime. Eat that same apple and work outside all day, I bet you are feeling weak in the knees before noon. The same principle applies here, except when you are away from a sufficient alternative energy source, the drain might very well kill you."

Dread filled Stephen's stomach. "Wait. Are you saying we are stuck here now?" Finn's warning didn't make sense. If Finn needed them to go and get the wand, shouldn't he have waited until they returned to remove the block?

Finn shook his head. "No, I don't believe so."

"You don't *believe* so? You mean you don't know?" Stephen bit his tongue in fury.

"Well, it affects everyone in different ways."

"Oh, that makes me feel so much better." Finn's fingers twitched, and his expression hardened. Stephen thought of the other so-called Sorcerers and what they'd demonstrated on the barricade. An icy knot built in Stephen's stomach. *Nice work. You have no idea what this man is capable of*, he thought. *You took him at his word because you wanted to believe, but his people could have killed that man the moment you walked away.* Ed's advice not to trust anyone once again echoed in Stephen's mind. *But yeah, go on and irritate him. Genius.* He tempered his tone. "I mean to say, what makes you so sure?"

"Isn't it obvious?" Finn gestured at the two of them. "Because you are both still alive."

"But isn't that because we didn't know how to do any of this before today?" said Bean.

Finn tilted his head and glanced at Bean before answering. "Just because you were unaware of what you were doing, doesn't mean you weren't doing it. The difference is now you know, and the reason I'm confident you can complete this task is the fact you wouldn't be standing here if you hadn't already figured out how to protect yourself at an instinctive level. Not everyone is so lucky."

"The plague." Stephen's eyes widened as he connected the dots.

Finn nodded. "Yes. The plague."

Stephen frowned. He'd always assumed the plague was something common, like a new strain of the flu. The worldwide economic collapse and fall of much of the power grid hadn't helped either. "If people knew its cause, why couldn't they find a cure?"

Finn held a finger up. "The first thing you need to understand about who we are and what we can do is that it's not a disease but a gift."

Bean snorted. "Some gift."

"So back to this whole mission, or quest, or whatever you want to call it. Are you going to tell me where I am supposed to go to find this wand thing?" Stephen asked.

"It's not far," replied Finn, removing the finger from his lips to inspect its nail. "In fact, I'll even give you a map."

Stephen's head throbbed and his skin itched as a map unfurled across his vision as if suspended in the air. His eyes might have bulged out of their sockets at the display if his stomach hadn't taken that moment to growl loud enough to be heard by everyone in the room.

"You should have spoken up." Finn wagged his finger. "As I mentioned before, never let yourself go hungry." An unfocused look flashed across Finn's expression. Within moments, the stairwell door opened. A girl Stephen hadn't seen before appeared carrying a bag of brown rectangular packets of varying sizes wrapped in plastic. Dropping the sack by Finn's feet, she disappeared with as little fanfare as she had arrived. Finn pulled out one of the packets. "Fortunately, I knew about a large cache of these well before the panic set in." He returned the packet to the sack. "We haven't needed them thanks to the gardens we keep on the upper floors. Take these with you."

"I still don't… Will I be able to… How did you?" Stephen couldn't help asking.

"It's the same as in the game you like to play. One computer connects to another. Except for the computer in this instance is your mind." Finn gestured to the bag, which appeared stuffed to its breaking point. "Now eat. Never forget what I said. Once you leave this tower, you will need to make sure to always keep your energy levels up."

"But what if I can't?" Stephen asked as he ripped into one of the smaller packets near the top containing a bar the color and flavor of mud. "I mean, I've never accessed the data stream or whatever you want to call that…that…" Stephen gestured in the air, unable to come up with another term to describe the flood of information that had assaulted his senses earlier.

"It will come to you," Finn answered in a flash, "if you let it." He took a deep breath. "I know what it must be like, for this to all be strange and new." He shook his head. "The more time that passes before you master control will make it that much more difficult. Even now, I suspect your mind is trying to create another barrier. It's afraid. It's coming up with reasons why none of what you've seen or heard is true. It doesn't have to be that way. Retrieve the wand for me, and I'll make sure you and your guardians never live in fear of the Watch again."

Eighteen

A bead of sweat crawled down the length of Stephen's spine under the weight of a backpack loaded to its seams. The street in front of him was empty of people but littered with abandoned cars, making the way somewhat more challenging. "Should we take the bridge or tunnel?" he asked Bean, seeking to fill the unnatural quiet. *Who would have thought that life in the middle of nowhere would be noisier than the big city?*

Bean paused in mid-stride as her gaze glazed over. Bean had been all too eager to take advantage of their new abilities. She surprised him by how ready she was to access the data stream, especially after Finn's warning about the energy drain it could cause, but when questioned, she shrugged him off. "All the more reason to master it before we leave the island."

Stephen remained less… He struggled to think of the word that would describe the feeling. *Enthusiastic.* Stephen nodded to himself. Enthusiastic was a good word. Finn was right. He didn't want to believe him, but not for the reason Finn suggested.

"Neither."

Stephen almost jumped out of his skin as Wes stepped out from one of the abandoned buildings. "You could have given me a heart attack."

"Not my fault you don't pay attention," Wes said as he joined them in the middle of the street. "I thought you could use a guide." He glanced up to the sky, tracking the position of the sun. "By the looks of it, I was right."

Stephen's lips twisted. Something about their mission gnawed at him and had since the second they left the barricade behind. It solved too many problems. *If a deal is too good to be true...* What he couldn't figure out was what Finn stood to gain other than a piece of tech. Why take the risk with relative strangers when there was a good chance it didn't even work anymore?

He took a closer look at Wes. His eyes narrowed. Had Finn sent him to keep an eye on them? If so, then why? Did Finn not think they'd hand the wand over? He ground his jaw. Handing over the wand was the best chance he had of defeating the Watch and rescuing Ed and Helen. *Or maybe Wes is your friend and wants to help because that's what friends do.* He remembered how pale and tired Wes had looked as they had gotten into the boat. Stephen had assumed at the time that his appearance was a result of city living, but if Finn had been telling the truth, the energy drain might have already begun taking its toll, and yet he'd still risked it to find him when he'd missed their game. "Are you sure you can make it?"

"Finn doesn't have a monopoly on ideas around here. I believe you just need the right sort of antenna." Wes smiled and reached into his jacket. He pulled out a narrow metal rod affixed to a wooden handle and brandished it about. Its tip was covered in a small sphere of crunched-together aluminum foil. "I call it, Insurance."

"Another wand." Bean laughed, her gaze sharp and focused. "Don't you think you are taking the whole Sorcerer thing a bit far?"

Stephen looked at the rod again and had to agree it did resemble a magic wand. That is, a magic wand made out of garbage. "I'm not sure electricity works that way."

"Laugh all you want"—he waved the rod in the air—"but I'm the difference between you sleeping outside for the next day or two, or getting us where you are going in a matter of hours."

"What are you going to do?" Bean wiggled her fingers. "Say alakazam and get us there in a puff of smoke?"

"You'll see," Wes answered with a smile.

The straps of the pack pulled at Stephen's shoulders. While it seemed there were more than enough supplies now to go around, Stephen wasn't confident there would be enough for three on the road unless Wes did have a way of reducing their travel time. He looked at Wes, at his pale skin, which couldn't have spent more than mere minutes in the sun up until now, and at his narrow frame. Stephen would bet a ration of water that Wes had even less experience in the wilderness than he had. *Didn't stop you.* He pushed out his chest at the thought while redistributing the weight of the bag across his shoulders. "Okay, oh great guide, which route should we be taking then?"

"Easy. The rail."

"Okay, so we walk it?"

A coy smile inched up Wes's face.

Stephen's forehead puckered. "You mean, the trains are still running? But I thought the tower couldn't power more than just the lights and the water."

"Not the tower and not all of them. But lucky for us, we only need one to get where we are going."

Stephen and Bean followed Wes as he navigated city streets further cluttered with the rusty shells of abandoned cars and broken glass the further they went. "We cleared the roadways while we were building up the barricade," offered Wes. "Seemed like a good idea. Two birds with one stone and all." Wes threw out his arms as if they could somehow stretch from street corner to street corner. "The thought was allowing the rest of the place to go natural, so it would act as its own sort of obstacle course. Most of us don't even bother coming up this way anymore. I wouldn't be surprised if the others forgot about the rail altogether."

Wes turned and entered a squat building made of a tan stone; it was streaked black. Large panes of glass in the building's windows were either missing or broken, making the entire structure seem all the more ominous. Stephen's misgivings grew stronger. He shook his head again. Life had been so much simpler before he'd allowed Ed's paranoia to enter his mind.

Bean followed Wes, showing none of the same doubts that were plaguing Stephen. *And when did you start trusting her?* he wondered. *The marina,* his heart answered. He remembered how she'd looked at him like she could see into his soul and him, hers. Stephen buried that last thought deep down. *Don't confuse the whole shared survival thing for more than it is,* his brain reminded him. *She's going with you because she has no other place to go.* Stephen muttered a curse as he raced to catch up before the pair were too far out of sight.

"So, Bean?" Wes asked as they maneuvered around a pile-up of one-time luxury cars, now rendered into garbage. "Interesting name. Let me guess, your father's name was Frank. As in, Frank and Beans. You get it, right?"

Bean shot Wes a look. "I can think of a few worse names to call a person."

Wes snorted as he scouted ahead, disappearing behind the remains of a bus.

"You know, your friend can be a bit of a jerk," whispered Bean.

"He's not so bad once you get to know him," replied Stephen. *Do you know him though? Do you really?*

Bean added, still soft enough that the words wouldn't carry, "My real name is Beatrice, but my sister couldn't say it when we were kids. Called me Bean instead. It stuck."

"That's cute." Stephen attempted a wry smile. It must have been nice to have other kids to grow up with. "Where is your sister now?"

Bean's jaw tightened. "Not here."

Way to step in it again. Wes reappeared in that moment, gesturing for them to turn right and follow him into a building that looked as if it wouldn't be standing much longer. Once in the building, each footfall echoed like a gunshot causing the hairs on the back of Stephen's neck to stand on end. What few panes of glass remained in the windows were long since darkened with grime, making the light that did pass through seem diseased. Movement low to the ground and fast caught his eye. Stephen suspected it was a rodent and shuddered.

"This way," Wes's voice boomed, startling some other creatures that had made the building their home. Stephen looked around, trying to locate the voice's source. The play of acoustics made it difficult, but he managed to catch sight of Wes's shirt as he began descending a flight of stairs. Bean, however, was nowhere to be seen.

"Bean?"

"Over here," she answered, materializing out of the shadows like a ghost. While Finn had been generous with the food and water, his generosity had not extended to giving either of them the color-shifting shirts, but it would seem Bean didn't need it. His skin prickled at the thought of what sort of damage she might inflict on those that threatened her. *Good thing she is on your side*, Stephen thought.

"How did you do that?"

"Do what?"

"Are you two waiting for an invitation?" Wes called from the base of the stairwell. Light shone from his palm stretched above his head, cutting the otherwise perfect darkness and illuminating the ground around them. "Please mind the gap," he laughed. Stephen raised an eyebrow. "What? I had to look up a bunch of videos about subways to get her up and running. It's funny."

Stephen shook his head.

A screech of metal covered any other words they might have spoken as a train car pulled to a stop across from Wes. Wes patted the metallic cylinder as one might an animal. "It took me two years. Switching the power supply over was brutal. I almost electrocuted myself, but I didn't want to connect it to the tower's grid. She wouldn't be my little secret anymore. Then one day, just as I thought I'd run out of options, it sort of clicked. She's my secret awesome machine. I call her SAM."

"So if not the tower, then what is powering it?" asked Bean, running her hand over the metal surface.

"My guess? It has something to do with those things." Stephen pointed to several large rings wrapped in coiled wires mounted along the base of the car. "What are they, some kind of battery?"

"Sorry." Wes shook one finger before tapping his forehead. "I'm not sure I want that secret getting out." He nodded his head toward the vehicle where Bean was examining one of the rings.

Stephen rolled his eyes. "Who would we tell?" The light emanating from Wes's outstretched fist blinked out of existence as the train car's door slid open. Warm light welcomed them into its interior. Wes took a seat, gesturing for Stephen to take the one across from him while holding onto one of the car's metal railings. The doors closed with a soft whishing sound. Bean stood in the center with her hand wrapped around a support rail.

"How does the Watch not know about this?" Stephen wondered aloud.

"They aren't the only ones." Wes's grin threatened to break his face in two.

"But it's a train. A functioning train," Bean stated the obvious. "Isn't that a little hard to miss?"

Wes's smile evaporated. "Well, yeah, they might have noticed if I'd ever tested it further than the service tunnel."

"So you don't know that it will get us there." Bean tensed and made a move as if to exit the train before it started. She frowned once more at Wes when the door didn't re-open. "Forgive me if I'm not a super fan of the idea of being buried alive down here when this bucket of bolts fails."

"Oh, she'll get us there." Wes patted the metal bar as he had the car's exterior. He muttered more under his breath, but Stephen couldn't catch the rest. The car lurched forward, and Stephen decided to let the comment go. Even if the furthest the train could manage was one or two miles, it was better than walking.

Stephen blinked as the train exited the service tunnel. His eyes, blinded by the light, did not adjust to the brightness of daylight right away. The car continued its acceleration until the streets were passing like a blur. Then darkness blanketed them again. Stephen's ears popped as they burrowed deep under the waterway through another tunnel. Stephen looked over at Wes. Were the cabin lights bleaching out what little color Wes's skin possessed? Or was the drain already taking its toll? He looked over at Bean. *We're supposed to have some built-in resistance, right?*

Her skin looked grayer, too, although not to the same extent. *It must be the lighting then.* Forcing himself to look away before she noticed, he shook his concern away.

"Did you ever watch a game?" Wes gestured at a faded poster hung above one of the windows featuring a helmeted man clad in heavy pads.

"Nah," replied Stephen. "At least not any that I can remember. Did you?"

"I've watched the replays." Wes sighed. "Dad was a major Sharks fan before all hell broke loose, with season tickets and everything. You would have thought he was an owner of the team. Or you might have, before…" Wes's expression dulled. A muscle in his jaw twitched. "I forget the point I was trying to make."

"That's okay. I wouldn't have gotten it anyway. My Ed wasn't big on sports."

Wes leaned back into his seat. "Yeah, I guess I can't blame him. Even my dad had to admit the players on the teams weren't exactly playing fair. Especially not during those last couple seasons." He shook his head. "I don't care how much money was on the line, you couldn't pay me to turn myself into a monster like that."

Bean yawned and shifted her stance.

I bet Bean knows what he means. Might as well turn in your guy card now. He waited for information, which could offer a hint at what Wes meant to pop into his brain like the definition of biometrics had, but all he could think of was Ed and Helen being held against their will, and all he was doing about it was sitting on a train discussing a profession that no longer held any relevance. "Yeah, roid-rage," he offered. *Lame.*

Wes nodded in the direction of the poster. "If only. I'm not talking about steroids. I am talking about people turning themselves into real live monsters. Like tusks and stuff.

Anything they could do to intimidate or get ahead, and all of it was legal. Man, it used to scare the crap out of me watching the players take the field, but Dad ate that stuff up. I mention it because that's where we are going. Shark-fan central."

The sunlight bathed the world outside the car with a rose golden light as the train began its deceleration. Its hue made Wes appear jaundiced. "You're not looking so good," said Stephen, giving voice to his growing concern.

Wes's lips narrowed. "Bit of motion sickness," he answered. He pulled out the narrow metal rod from his jacket, clutching it in one hand so tight his knuckles were white.

Bean turned and took in Wes's appearance beginning at his feet and resting on his face. "You should go back home. After all, Finn sent us, not you."

Wes waved the comment away with a flick of his wrist. "We're almost there." The car continued speeding its way along the track. More sunlight flooded the cabin but did little to improve Wes's skin tone. "Besides, you're going to need me unless you feel like walking back. SAM is mine, remember?"

"Keep her," said Bean. "I'm still shocked that this can on wheels made it this far."

"I'd prefer to walk back than bury you," said Stephen in a low voice. The skin of Wes's hand was taunt and bone white where his fingers and the metal met.

He shivered. "I knew I should have worked on the climate control before taking her out. A cold front must have come through. You can't trust the weather out here. One minute it's summer and the next we're buried under three feet of snow." Wes's lips had taken on a blue sheen, emphasizing his point.

"Dude. Seriously. I think you should go back while you still can."

Wes's deteriorating condition was all the proof Stephen needed that Finn had been telling the truth, at least about the limitations of the Sorcerers abilities. *Your abilities now, too*, he reminded himself. Seeing that it had been an hour or two, Stephen hated to imagine how Wes would have fared had he not found them at the riverfront as soon as he had. The road might have killed him. *How* had *Wes found them on the waterfront?* A thought occurred to Stephen as he pulled the pack back onto his shoulders.

"You knew where we were before you even left the island?"

"What?" Wes replied through chattering teeth.

"It wasn't by luck when you found us the other day at the pier. You knew we were there and not crossing by either the roadway or the tunnel. How?"

A slight pink blush blinked into existence across Wes's cheeks before disappearing beneath his now waxy condition. "You called."

"The bench." Stephen's eyes widened as he recalled that moment of complete despair. Bean looked taken aback and almost lost her footing as the train swayed. *She must think I've lost my mind*, he thought. *Perhaps you have.* Looking at her, he explained. "According to Finn, I've been accessing these abilities for years without knowing what I was doing. I was thinking about giving up. I must have somehow sent out a call for help."

Bean's eyes softened and her body relaxed, if only for a moment. Her free hand stretched toward his. He held his breath as he waited to accept her hand in his, but then her arm stiffened and her back arched as she brought her hand up to cover another yawn. Then she shook her head. Her eyes were once again as hard as the iron rails. The train came to a stop and the doors slid open.

Stephen's cheeks burnt. "So that's what we'll do." Stephen stood and faced the door. The weight of the pack dug into his shoulders.

"Do what?" Wes's words were clipped. Stephen turned back. He didn't need to be a doctor to see that Wes's continued denial about his condition would kill him if he didn't start heading back to the island and the protection of the tower soon.

"I'll send you a message when we have the wand and are on the way back." *Assuming you figure out how you did it the first time that is.*

Wes started to rise in protest, but crumpled back into his seat, releasing his homemade antenna. His shoulders slumped, and his head bowed in defeat. "I'm sorry." His fingers twitched. "Take Insurance. You'll need it."

"It doesn't work, Wes. You have to know that."

"The faster we get off this train, the faster he can go back," said Bean, squeezing by Stephen and jumping onto the platform.

"Please."

Stephen's gaze remained fixed on the car as it pulled away from the station, as if Wes might attempt to return the moment it was out of sight. "If you chuck that thing over there, I doubt anyone will notice." Bean's words brought Stephen's attention back to the present. Large cracks in the concrete slab of the unwelcoming platform had given birth to weeds, and insect trails lined beams that once must have supported a shelter roof. A building no bigger than Stephen's farmhouse stood behind them, its windows long since boarded up. Brick buildings lining the other side of the road appeared equally abandoned.

Stephen turned the antenna over in his hands. The handle was narrow, only the size of his thumb and about a third as thick, and the metal rod was no longer attached. The two pieces had broken apart when Wes dropped it. Bean was right;

he should throw the whole thing away. The pack was heavy enough, but he'd promised. *Wes named it, after all.* He shoved the handle piece into his back pocket. Figuring out what to do with the metal piece was more problematic due to its size, but he managed to squeeze it into the pack. Fixing things other people viewed as junk was one of the things he could do best. Maybe when all this was done he could give Wes a new and improved model.

"You coming?" Bean shouted from the edge of the platform.

Stephen grunted as he adjusted the pack's straps and began walking down the center of the roadway. They'd arrived at their destination with a full pack and in a fraction of the time they'd planned. Now all he had to do was find the wand, return home, and take down the Watch, but with each step closer to his goal, he couldn't help feeling like somewhere along the line, he'd made a colossal mistake.

PART THREE

Nineteen

Stephen crumpled the leftover wrapper from a larger packet marked 'MRE: Meal Ready to Eat' and scanned to see if there was a fire-can or something similar where he might dispose of the rubbish. The food, if you could call it that, contained inside was about as satisfying for dinner as a cardboard box, but eating it or any of the other foodstuffs in the pack was a whole lot easier than foraging. *Safer, too.* Giving up on finding a place for the trash, Stephen shoved the garbage into a pocket.

Bean laughed. "What are you going to do when you run out of pocket room?" she asked. "Why don't you drop it? It's what everyone else here seems to want to do with their garbage." She gestured to a pile of water-rotted wood and moldy fabric laying nearby, which once served as a piece of furniture. "I'd bet you a steak dinner that no one would even notice."

The area between the island and their destination once supported one of the most populated parts of the country. Now the roads were lined with buildings long abandoned. It was a good thing they had their supplies. If any grocery stores still operated, they weren't exactly advertising operating hours. Even though he'd just eaten, the thought of food made his mouth water. There might not be grocery stores anymore, but that didn't mean there wasn't a hidden market like Jim's tavern nearby. A couple of the meal bars would be worth a good trade. Stephen shifted the pack's weight, easing his shoulders where the straps had cut into his skin. "Maybe it's time to take the main road?"

Bean raised a brow. "We'd risk getting spotted."

"Would meeting other people be such a bad thing? They could at least point us to where we could trade for that steak dinner or something. Doesn't that sound awesome right now?"

"I'm not so sure. What if those people don't trust strangers?" Bean argued. "They might alert the Watch the second they see our shadows." She stood straight as she flexed a glowing fist.

It wasn't the first time since leaving the train he'd caught her experimenting with their newfound ability. So far, she hadn't acted any more tired than usual. If anything, she seemed more vibrant now, as if not accessing their abilities before had been the more exhausting activity. He wished he felt the same. He shifted the pack again. Thanks to the train ride, it was still heavy with their supplies, but he had no way of knowing how long they'd last if Finn's energy drain did start having an impact. "Are you sure you should be doing that?"

"I'm practicing. I don't know about you, but I'm not in the mood to run anymore." Stephen didn't need Bean to voice the words to understand that she wouldn't hesitate to attack if threatened. He thought back to the decision he'd made at the pier before he'd recognized Wes. He'd convinced himself that he could do what had to be done, but could he if it came down to it? Could he really? He was no longer as sure. Up ahead, a worn sign read 'cester' as if the 'Wor' in Worchester had taken off in a panic with everyone else. One way or another, he suspected he'd soon find out.

Bean looked at him sideways, her lips hinting at a smile. "Welcome home?"

"This was never my home," Stephen grumbled. "Even if Finn says I was born here." He chewed on his lip as he scanned the empty street ahead of them. Nothing about it looked familiar. "Do you honestly think the townspeople are going to turn us in to the Watch the minute they see us?"

"You know as well as I do this is where it all started. If anyone isn't to be trusted, it is people from around here."

Stephen's lips tightened, but he chose not to argue with her as he scanned the streets ahead of them. Even if the people of this town weren't allied with the Watch, if he'd seen all the chaos they had, he wouldn't trust a stranger either. "Fine. You win. We take the scenic route."

Stephen blinked as the virtual map Finn sent him unfurled across his vision. Summoning it was the only thing he had been able to do related to their abilities with any confidence. He blinked again, and the map zoomed in and transformed into a three-dimensional overlay. A large red arrow filled the street. Street names and other details like business ratings and phone numbers floated over the top of the surrounding buildings. Stephen shook his head. As nice as it was to have a map of the area to help guide them, the overlay was proof the map was at least fifteen years old. Who knew what changes might have been made to the city since then? Stephen thought of the elaborate barricade that protected Finn's tower. Those remaining in this city might have attempted something similar if they felt threatened. There could be traps for uninvited visitors or mazes made of salvaged materials.

Once again, Stephen couldn't help thinking the object of their quest had to be long gone as they followed the red arrow, terminating at a checkered flag in front of a gray building. Unlike the buildings to either side, no additional information popped up across his augmented vision. "I guess this is it," suggested Stephen, waving toward the virtual entranceway.

"What is?" Bean asked.

"Our destination."

"A parking lot?"

Stephen took a step back to see if additional information about the building might appear. He wrinkled his nose. Something about the place nagged him. While the building's windows were blacked with grime, they were still intact. There were no signs of graffiti or other signs of structural abuse either. The hair on his neck prickled.

He waved his hand and the overlay dissolved. The gray building disappeared, replaced with an empty lot. *I knew this was a wild goose chase.* Frustrated they'd come so far to reach a dead end, Stephen picked up a rock at threw it at the lot. The rock bounced in midair, dropping to the ground in front of Stephen. "Did you see that?" he asked.

Beans eyebrows shot up. "Do it again."

Stephen picked up the stone and threw it again. Again, it fell after connecting with something Stephen couldn't see. He closed his eyes and reached out. Stephen's fingers connected with a warm flat surface. He brought the map overlay back up over his vision. The gray building reappeared. Stephen walked toward the entranceway and noticed a panel to its side illuminated as they approached.

"What are you doing?"

"The whole place must be camouflaged. Like those crazy clothes Finn's group uses. Use the map he gave us."

"Finn didn't *give* me anything," Bean grumbled. "Why else do you think I let you lead the way all this time?"

He placed his hand on it. A tiny portal in the building's wall opened, exposing a lens. "What is this place?" Stephen asked as the lens blinked and an indicator light blazed green.

He pulled his hand back as if burned. "I don't know what I just did, but I did something." Just as he was about to drop his hand, he heard the sound of a latch release. He caught Bean's eye.

She shrugged. "So, the lights are still on. Maybe it's like the tower and the people inside know where we can get fresh water around here," she said, gesturing for Stephen to continue inside. As they entered the building's hallway, a warm glow filled the space as they crossed a tiled floor clean enough to eat off its surface. The door behind them clicked shut.

An arrow reappeared in front of Stephen's vision. This time it was black and narrow. *There is no way a building like this is abandoned.* Stephen's neck hairs rose further with each echoing tap their footfalls produced. *Stay alert*, he focused the thought at Bean as if she could read his thoughts. *Be ready.* Bean raised one answering eyebrow, making Stephen once again feel like an idiot. Of course she's alert.

"Go on. Open it." Bean's voice nearly caused Stephen to jump out of his skin as they stopped in front of a rather nondescript office door.

"I'm not sure that's a good idea. We don't have any way of knowing what is on the other side. What if it's been booby-trapped?"

"Chicken." She picked up his wrist and placed his palm on another pad to the door's right. There was a hissing noise along with the sound of escaping air as the door swung on its own accord. The interior of the room looked as if its primary occupant had gone out for a few morning errands, expecting to return later that day. A coffee mug sat in the center of a rich mahogany desk in front of a black leather chair. Several university degrees, including a medical degree showing the name Camille Nadal, hung from the wall. A potted plant filled another office corner. The plant's emerald green foliage put

Stephen on guard as the surest sign yet that they weren't alone in the building—until he touched one of its leaves. They were artificial. He let out a breath.

Bean walked around the desk and rummaged through its drawers until she pulled out a rectangular piece of plastic.

It contained a copper chip on one end. "What's that?"

"A key card. Might come in handy."

"Any sign of a wand?"

"Not even close. Maybe it's down the hall." Bean shoved the card into her pocket and exited the office, not waiting to see if Stephen followed. Her pace increased as if she too experienced the same ill ease about the place. She led them further into the building's interior.

Few of the doors were marked by a sign or nameplate, and Stephen soon lost track of which they had or hadn't opened. A few of the rooms closest to the entrance contained bed-shaped contraptions lined with yellowed paper. Others contained plastic chairs whose arms were fitted with paddles and thick straps. Those rooms tended to also contain rows of empty vials fitted with multi-colored plastic caps. None contained anything remotely wand shaped.

"What do you suppose they did here?" Stephen asked.

Bean snorted, shutting the door closest to her. "Isn't it obvious?" The smile left her lips. "Oh, that's right. You wouldn't know."

Stephen peeked into another room. "Check this out." The size alone separated it from the others. Three rows of large work centers broke up the space, each with its own sink and storage areas. Strangely shaped glassware rested on top of the shelves, and large machines whose purpose Stephen couldn't guess lined the walls.

"Looks promising." Bean pointed at another door, this one made of glass, located in the back of the room. A line of metal cabinets, visible through the glass, lined the back wall of varying sizes. Bean pulled on the handle, but it refused to open. She pulled the card out of her pocket. "Maybe this is what the card is for." She waved it in front of the door. An indicator light flashed red. "Too fast?" Bean waved the card again. The red light blinked once more, followed by a bright white flash up above coming from a camera mounted from the ceiling. "I think this thing just took a picture." She handed the card to him. "This place is supposed to be keyed to you. Why don't you give it a try?"

Stephen scanned the door. With the exception of the hole for the indicator light, there wasn't much else to it. "What do you think I should do?"

"Try putting your hand on it or something. That seems to have worked so far."

Stephen pursed his lips. Holding the card in one hand, he reached out toward the handle. His fingers twitched as they came in contact with the cool metal. He scrunched his eyes shut, bracing himself for an alarm or another flash as he waved the keycard with his other hand. *Click.* Stephen opened his eyes. The red light in the upper corner now shone green.

"Who'da thought? Finn was right. You were the key." Bean grinned.

"It still doesn't make any sense. I mean, why me?"

"Does it matter?" Bean countered. "Now, oh mighty keymaster, why don't you go grab the magic wand thingy so we can get the heck out of this place before whoever might be monitoring that camera decides to come and investigate?"

Stephen crossed the room and opened the various cabinets. Some contained vials, while others contained small round trays. Most were empty. His hopes of finding the wand in this strange place were all but dashed as he opened up the smallest cabinet and pulled out a rod that was as long as his hand and as thick as his thumb.

"That's it?" Bean asked. "Doesn't look all that high tech to me."

"If it's not the wand, then we are in major trouble." Stephen swung his pack around to his front and tucked the rod into one of the pockets.

Bean had moved over to the larger cabinets and was peering into them. "What do you think the rest of this stuff was for?"

Stephen shrugged. "Don't know and don't care. Let's get out of here."

"But aren't you at least a little bit curious?" She started to reach out to touch one of the vials.

"I wouldn't do that if I were you."

She pulled her hand back and turned to look at him with a quizzical expression.

"You said it yourself, we're at ground zero. Do you really want to poke around and let loose another plague?"

She frowned but shoved her hands into her jacket pockets. "Ready?"

Bean turned to look at the row of cabinets one last time. Her shoulders slumped.

Stephen's senses were on edge as they navigated through the maze of hallways within the facility. With every footstep, every turn, he expected to find some sort of guard or obstacle, but none appeared, and before long, they were at the building's main entrance.

Stephen summoned the map once more to remind himself how to get back to the train station. His vision flashed red. "Now what...?" he began as the exterior wall seemed to disappear, giving him an unhindered view of a truck parked outside. *Well, that's a nice trick. I wish I knew how I'd done it.*

"What's wrong?" Bean asked as he struck out his arm, urging her not to open the main door.

"We've got company," he replied. "They're outside."

"Who are they? Can you tell? How many?"

Stephen scanned the area outside of the lab. "Does it matter?" Movement caught his eye. A figure approaching the building from the side. "I only see one." He looked for the tell-tale sign of a member of the Watch. What would happen to his folks if Dr. Lambda caught him out here? Would she realize he'd reneged on their deal?

"We can take him." She balled her fist.

"No wait, I can't see that far out. There could be more of them."

"We take them out, too." Stephen didn't need to look in her direction to know that lightning once again danced between her knuckles. He thought about the cameras and indicator lights and wondered if the same network that protected Finn's people from the energy drain was in place here. Maybe the whole town was still powered somehow. That might explain why he hadn't tired by utilizing the map as they navigated through the streets or why Bean hadn't demanded more than her share of rations. The man turned to the side and raised a fist. There was no mistaking the cloth that wrapped around the man's arm below the shoulder. *You can't let them find you here.* Stephen pushed her wrist down. "Too risky."

"Maybe for you, but not for me."

"This place screams mad scientist. Who knows what other chemicals or gases are floating around in the air by now. That lightning of yours could cause an explosion."

The light winked out. "What do you suggest we do then?"

"We don't have a choice. We're going to have to find another way out."

TWENTY

The crash of breaking glass pierced the silence as they made their retreat down the corridors of the lab. "They're in."

"You think?" Bean replied, then winced. "Sorry."

Stephen had grown to expect Bean's sarcastic outbursts. If anything, her attempt at an apology was more out of character. He looked at her and remembered her face the night they met, bathed in moonlight as he explained why they would have to leave the road. *She's scared,* he realized. *She doesn't want to fight them any more than you do.* Stephen remembered the emotions that had swirled around him when he readied himself to take another life. Once the deed was done, there would be no going back. "It's okay."

"No, it isn't." She paused. "Stephen, I'm not… I mean to say, there is something I think you should know."

The halls echoed with the sound of more glass shattering. A loud curse echoed followed by several other muffled voices entering the mix. The hallway took on a purple glow. Lightning danced across Bean's balled up fist. Stephen's gaze locked into hers and saw steel resolve reflected back. The look terrified him more than the voices down the hall. He reached out and touched her shoulder. "Whatever it is, it can wait. We just have to find a back way out of here like we did at the tavern."

"It sounds like one of them was hurt coming in. We should take them out now. Maybe not with lightning, but we can still do some damage while they are distracted."

"And what if it doesn't work?" Stephen whispered, nodding his head at Bean's clenched hand. "What then?" He saw her knuckles were white. The more he thought about it, the more convinced Stephen became that the Watch wasn't here for them, which could mean they were after a different target. *The wand. They must know it is here. But how?* He recalled the camera's flash in front of the glass door. What if the security camera did more than take a single picture? What if it kept recording after that initial flash? Anyone monitoring its feed would know the wand was now in play. *And who took it.* "And what about the wand? I don't have a clue what it does, but I'm pretty sure the Watch shouldn't get their hands on it."

Bean stumbled and overcorrected. Her movements became sluggish and she no longer kept up with his pace.

Not the drain. Not now. A fourth voice entered the mix. While he could not make out the voice's exact words, it was clear this individual was in charge, as the other voices went silent. *He knows we are here*, Stephen thought as his gaze darted around the room in search of another exit. "Just a little further. Okay?" He placed his hand on her shoulder. "Don't make me carry you again." The sheer thought exhausted him, but he knew he would do it again if he had to.

Bean glanced at his hand and then down the hallway in the direction of the lobby. Her shoulders rose and sagged. "I didn't make you the last time."

They continued toward the end of the hall, making as little noise as possible. With the exception of the glass room, most of the doors they passed looked much the same as the office where they'd found the keycard. However, soon the hallway ended with nothing to indicate another way out existed.

"Guess it's a showdown, after all," Bean whispered, clenching her fists.

"Not necessarily," replied Stephen, pulling up Finn's map overlay. A sign with lettering as clear as the day it was first printed showed the word 'EXIT.' An arrow printed under the letters pointed to their right. "This way," he said, pulling her toward an even less descript door than the rest.

"The janitor's closet?" Bean asked. "Isn't that a bit cliché?" Her eyes tightened as she looked in the direction they'd come. "If we are going to hide, why don't we go into one of the other offices? That way if they do come this way we at least have some fighting room."

Voices murmured from the down the hall, followed by heavy footsteps. They were running out of time. "It's not a closet." He opened the door.

"Sure looks like one to me," Bean replied, stepping around Stephen. She raised her fist, glowing like a firefly rather than lit by sparks of electrical discharge. The light caused shadows to dance across the row of shelves stocked with bleach and various spray bottles as she moved. "I suppose we can hide behind this?" she added, pushing a yellow pushcart to the side. She turned, causing the shadows to shift once more, and Stephen noticed a line in between the shelves and the back wall.

"It's another door."

"What is?"

"The shelves." Stephen grinned as he reached toward the back wall. "More camouflage." He stifled a laugh as his fingers found a pull hidden behind one of the spray bottles. "Who builds a place like this?" Stephen asked more for himself. The janitorial shelves swung out with ease, revealing a spiral staircase leading down into nothing but darkness.

"Where do you think it goes?"

The map overlaid across Stephen's vision didn't reveal any additional information, and the effort of maintaining it was beginning to give Stephen a headache. "I have no idea," he answered, banishing the map once more.

"Well, I suppose I should lead the way then," offered Bean, raising her fist up high.

They'd found another door at the base of the stairs, which opened to an empty railway platform. A tunnel lined with brick arched above either side. "Where do you think it goes?" Stephen let his hand drop from where it held the door ajar to gesture at the open tunnels. Realizing his error, he spun to catch the door, but he was too late. The sound of the latch engaging was all too clear. "Just great," he muttered to himself.

"Guess we're going to find out. Come on." Bean offered and took the first steps. "Maybe it leads to another way up."

Stephen shifted the pack's straps once more. *She's right*, he told himself. At least they shouldn't have to worry about the Watch finding them any time soon.

The thought that the rail could still be electrified didn't hit Stephen until they were well on their way. They'd been walking for what felt like an hour on top of the rail without spotting a ladder or other way out when they came to another arch. Stephen and Bean shared a glance but passed through it without comment. The air seemed to shift. Before, the air had resembled that of the lab above. Sterile. However, the air smelled of dirt and mold. It was as if the archway had acted as a sort of airlock. They found another concrete platform on the other side. Stephen suppressed a grunt as he removed the pack from his shoulders and hoisted it onto the edge of the platform. After pulling himself up, he reached out to help Bean. The pale glow emanating from Bean's palm dimmed as she grasped his outstretched hand.

It occurred to Stephen that Bean had been maintaining that glow for the entire time they had been in the tunnels. He tried to think of the last time he'd seen her eat. "I think we can take a break," he offered.

"I can keep going," she replied.

"What about upstairs? You were exhausted."

"I caught my second wind, okay?" The light from her hands increased in intensity.

Stephen tried to hide his disappointment as he looked around. When he'd seen the platform, he'd hoped they might find stairs to the surface, but It appeared the platform led to another tunnel. They'd have to navigate the darkness a while longer. He caught sight of Bean's face. It was difficult to determine if she had grown any paler than usual, but he'd known her long enough to recognize she'd be the last person to admit weakness. "You might be all set," he countered, "but I'm starving." He rummaged through the pack by his side until he found a meal bar he imagined tasted much like the combination of clay and ash might. It was one of the better recipes. "Here, I got you some dinner."

Bean smiled as she took the bar from him. "Aw, honey, you cooked." The light from her hand diminished as she tore into the wrapper. They sat there in shared silence as Stephen tried to pretend the bar he was eating didn't smell like asparagus pee.

"You ready?" Bean asked.

Stephen sighed and pocketed the wrapper with the others. "I guess so."

Once again, the purple light bloomed into view as Bean launched forward into the platform's tunnel while Stephen returned the remaining meals to the pack and repositioned it on his shoulders. Bean had gone a few feet ahead when the light came to a stop. When Stephen followed, he saw why. A mountain of black and gray rubble mixed with twisted steel beams filled their view and blocked their path.

"You have reached your destination. Now ending route guidance." Bean's voice sounded robotic, and her eyes appeared glazed over. Bean shook her head. "Did you say something?"

"Not me." Something tickled Stephen's nose, distracting him from her comment. He swat at it and noticed a dark smear on his hand. *Spider,* he thought. *Fantastic. You got away from the Watch just to get taken out by poisonous spiders.* Stephen turned to go back the way they came. They'd have to follow the rail tunnel to its next stop.

"I think I found something."

Stephen looked where Bean pointed. Down near the base of the debris was a hole, large enough for a mouse to pass but not much more. Its edges appeared jagged, and dark shards lay on the ground beneath it. Stephen reached down and touched one of the shards. It broke apart in his hand.

"Wood?" It didn't make any sense that wood would be among the debris...unless? Stephen looked at the slabs of concrete and twisted beams again. *What if this wall is only supposed to 'look' like a cave-in?*

Stephen clenched his jaw and gestured for Bean to raise her hand, better illuminating the surface. A rusted metal pole protruded from the middle, confirming his theory.

Stephen reached down to the hole in the door and pulled. A large piece came loose in his hand with a snap. The smell of rotten wood assaulted his nostrils. Whoever built the series of secret doors and passages had forgotten to factor in the environment's effect on their design. His nose tickled again. Stephen's eyes watered with the effort to hold a sneeze in, but it was to no avail. The sound echoed in the tunnel. So not camouflage, but it still might be a way out.

Stephen yanked apart another piece of the door, barely registering splinters as they entered his flesh. The light from Bean's hand dimmed as she joined in the destruction. Together, they pulled until Stephen estimated the hole had to have increased in size large enough to allow their bodies to pass if they crawled.

It wasn't quite enough. The backpack caught on a portion of the opening as he attempted to follow Bean through. He heard its fabric tear as he forced it through the remainder of the way and hoped their supplies within hadn't been damaged, too.

Together, they inched forward in the darkness on their hands and knees. Only when Stephen stopped hearing the pack scraping the debris above did he risk standing up again. He took another step and hit a solid wall.

"Watch your head," said Bean as she stood beside him.

Stephen's hand explored the wall until it touched something cool and angular. He could feel bubbled ridges, which had to be the result of rust. This had to be another door. He pulled. There was no movement. Bean must have noticed his muscles tense in the poor light as her hand joined his. Together, they pulled on the handle until it gave way. The door opened an inch, and as it did, a corner scraped at the ground below. Stephen closed his eyes, wishing he could do the same for his ears as he tugged more until the door opened further. Bean squeezed by him.

The door's closing was smoother, and the light from Bean's hand blazed at the sound of the latch making contact once more. They found themselves at one end of a massive room. The ground beneath them was covered in stone tiles, which sparkled in the reflection of Bean's light as they inched forward. Then her light was joined by another. Stephen turned to identify its source. A large rectangular panel dangled from the ceiling just a few feet away.

As they walked further into the room, another panel began to glow. Bean shook her palm, and the panels became the room's only light source. "How are they still working?" she wondered aloud.

Stephen shrugged, thinking that Bean didn't expect an explanation.

A third panel started to glow overhead. Then there was a popping sound, and the panel went black. Stephen pushed Bean to the side.

"Hey," Bean exclaimed before covering her mouth with one hand.

"I don't know about you, but I'd prefer not to be under one of those things if the wiring is bad." Stephen kept his voice just above a whisper.

Stephen watched as Bean glanced back to the first panel. A narrow cord was all that connected the thing to the ceiling. It swayed in the breeze created by their passage. By the look of it, it wouldn't take much to send it crashing down. He fought his lips from curling into a smile as she scurried further to the side of the room and away from the additional lighting fixtures, even though those remained dark.

Even still, there was now enough light in the room to see a large dais on the other side. Chairs were strewn about in front of the dais, as if a performance had been interrupted at the time of the explosion. On the stage, were several white and coffin-sized chrome cylinders lined against the wall. They beckoned him.

He climbed the stairs of the dais, two at a time.

"What do you think they were supposed to do?" Bean asked as she followed behind him.

Stephen shook his head, but couldn't turn away. One of the cylinders caught his attention, begging him to inspect it first. His feet had their own ideas, taking him over to one of the others located more in the middle.

His feet stopped by its side before his brain processed the walk. His hand ran across the cylinder's surface while pressing down. A door in the cylinder's side opened, exposing a keypad, display, and green indicator lights.

"I don't think you should be…" Bean began.

Stephen's eyes widened. "I didn't. I don't." His fingers began dancing across the keypad on their own volition. "I'm not," Stephen realized, in growing terror, that he no longer controlled his own body.

Bean raced to his side and grabbed his wrist. Stephen's other hand shoved at her as his fingers continued to type in commands. "Sorry. I didn't mean to do that. I don't know what is happening," he said, pleading with his eyes for her to understand.

He willed his fingers to stop moving, and as he did so, his peripheral vision caught sight of the cylinder closest to the edge of the dais. Unable to continue to meet Bean's eye after he shoved her or watch as his hand move on its own, he focused on the tube while urging his fingers to stop.

Bean approached him again, touching his sleeve. He didn't know how, and he didn't know why, but she understood the panic going through his mind at that moment all too well. She touched his wrist again, and he focused on the warmth of her touch on his skin until his fingers finally stopped moving.

A beep brought his attention back to the cylinder in front of him. The display flashed 'DEACTIVATE.' Bean drew Stephen back toward the edge of the dais as the cylinder creaked. A gap opened in its side, releasing a gas from within. A large portion of the tube lifted up and slid out. More gas exited. Stephen released the breath he was holding as the mist dissipated into the air.

Then nothing.

Stephen's curiosity got the better of him, and he took a step forward to better see the contents of the tube. Bean's hand encircled his as she followed. Together, they peered over the edge.

"Is he dead?" Bean asked.

Contained within the tube lay a dark-haired man.

TWENTY-ONE

"He looks awfully well-preserved for a dead guy," Bean said as she backed away from the cylinder.

From what they could see above the man's clothing, his skin tone was an unnatural alabaster white, but Stephen had to agree with Bean. There were no signs of decay and no smell of death. "But he can't be alive either. Can he?"

"If he's alive, he really doesn't like the sun."

Stephen glanced back at the door from where they'd come. It didn't appear as if anyone had traveled this way in a very long time. He spotted the outline of another door centered in a recessed portion of the back wall. With only two of the ceiling lighting fixtures working he hadn't noticed it before. Was there another way out? He clung to the hope.

"Water," a man's voice muttered.

Stephen almost mistook the sound for crumbling paper, but Bean screeched as she jumped back, stopping herself inches away from falling off the dais. Purple lightning danced across her fingertips and up her lower arm. Stephen tensed into a flight or fight pose, ready for either.

"Water…" the man spoke again. This time there was no mistaking that the words were coming from the man within the cylinder. As Stephen stared in shock, a single white finger lifted out of the tube and curled around the edge, followed by another. "Please," he added.

Though the voice was weak, it possessed a tone of command. Stephen was digging through his backpack in search of the canteen before he knew what he was doing. *At least he isn't calling out for blood*, thought Stephen as he twisted open the top. With his white-blue skin and sunken eyes, the man's vibe was too vampire-like for Stephen's comfort.

Stephen poured a bit of their water into a cup and approached the cylinder. The eyes of the man inside were open but darted around as if in search of focus. Unthinking, Stephen reached into the tube and pulled the man upright with one hand while holding the cup to the man's lips with the other. Wires and plastic tubes hung from his torso and his limbs like tendrils.

"Ah…" The man closed his eyes after taking a sip. "Much better." The cylinder vibrated as the tendrils released the man and retracted back into its hull.

Color returned to the man's complexion. Though his skin remained pale, it no longer appeared as white as the cylinder surrounding it. His appearance suggested he was somewhere between his twenties and thirties, although it was hard to tell for sure. When his eyes opened once more, they made him seem decades older. *Like Finn*, thought Stephen.

"How?" Bean whispered behind Stephen.

The man blinked twice more, and his gaze became steadier, focusing in on Bean.

"Well, this is a nice surprise." He smiled. "And you are?" His voice became livelier along with the rest of him with every passing second.

Stephen knew without looking that Bean would be frowning at the compliment and forced himself not to smile.

"Someone who doesn't trust reanimated corpses," she replied.

The man shook in Stephen's arms. At first, Stephen thought that he must be having a seizure, only to realize after a few moments that the man was laughing. "Delightful. Please accept my humblest apologies," the man offered. "I suppose my appearance must indeed come as quite a shock."

"Who are you?" asked Stephen.

The man frowned at the question. "You don't recognize me?"

Stephen's eyes narrowed. "Should I?"

The man sighed. Lifting his other hand out of the cylinder, the man grabbed onto the tube's side and pulled himself up until he was in an upright position without the need of Stephen's support. Stephen took a step back to give the man more room to maneuver as the man wiggled one leg then another. "Based on your age, I suppose not. Still, one always hopes." The man grimaced. "Do you know that pins and needles feeling you get whenever you allow your limbs to fall asleep?"

Stephen nodded.

"Well, what I am currently going through feels like that." He wiggled his leg again as his frown deepened. "Except a thousand times worse." The man twisted at the waist as he lifted one leg over the edge followed by the other. He looked at his legs as if they were the worst kind of scum for not behaving. "Would you mind helping me a bit longer?"

Stephen stepped forward and helped pull the man out of the cylinder, supporting his weight with his shoulders while the man touched the floor with each foot a toe at a time. He didn't speak again until he was satisfied that his legs weren't in danger of collapsing out from under his body.

"I'm Dr. Alan Dronigh." A cocky smile returned to his face.

Stephen fought from glancing at Bean as she sucked in her breath. The man could be any number of people, but Stephen was convinced his biological father couldn't be one of them. *Unless he's been here this whole time.* Stephen silenced the voice in his head. The man had an air of charisma about him, that much was true, but he was either delusional or a liar.

"This is the part when you tell me your name."

There was no way he could be the same person. "I'm no one," Stephen finally replied. *But how common is a name like Dronigh?*

"Well No One and Ms. Someone Who Doesn't Trust Reanimated Corpses, would either of you be so kind as to tell me where we are?"

Stephen summoned the map overlay again. Stephen blinked. "That can't be right," he muttered to himself. To the others, he replied, "If the map is correct, we're under what used to be the DK Ventures Tower. At least what is left of it."

The person claiming to be Alan looked around the room. "Ah, I hoped for something different. I thought I smelled peanut butter."

"Peanut butter?" asked Bean. "All I smell is dust."

"Where do you think you should be?" Stephen asked.

"It doesn't matter. We are here now."

"Would have helped if the front door was more accessible." Bean gestured with her thumb up at the ceiling. "It's more mountain up there than building. I doubt anyone bothered to look for survivors."

"I told Damien he wouldn't regret the expense of reinforcing the structural supports in that area. The foreman bragged it could survive a bomb." Alan chuckled at the comment before looking at their faces and then scanning the contents of the room. "I guess Damien should have paid him more. I'll tell him myself as soon as you take me to him."

Stephen's lips tightened into a fine line. "We don't know any Damien, and we definitely aren't taking you to him."

Alan's smile slipped. "But of course you are." He frowned, and his eyebrows knit in confusion. "Didn't he send you?"

"No one sent us here. We found it by accident."

Alan's frown deepened. "No." He shook his head again. "No, that can't be right. Damien sent you. That was all part of the plan."

"What plan?" asked Bean.

"What plan? The plan, of course." Alan started to shake. This time wasn't caused by laughter. Alan's head began to roll from side to side as spittle began to form at the side of his mouth.

"What's happening?" asked Stephen.

"Like I have any idea," replied Bean. "Maybe it's a side effect from being in whatever that thing is." She took another look at Alan, and her eyes widened. "Lay him on the ground," she ordered.

Stephen lowered Alan to the floor and took a step back to give him air.

"Quick," demanded Bean. "Giving me something I can put in his mouth so that he doesn't bite off his tongue."

Stephen glanced around the room in a panic. A narrow piece of debris caught his eye. Picking it up, he rushed back over to Alan and stuck it in Alan's mouth.

"If he's the real Alan Dronigh, then he's like us, right?" asked Bean, tucking errant strands of hair behind her ear as she looked down at the man on the ground.

"So?"

She touched Alan's arm and closed her eyes. Alan continued to shake on the ground. She frowned. "I can't. You try."

"Try what?" asked Stephen, perplexed.

"You're supposed to be the network expert. Pretend his brain is just another computer and connect with it. See if you can settle him down. Like I had to do for you when you first accessed the data stream."

Stephen's brows knit. "But I don't have a clue how you did that either."

Bean reached up and touched Stephen's cheek. "You have to stop fighting so hard. Open your mind like Finn told you to." She pointed at the man convulsing on the floor. "At least try. He is your father."

Stephen crouched to the floor next to Alan's convulsing body and placed his hand on the man's forehead. "He's not my father," he grumbled, but closed his eyes and imagined reaching out with his mind as if it were his arm. As he did so, a pressure built up behind his eyes, as if there was another presence in there with him, fighting him not to do this thing, breaking his focus, and blocking his effort. It was as if the other presence was encouraging him to let the body before him die. "This is pointless." He opened his eyes.

"He's not breathing. Try again."

"I told you I don't know how."

"I don't care. Now focus."

He placed his fingers on either side of the man's temples. The skin beneath his fingers was damp with sweat and twitched in a racing pulse. The pressure returned ten-fold. Like that first experience with the data stream, a wave of thoughts that weren't his own rushed across his consciousness. Stephen closed his eyes, tightening the lids as moisture threatened to escape. A comforting warmth spread on his arm where Bean's hand rested. *Pretend it's another node on a network.* He imagined he was back in his hidden nook in the barn staring at his rebuilt console. His fingers flew across the man's forehead with light taps as he visualized entering commands on a keyboard.

The pressure eased as if startled. He pushed through, forcing himself through it much as he had forced the bag through the opening at the top of the stairs. However, just like he'd experienced with the bag, he felt something in his mind tear. Then the pressure fell away, and Stephen pushed his mind and his will forward.

His vision shifted. When he opened his eyes, Stephen was lying on the floor looking up at Bean and his own face. His eyes appeared dull and unseeing. It was as if someone had positioned a wax figurine above him. "What's happening?" he attempted to yell, but there was something in his mouth, blocking the words. He spit it out. The piece of debris. "Bean?" he whispered. "Something's wrong."

"How do you know my name?"

"You told me. Short for Beatrice."

She met his gaze, her lips parting as her eyes widened. "It will be okay." She placed her hand on his forehead. The sheer size of the whites in her eyes betrayed her lie. She looked at Stephen's body. "You're not breathing," she murmured. It was true. His chest was just as still as his face. Turning back to face him, she said, "You were supposed to find his mind. Not take it over."

His panic rose. "What do I do now?" His vision started going black.

"Focus on me. Just me." Darkness framed his vision of her, but at the same time, that growing darkness allowed him to ignore everything but her. Strands of her blonde hair had escaped from behind her ear. He wanted to reach out and sweep it back where it belonged, but the hand that moved was not his own. As he watched, her eyes filled with unshed tears. "Good. Now try to find your way back," he heard her whisper.

He closed his eyes and imagined Bean. She became a flame on a candle in his mind, full of light and warmth, but flickering as it danced to an imagined breeze. He should be fighting to calm himself, but all he could think of was protecting her from the wind. The panic in his chest subsided as the flame straightened. Then he felt a hard shove as if someone had snuck up and pushed him from behind. His stomach lurched as if he fell.

When he opened his eyes, he was looking down on Bean's hunched over form. He attempted to reach out to touch her back and was pleased to see his arm obeyed his command. Bean looked at him at his touch. Narrow lines of moisture streaked her face. His lips turned up. "You do care."

She jumped up and walked away. "Don't you ever try that again."

Stephen looked at Alan lying prone on the floor. The convulsions had stopped, but his eyes were still closed.

Alan groaned. "Don't worry, I'll make sure there will never be a second time. Excuse me." He twisted his body so that he was propped up on one elbow facing away from the others. His torso shook as bile created a puddle on the floor.

Bean wrinkled her nose and took a step back. Alan frowned. "Unfortunately, it would seem that I still require a little more recovery time. If you aren't going to take me to Damien, would you at least move me somewhere a little more comfortable? My head feels as if it might split in two."

Stephen nodded and pulled Alan upright, bracing Alan's body with his shoulder. Bean looked at them and then at the other cylinders on the dais. "Are there any others like you down here?"

Alan turned his head following Bean's gaze. His eyes twinkled under the swaying light. "No." His lips curled. "Rest assured, I am quite unique." He turned back toward them and met Stephen's eyes. "As I am beginning to suspect, you are as well."

TWENTY-TWO

Stephen attempted to shift Alan's weight while checking out the pair of recessed doors on the other side of the room. "Do you think it's a way out?" They had to find a way out. They'd spent too long down here already.

Bean glanced at him, cocking her head in unvoiced question.

"Over there. I think it used to be an elevator," replied Stephen, pointing in its direction. Considering how well-preserved this room was, he had to wonder if the elevator shaft might have also survived intact. He had no idea how they would be able to scale such a thing, but figured there had to be a service ladder or something similar inside. Each minute they stayed down here was another minute he risked the Watch returning to the tower. *Assuming they haven't already figured out you aren't there.*

Alan followed their gazes. "I'm afraid that's not an option."

"It could be," Stephen argued. "I mean look around this room. Look at the lights. They survived. Maybe the elevator did, too."

"Ah, I see why you might think that, but no." The corner of Alan's lip turned up. "I'm quite certain we'd find the way blocked."

"You don't know that."

"Yes, I do. The initial explosion took place in there. I'm not sure of the exact location of explosions that followed, but there were more than a few." Alan shrugged. "That's why I went into the pod to wait it out rather than trying to go up."

Stephen took another look at the elevator. He imagined the pile of rubble that in all likelihood still lay above them. "Do you know if anyone was in it? When the building came down? The elevator, I mean." Stephen asked as he repressed a shudder. Anyone trapped inside would have spent their last moments in terror as they ran out of food or water. It would have been awful.

Bean looked at the pair of doors, and Stephen noticed she hesitated just a step. "Do you think it was quick?"

"It was quicker than he deserved," Alan's voice cut through Stephen's thoughts. He gestured at the debris and hanging wires. "You recognized the building's name. What do you know about what happened here?" Alan shifted again.

The change in weight distribution caught Stephen off guard, and it was all he could do not to stumble. *How did I get stuck with this job?* "Not much. I do know this building is pretty much the center of where it all started. As in, ground zero." He scanned the map's information. "Oh, and it once housed some sort of think tank."

Alan snorted. "Some sort of think tank," he repeated. "Oh, we did so much more than that here." Alan swept his free arm, as if to encompass the room. "We didn't just come up with ideas. We took them further, pushing the limits of the human experience. We found ways to eradicate diseases. Make people better, faster, and stronger than they were before. We were maximizing life's every potential."

"So says the man who can't walk on his own," said Bean.

Alan's lips tightened, and his arm returned to his side. His eyes took on a distant look. "There will always be those who fear or can't handle change, and even more who value their profits over the greater good. Unfortunately, those people joined forces." Alan shook his head as he motioned for Stephen to stop. He took a hesitant step on his own. "Ground zero." Alan seemed to chew on the word. "We can discuss that term later, but first, do you happen to know if there were any other survivors? From my so-called think tank, I mean."

Stephen frowned and tried to think of anything Ed or Helen may have mentioned over the years, but his memory drew a blank. The beginning of the end of life as they knew it just didn't come up in their regular conversation. He imagined tapping into the data stream. It offered even less help. Its information stopped at the beginning of the panic.

"If any did, they kept their stories to themselves," replied Bean before Stephen could answer.

"Pity." Alan smiled. "But that doesn't necessarily mean there weren't. Discretion was everything in our business, and we tended to bring on those who knew how to keep sensitive information a secret." Alan took a couple more steps, each more confident than the last. Stephen stayed back and crossed his arms. "So, if there weren't any other survivors and you didn't come here to rescue me, I must ask, why are you here?"

Stephen glanced at Bean and then at the roof above them. It was well past evening by now.

Alan wobbled. "Ah, I understand you want to keep your secrets. As I said, we are"—he paused to look at one of the hanging light fixtures—"or *were* a discreet group." Alan patted Stephen's hand, before shaking it away. "How about we talk about something else while we get to know one another better? Like why you call this place ground zero."

Bean spoke first. "My parents lost their jobs. So did everyone else. Some company that everyone thought was too big to fail, did. My parents waited around. They thought it was only a matter of time until things got better, but things didn't get better. Kids started dying instead." Her lips twisted. "My parents were stupid."

Stephen realized how lucky he had been to reach the farm with Helen and Ed so early in the initial crisis. If his guardian's hadn't connected the dots between events, weeks if not months before the rest of the population, they might never have reached the farm before the real global panic set in.

"Then things really got bad. When people realized that no government was coming to help them, they took matters into their own hands."

"So who is in charge now?" asked Alan.

Bean shrugged. "Big picture? Who knows? But a group called the Watch sure thinks they are around here." Alan's lips twisted. Stephen found himself yawning. Bean, noticing, yawned, too. She asked, "How long do you think we've been down here?"

"Three, maybe four hours," he guessed. *Three or four hours they could have spent on the road back to the tower.* He yawned again. That would mean the time was long past midnight by now. Stephen's back ached from their walk through the tunnels. He looked back into the open room.

"Maybe we should camp here for the night before setting out again."

Stephen's shoulders tensed at Bean's suggestion, but he yawned again anyway. As much as he wanted to be on their way, she was right. *But where?* Stephen frowned. His eyebrow rose as an idea sprouted in his mind. "I guess we could sleep in the pods." *Worst case, we can leave Alan in one.*

"What? The pods?" Alan pulled back. "That's a terrible idea. We can't. Why would you even suggest something like that?"

"Of course we can." Stephen plastered a smile on his face. "They protected you for, what, fifteen years? What's one more night?" They'd reactivate Alan's pod and be on their way first thing in the morning without him. It was a great plan. Then, after delivering the wand and freeing his folks, he'd come back for him or send someone else to do the job. *Maybe*. "They are perfect."

Bean glanced back at the cylinders. She pulled Stephen to the side. "Are you nuts? What if you lose control again?"

"I won't." Stephen scowled in an effort to mask the feeling of helplessness her words brought back.

"Why don't I believe that?"

Alan arched an eyebrow. "They *were* perfect." He nodded his head in the direction of one of the more damaged pods. "Not so much anymore. What if you got in and it sealed itself? We might never get it to re-open."

Stephen turned his attention to Bean. "We need to be out of sight. What about the people back at the lab? What if they found the door? They could be almost here by now." The excuse wasn't even a lie. Stephen glanced at the door. If the Watch knew someone had taken the wand, they could still be out there tracking them.

"You poor things," said Alan. "I can't begin to imagine what an ordeal you must have gone through." He also focused his attention on Bean. "The world ends and you are on the run. No wonder you are both terrified." Alan's voice had smoothed into a near purr.

Stephen smirked as he waited to see how Bean might respond. *This guy*—he still refused to accept that Alan was his biological father—*might think he knows how to talk to women, but he doesn't know Bean.*

Bean bristled like a cat. "I. Am. Not. Terrified."

Alan laughed, "I stand corrected. You remind me of a colleague of mine named Sarah. She was a tough one, too."

"Do you think she was tough enough to survive that?" Bean pointed at the light fixture still hanging by a cord, which looked lower to the ground than it had upon their initial arrival.

The smile fell away from Alan's face, but the laughter never left his eyes. "It wouldn't surprise me in the least."

"So, back to tonight," Stephen interrupted. "I still think our best bet is to spend it in the pods. We just leave them open."

"No." Alan's pronouncement boomed across the space. "No. And that's the end of the discussion."

Stephen raised an eyebrow. He'd use the same tone of voice as Ed had used on him whenever he'd been particularly stubborn. "Fine, we'll sleep somewhere else, but we take turns," he said to Bean. He thought of the screech the access door had made as it scraped across the floor when they'd entered. *At least no one is going to be able to sneak up on us through that thing,* Stephen thought.

Alan's lips curled up. "Something I am more than happy to do. I'll even take the first watch."

Stephen clenched his jaw. He hadn't intended to include Alan in the rotation.

"You both look dead on your feet." Alan pointed at the pods with his thumb. "I've been asleep for…what was it?"

Stephen turned away and scanned the room for another location. "Fifteen years." A large section of ductwork lay on the ground nearby. It could shield them from view.

"Well, then I think I can manage to stay awake for a few hours. If it makes you feel better, I'll even keep watch here while you two get some rest over there."

Once they were behind the ductwork, Stephen unzipped the backpack and pulled out the tight roll that served as their sleeping mat, and he whispered to Bean, "I'm sorry."

Bean paused. "For what?"

"For, you know"—he nodded his head in the direction of the fallen ductwork—"all of this. What your family had to go through afterward. I had no idea it was like that."

Bean snorted. "That's hardly your fault."

Stephen stood, and as he shook the mat out, he caught a glance of Alan at the wall. Alan's eyes were focused on the dais. Shadows cut across his face, so his expression was hard to read, but it appeared his lips were pulled in a smug smile as if amused at a joke only he understood.

Alan turned his head, matching Stephen's gaze. *That's not creepy at all*, Stephen told himself. He broke eye contact first, crouching behind the metal as he smoothed the mat across the floor. As he did so, he noticed his shadow against the tubing's surface. It was almost identical in height and form to Alan, and he found himself for the first time beginning to accept that Alan might just be his biological father.

Twenty-Three

Stephen opened his eyes to darkness. He hadn't intended to fall asleep, not wanting to trust their safety to some guy they'd pulled out of a metal tube, even if that guy was his birth father, but it would seem his body had other ideas. As he listened to Bean's rhythmic breathing by his side, he was tempted to turn over and slip back into unconsciousness. Then he heard a scratching noise from the direction of the subway access door. Stephen shot up, banishing thoughts of sleep from his brain. As he did so, one of the lighting fixtures came back online. *They must work with some sort of motion sensor*, he thought. As the light expanded and intensified, he looked around the room, but Alan was nowhere to be seen.

I knew we shouldn't trust him. Stephen reached over and tapped Bean's arm. Her eyes opened in an instant. She rolled into a defensive crouch with one hand clenched into a fist, as if readying to do battle with the other flat on the ground.

A blinking green spot the size of a gnat appeared in his lower vision. Stephen swat at it. *Weird bug.*

"What is it?" Bean's lips hadn't moved, and yet the words in his mind were spoken in her voice.

Stephen frowned and tried to formulate a response in his mind. He imagined a 'send' key and pressed it. "Alan's gone."

"Gone? What do you mean gone?" This time, there was no doubt that her words were in his mind. A grin spread across his face in light of this newest skill, his irritation forgotten for the moment.

"He couldn't walk more than three steps on his own last night. How could he be gone? Where *could* he go?" he heard her say.

Stephen shrugged as his annoyance with Alan returned in full force. *Maybe he really is dear old dad, after all. He sure does have the disappearing part down.* "I don't know. Maybe he knew about another way out of here." This time the words were much easier to send out. As annoyed as he was, Stephen was more than a little relieved that they didn't have to worry about the man anymore. It also meant an exit could be somewhere nearby.

He heard a muffled scratching, scraping sound again, and Alan's whereabouts became the least of his concerns. *The Watch,* Stephen thought. *They must have found the entrance, after all.* If so, they had minutes before the Watch found the door to this room. *Or it's rats.* Stephen shuddered as adrenaline flooded his system. Stephen turned his hand so that his palm was face up and brought his fingers together until they were just shy of touching, as he'd seen Bean do so many times before, and he concentrated. *Think of it as another program*, he thought, focusing in on the ridges of his fingerprints. *Run electric eel 2.0.* A flash of purple light jumped from his thumb to his middle finger. *Yes.* The light winked out. He'd let the joy of his accomplishment break his concentration. He focused on his hand. The purple light flashed again, this time from thumb to pinkie and then from the ring to the index finger. His fingertips tingled as the light continued to jump across his skin, faster and faster, until it appeared to consolidate into a ball hovering just above his palm. *I am Zeus, God of Thunder.*

"It's about time you figured that out," Bean's voice in his mind broke his concentration once more, and the orb blinked out.

He now understood why Bean was so quick to accept the lessons Finn had taught her while not worrying about the risk of the energy drain. The knowledge that he would never again be without defense was intoxicating. He flexed his fingers again, and the light returned on command. He opened his fingers, and the light went away in an instant. Why had it been so hard to believe in what he could do?

"Did you know that the man who first discovered how to do that particular skill thought it little more than an amusing party trick?" Alan's voice echoed in the room. Stephen spun, searching for the source of the voice. "Did I startle you?" continued Alan as he stepped out of one of the room's remaining shadows. "My apologies. After the feeling came back to my legs, I found I could no longer sit in one place, so moved where I hoped I wouldn't disturb you. I also turned off the lights."

How had I missed seeing him? Stephen wondered. The shadow had wrapped itself around him like a blanket. Stephen also noticed Alan's stride no longer showed any semblance of weakness. "How…?" Stephen started.

"I reprogrammed the control to ignore my movement so that you could get some sleep. I thought it was the least I could do."

Alan spoke of accessing a nearly ruined control panel and wirelessly updating the code with a mere thought, as if it was the sort of thing a regular person could do any day. Stephen blinked as it dawned on him that as far as Alan knew, everyone still could.

"No, I was going to ask how long were we asleep?"

Alan smiled. "Oh. I'd say about nine hours."

"Nine hours?" Stephen exclaimed. "Nine?" he repeated. He cursed. If they had found an access ladder, they could already be at the train station on their way back to the island by now. "Why did you let us sleep that long?"

"Because you needed it."

Stephen clenched his teeth. "Don't you get it?" He pointed at the door. "There are people after us. People we might have gotten away from in that amount of time who we are now going to have to fight our way past, all thanks to you."

Alan raised an eyebrow. "Must you? Fight them, I mean."

"Listen, I know this must be hard for you to accept. The world was a different place when you got into that pod. But now, we do what we have to do to survive."

An ear-piercing scrape silenced further debate as the door started to open. *Not rats then.* Alan took a step toward it. Stephen stifled a curse. An incautious man was a dead man, and as much as he wanted to be rid of Alan, he didn't want that on his conscience. He grabbed Alan and pulled him down behind some fallen ductwork while Bean followed suit. They might not have any option other than to fight, but at least they might still be able to take whoever it was on the other side of that door by surprise.

Alan started to say something. Stephen covered Alan's mouth with his hand and shook his head. Alan arched an eyebrow, then shrugged. Interpreting the gesture to mean that Alan would follow their lead, Stephen risked a glance around the ductwork.

A man stepped out of a doorway's shadows. His skin appeared paper thin with age spots dotting his balding scalp. He wore a jersey, which hung from his frame as if purchased once for someone twice his size. Most of the paint that once proclaimed the team's name and player's number had flaked off to illegibility. A thin chain with an egg-shaped pendant hung around his neck. Stephen did a double take as the lamplight hit the man's face in full. His nose was broad and flat with nostrils that flared like a beast's. Gaps where teeth should have been made him appear to possess fangs. *Then again...* Stephen took another hard look at the man's mouth. *They might very well be actual fangs, or were they more like tusks?*

The man took another step into the room, and Stephen noticed he walked with a limp. *Don't freak out. He's just an old man with a bad leg in serious need for a trip to the dentist.* The old man's nostrils flared once again as his lips curled up. *Tusks,* thought Stephen. *Definitely tusks.* "What are you playing at? Hide-and-go-seek?"

The old man laughed or at least produced a sound that Stephen interpreted as a laugh. It was low, and rough, and could have passed for the bark of a dog. "Not much of a game. You stink, you know." Stephen watched as the man grabbed his less favored leg and twisted. The act made a sickening snapping sound as the leg seemed to rotate into an unnatural position. The man dropped down onto all fours, looking like a bull readying for a charge. "Ready or not, here I come." He scraped the floor with the unnatural leg, now appearing anything but lame. The ground shook with each step.

Seconds that seemed like years compared to the beating of his heart passed. Not wanting to give their position away until they had to, Stephen's hand remained flesh-colored, but his fingers were curled, ready to summon the lightning in an instant. What had Alan called it? A party trick? Dr. Lambda's word for what they could do came back unbidden. *Delusion.* What if that's all it was? Was he really willing to trust his life to something the original creator described as a trick? The man at the barricade had been weak already. Even if the lightning wasn't a figment of his imagination, it wouldn't have taken much to knock him down. This man, this monster, was different.

As the old man's steps grew closer, Stephen became more convinced trusting in their abilities was a mistake. He turned to warn Bean, but she had disappeared. His heart caught in his throat. He wanted to call out but worried the old man might sense projected thoughts as well as audible calls. There was no telling what a person who'd been physically modified like that could do.

Then the footsteps stopped. Stephen risked another glance around the ductwork. The beastman lay in a crumpled pile on the floor, his unnatural legs twitching. Bean stood above him, her fist clenching purple lightning like an avenging goddess. A beautiful, magnificent, all-powerful avenging goddess. *The lightning trick had been enough.* Or maybe Bean was just that good. *Be glad she's on your side.*

Stephen's heart skipped a beat as Bean nudged the man with her toe. The man's leg spasmed, but there was no other evidence of consciousness. Satisfied he was no longer a threat, she left him there and returned to where Stephen still crouched. "I believe this puts me ahead again."

"Ahead of what?"

"Oh, don't pretend you haven't been keeping score."

"I don't know what you are talking about," Stephen murmured with a smile. Bean's eyes seemed more slate than jade and her skin grayer than it had before, but that didn't stop Stephen from wanting to touch her if only to assure himself she was safe.

"Yes, you do. You've been keeping track of how often you've swooped in and saved me." Stephen started to protest but stopped when Bean held up one hand. "Don't even try to say you haven't. You're a terrible liar." Bean's eyes softened as she placed her hand on his chin. "I like that about you," she whispered as she traced her fingers across his jawline while coaxing his gaze to meet hers once more.

Then her lips met his, and all thoughts of their mission, the events of the last few days and even the recent danger, fled his mind. Lost in sensation and focusing on the heat of her skin where it touched his, Stephen forgot they weren't alone until he heard a cough. Bean pulled away, and a shy smile played across her lips. Her cheeks were rosy and her eyes sparkled. Gone was any trace of the shadow he thought he had once seen, and he weakened in the knees to look at her.

Her smile vanished. She took another step back, touching her lips with her fingers. "I—"

Worry took root in Stephen's stomach.

"If you two are quite done," Alan started, jolting Stephen back to the present. "I'd appreciate some help, here." Alan knelt on the ground next to the man.

"Good idea. We should move him before any more of his friends get here." Stephen came over to Alan's side and bent over to pull the old man up.

"And why should we do that?"

"So we can surprise them, too. It's our only advantage."

Alan rolled his eyes. "I told you before we didn't have to fight anyone."

"And I told *you*, we don't have a choice. Look at him." Stephen nodded in the direction of the old man's face. The old man's limp jaw opened as Stephen pulled him upright, allowing ample view of his long canine teeth. "Do you think a guy who looks like this is interested in talking? I mean, do you think he was born that way? Because I sure don't. Who does that to themselves anyway?"

"Any number of the Sharks. They thought it made them look more intimidating to the other team. Based on your reaction, I suppose they are right."

"Sharks."

"Yes, Sharks. As in, the football team. You should see some of the others. Rotledge might have spent more time on the bench than on the field, but you could never fault his enthusiasm."

"You know him?"

"I should hope so. After all, I asked him to come here."

TWENTY-FOUR

The beastman didn't so much as make a woof as Alan opened the door to the subway access tunnel. Stephen blinked as his eyes took in the beam of natural sunlight shining down from above. His chest ached as he filled his lungs with a deep breath, savoring the scent of fresh air, even if that air was mixed with dirt and a hint of rust. A hatch in the ceiling made invisible in the dark now lay open, exposing a ladder to the surface and freedom from the tunnels.

Bean cocked her head as she watched Alan reach up and pull the bottom rungs down to their level. "I don't get it."

"Get what?" replied Alan as he shook the ladder as if testing its strength.

"Why go in the pod? I mean, if you knew there was another way out, why didn't you take it?" Stephen grinned as Bean asked the question that gnawed on his mind since they'd settled down for the night. It was as if he and she had been connected long before ever accessing the data stream.

Alan stopped his inspection and turned to face them both while keeping one hand on the rung. "I would think that would be obvious." He nodded toward the rock and twisted metal that lay around them. "A group of anti-technological nut jobs had the building surrounded. I thought it best not to give them an easy target."

Alan returned his attention to the ladder and took a step. "And before you ask, I also couldn't possibly know if this access point remained open all the way to the surface, which is why I called for Rotledge to come and clear it for us."

"What should we do about him?" asked Stephen.

"Do?"

"About Rotledge? Should we wait for him to wake up?"

The corner of Alan's lips turned up. "After the thanks you gave him, I very much doubt you want to be anywhere near him when he wakes up."

"But we can't just leave him down here," Stephen protested.

Alan shook his head. "Of course we can."

"But he's your friend."

Alan paused and looked at Stephen. "In addition to our business projects, my company is…er…*was* invested in the success of the Sharks. He's a former business associate. Never confuse the two. Now, are you ready to return to the surface, or do you want to take your chances with whoever you think is following you down here?"

Seeing no other choice, Stephen followed Alan up to the surface, hoping he hadn't just traded one monster for another.

As they made their way outside and back down the rubble mountain, which had one time served as an office building, Alan picked up a clump of dirt and small pebbles at the base of the pile and began rubbing it across his clothing.

"You don't need to do that," said Stephen as he gestured to the empty open road below. "I mean, if you want your clothes to get dirty, they'll get there on their own."

Alan scraped harder. "Exactly, but that will take time. Until then, if everything is as you say it is, then I'm going to stand out, which is never a strategy for success if survival depends on blending in."

Bean picked up a wad of earth and threw it at Alan. "Here, let me help."

You don't have any reason to be jealous, Stephen told himself. *She likes you.* He paused as he watched the exchange in front of him. *Doesn't she?* Stephen frowned. There hadn't been a repeat of their kiss. In fact, she hadn't even touched him since then. Had it only been a response to her victory over Rotledge? A knot formed in his stomach that had nothing to do with the last meal bar he'd eaten. "Something else has been bothering me," interrupted Stephen.

"Oh?" asked Alan as he continued to rub dirt into his previously pristine clothing.

"You." Stephen glanced in Bean's direction for support but was unable to make eye contact as she scooped up another bit of dirt and handed it to Alan. "This is going to come out the wrong way, but you don't look anywhere old enough to be who you say you are, even if you've been asleep all this time." Stephen glanced Bean's way. "Er...I mean, you look my age, which would make you like twelve when you...you know"— Stephen chewed his lip to keep from saying the words *had me*, which rattled around in his head—"discovered stuff," he finished with instead.

A dazzling smile returned to Alan's face. "What can I say? I have good genes." Alan chuckled. "You kids might not yet appreciate the humor in that phrase, but one day you will realize it is one of the world's biggest understatements."

Bean shrugged and stepped back to admire her handiwork. "Satisfied?"

Alan looked down at his attire now stained brown with streaks of yellow-green where weeds had mixed in with the dirt clump. He sighed. "I suppose it will have to do." He walked down the street without waiting to see if they would follow.

Alan's connection and command of their abilities had gotten them out of the tunnels. Who knew how long they might have continued without seeing the light of day within him? *Don't give him too much credit. It was the guy he summoned who opened the door.* Stephen thought of his call to Wes across the water. *I wonder what sort of range we have.* Stephen wrinkled his forehead, focused his thoughts, and mentally pushed them until he thought he might give himself a headache.

Alan chuckled. "What exactly are you trying to do?"

Stephen's shoulders drooped. "I was trying to send a message to a friend letting him know that we were on our way back. Like how you called Rotledge."

"Was that what you were doing? From where I stood, it looked like those meal bars you've been inhaling weren't agreeing with you. I was feeling rather glad not to have tried them." Bean laughed at Alan's comment.

Stephen looked at anything but their faces as he sought to come up with a response. *You are such an idiot. Listen to her laugh. She's not interested in you. You were just in the right place at the right time. End of story.* His eyes landed on a pair of boarded-up windows belonging to what once had been a service station. Large swathes of faded red paint swirled across their surfaces, but the graffiti had long since fallen into a state of neglect.

"I give up." He threw his hands up. *Might as well ask. They can't think any less of you.* "How does this mental telepathy thing work over distances even when so much else doesn't?" Stephen gestured at the building to illustrate his point.

Alan glanced at the service station and then back to Stephen. He cocked his head. "Ignoring the simplistic use of the term 'telepathy,' I fail to see why you might think a failed business has any impact on our ability to transmit and receive information."

"A few weeks ago, I was living in the middle of nowhere, and my only contact with the outside world was done by computer. If our windmill stopped working, it was radio silence."

"How inconvenient for you."

Ignoring Alan's commentary, Stephen picked up a broken piece of asphalt. "Take this rock." He threw it up and caught it with hand. "Here, Bean, catch." Stephen threw to Bean's outstretched hand. "Now throw it back." Bean compiled. "I totally get that she and I might be able to communicate. Well, maybe I don't get *how* we're doing it exactly, but at least I'm guessing it is because I'm near enough for her to pick up whatever sort of signal it is I'm generating." Stephen tossed the rock again, this time further down the street, not caring where it landed. "But there's got to be some limit to my range, and without connecting to another computer, or node, or whatever to power the signal, how does the information get where it is going? It's not like the grid still works."

Alan stepped closer and placed a hand on Stephen's shoulder. "Is that a fact?" Alan walked over to the service station. After studying the window for a few moments, he reached forward and pulled at the boards. "The first thing you need to know is you were lied to. There is no grid, at least not like you think there is." They came away easy, falling to the ground with a clatter. Alan placed his hand on the glass and closed his eyes. Stephen watched as Alan's chest rose and fell twice while the rest of his body remained motionless. A glow began to expand from inside the shop. A sign near the door blinked on, showing the words 'open all night' in blue and red LEDs.

Bean gasped. "How is that even possible?"

"There are embedded power cells in the glass and nanoelectronics in the brickwork full of all sorts of sensors and processors, grouped under the generic term nanobots. The bots are in everything. Walls, streets, everywhere, even a person's blood. They are what gave people who could afford it access to the data stream with a thought. It was one of the very few things that the Evans family and their company ever got right. Now, all you have to know is how to take command and redirect the current."

"The who?" asked Stephen.

"The Evans family." Bean's lip curled. "As in, Louis Evans. The owner of ACI. The idiot who decided technology was bad and let his business go under."

"It seems I'm not the only one less than impressed with his leadership."

"But why not let people know there was still power?" Stephen asked. "People panicked when they were told the grid wasn't coming back online. Cities fell. Tons of people died. Why would anyone lie about something like that?"

"But that means…" She took a step back from the building. "All this time…" A violent swirl of rage and sorrow tore through Stephen's brain like a tornado. His knees threatened to buckle under its weight. He blinked as he regained equilibrium. It was a feeling so raw, Stephen wondered if Bean was aware she'd projected it and decided it was better not to ask. Her eyes were hard, and her cheeks showed no signs of shed tears. She might have shared her true emotion with him, but intentional or not, it was not something she was willing to share with anyone else. Then another of her sensations blossomed in his mind. It was hatred so fierce, Stephen shivered in response.

Alan shrugged. "Ignorance? A play for power? Greed? I can think of any number of reasons. The question you should be asking is why has the lie continued?" Alan examined his fingernails as if inspecting them for dirt picked up from his demonstration. "The answer that comes to my mind is because the wrong people are still in charge. Which is unfortunate, but in my experience, not unexpected. Now, shall we continue on?" He gestured at the road ahead. "Or do you have more questions?"

Alan stepped away from the storefront. As he did so, the lights from the open sign went dark. Stephen noticed Alan hesitated for a fraction of a second before continuing but did not look back. *He didn't turn the sign off,* thought Stephen. *Maybe it isn't quite as black and white as he wants us to believe it is.*

Twenty-Five

"And just where do you think you're going?"

Stephen spun at the sound of an unknown voice. A man stepped out from what remained of a coffee shop, based on the sign that hung above the door. The man smiled, showing teeth that were far longer than any naturally born human's ought to be. He took additional steps forward in a lopsided sort of gait that reminded Stephen of a fox or a coyote making its way through the forest. *Or a werewolf.* Stephen's forehead puckered, reminded of Jim's story. *Maybe Jim had seen something or someone in the woods that night.* The beastman's smile deepened as if sensing easy prey.

Alan spared Stephen a sideways glance. "One of these days, you will realize you can't judge people by their appearance alone. You'll find you are often wrong." Alan raised a hand in greeting and called out "Shaw." The man froze in mid-stride and cocked his head. His nostrils flared, as if picking up a scent.

"Dr. Dronigh?" The beastman's threatening smile was replaced with one of delighted wonder. "When Rotledge said it was you, well, we… You look great." He grabbed Alan's hand and shook it with gusto. "Especially for a dead guy."

"The reports of my death have been greatly exaggerated," chuckled Alan.

Alan's words were met with silence. He turned to look at Stephen with an eyebrow raised. "That was a reference to Twain." He looked at Bean when Stephen failed to react. "You, too? Mark Twain? No?" Bean shrugged. Alan sighed again. "Well, I guess when society as you know it is brought to its knees, the first thing that goes is a proper education. I suggest you look him up some time on the data stream." While still clutching the man's hand, Alan turned to face them fully. "Bean, Stephen, I would like to introduce you to Shaw McMillan, one-time All-American All-Star Quarterback to the Sharks."

"It's two-time, All-American." Shaw grinned, dropping his hand.

Alan waved the comment away. "Well, to be fair, you only achieved that once as a Shark, and really, that's the only team that matters. How is, what's her name? Amber?"

Shaw guffawed a sound that was both distinctive and displeasing to Stephen's ears. A quick glance in Bean's direction told him she was equally unsettled. "Nah, Amber and I split before the last playoffs. She cramped my style. You're thinking about Ginger."

"Ah, yes, Ginger." Alan tapped his forehead. "Gorgeous woman. How's she?"

"Long gone and good riddance. I caught her trying to pawn off some of my old trophies. Dumb bitch. She didn't realize the only currency that still has any value is muscle." Shaw flexed his biceps. "And that's something she'll never lay her claws into again."

"No doubt. What about the rest of the team? What are they up to nowadays?" Alan asked.

"Ah, a little this, a little that. Most of us stuck around the town when all hell broke loose. We couldn't let our fans down by leaving them unprotected."

The smile slipped from Shaw's face as his gaze slipped behind them. "Where is Rotledge anyway? He ran off saying he got a message asking to rescue you from some sort of pit of doom."

Alan's smile turned sheepish. "He's fine. Sleeping off what will no doubt be a monster of a headache. These two tazed him before I told them he was there for us." Alan clicked his tongue. "Rotledge has slowed down since his retirement. I would have expected better."

Shaw's face changed from threatening coyote to wounded pup. Stephen thought he even heard the man whimper. "Yeah. We all have. You don't know what it has been like. Had we known that last season would be the last…"

Alan's expression softened. "The years have been tough on all of us." Stephen's eyebrows rose at Alan's comment. Clearly, Alan wasn't going to share with Shaw that he'd effectively slept through all of them. "But you've always struck me as someone who knew how to make the most of whatever was thrown at him. I'm assuming you and Rotledge didn't take up a new career in the protection industry for free."

Shaw slapped Alan on the back. "As I said, muscle is the only currency left in town. You interested in signing up? The boss might appreciate an extra brain on the team."

"I was expecting to meet up with an old friend, but since he hasn't shown up, I would be up for a chance to say hello and catch up with anyone else who remains from the team. It's been far too long."

"That, I'd be happy to arrange." Shaw leaped into motion, the wounded pup now like an eager dog.

Stephen smiled when Bean didn't follow Alan and Shaw as they continued down the road. *Good riddance,* he thought. Now all he had to do was get the wand back to Finn, save Ed and Helen, and maybe—if he was lucky—win the girl. His cheeks blushed at that last thought, but he couldn't help asking, "Do you want to go with him?"

"Why would I do that? We got what we came out here for."

Stephen's relief was interrupted by a loud growl.

"I think that was just your stomach. Again," said Bean with a laugh. "Seriously, how did you not starve before?" She came over to his side. "I'll get you something to eat."

She pulled on the backpack. Its straps cut into his shoulders as she stood on her toes and rummaged around.

"That's okay. I can get something myself." He swung the pack around and opened its pocket. Stephen paused as his eyes saw a handful of empty wrappers and the larger half of Wes's antenna. "Where is it?" He dropped the bag to the ground and emptied its entire contents onto the street.

"Where's what?"

"The wand." Stephen managed to bark out as his hand touched the pack's bottom without coming into contact with the metal rod. "It's gone."

"What do you mean *it's gone*?"

"I think he took the wand," Stephen whispered. "Alan." The smile fell from Bean's face. "He must have gotten into the bag while we slept." He rubbed his temples. He *knew* he shouldn't have trusted Alan. He *knew* it. Their entire mission was a failure. Stephen kicked the empty bag, wishing it was the Watch. "What's so important about it anyway? Dumb stick. Probably doesn't even work anymore."

"I'm guessing Alan knows."

"Knows what?"

"What the wand does. Or at least he knows why it's valuable." She pulled Stephen back from the pack before he could damage their remaining foodstuffs. "Why else would he take it?"

Because he's a selfish jerk who doesn't care about anyone. That's why.
"So now what?"

"We get it back."

"Right. We just run up to Alan and demand it back. Yeah, I can imagine how that works for us." If Alan wasn't feeling cooperative, he might use it against them. *No*, Stephen shook his head, correcting himself. Alan didn't need to use the wand on them. All he had to do was call them liars and turn one of his beast friends on them. Stephen looked down the empty road leading back to the train station and the city beyond. His folks would spend the rest of their lives wondering why he'd abandoned them to their fate.

"So we don't ask."

"He knows he stole it. He's gonna be ready for us to try to take it back."

"Not if we act like everything's fine." Stephen's brow wrinkled as he tried to follow her logic. "Like he's welcome to it. You said it yourself. We have no clue what it does. Why should it be any more valuable to us than any other piece of garbage picked up from the side of the road?" Bean pointed the remainder of Wes's antenna mixed in with the pile of bars surrounding the pack. "We don't have to act right away. We can wait until his guard is down. It could totally work."

"So what's our story then?" asked Stephen. "He knows we are on the run. Why would he want us to go wherever it is he is going?"

"Tell him you recognized him after all and that you are his son. Tell him you want to get to know him better."

Stephen pursed his lips. "That's not happening."

Bean rolled her eyes. "If you have a better idea, feel free to share it."

Stephen bent down and grabbed a rock. He flung it at the closest building. The sound of glass shattered echoed down the street. Dogs barked in the distance. "He knows someone is after us. It would make sense for us to look for safety in numbers."

Her eyes twinkled as she began stuffing the bars into their bag. "And here I was beginning to wonder if the only suggestions you listened to were your stomach's."

He bent over to help her, and his hand touched hers. She straightened, leaving him to finish cleaning up the mess on his own. "You heard Shaw. This is his neighborhood. They can't be going far, but we're going to have to sprint if we want to catch up.

Once their supplies were returned to the pack and its straps lay across his shoulders, they took off in a run after Alan and Shaw, finding them a few blocks away. While Alan looked like he didn't have a care in the world, his gait remained slow and tentative. Shaw walked several paces ahead. "Shaw," Stephen called out as they reached Alan. His side cramped. "Wait up." Shaw cocked his head at the sound of his name but didn't stop, like a dog listening for a command.

"Shaw." Alan's tone, infused with command, stopped Shaw in his tracks. "I believe the kids are asking us to stop. I could use the rest, too. Not all of us were born into athletic dynasties like you were."

Shaw shrugged and wandered over to a brick staircase that no longer led to anything habitable. Shaw turned in a circle three times before sitting down. Stephen's eyes met Bean's as she raised one eyebrow before joining Shaw on the step. Stephen removed a canteen from the backpack's supplies and offered her a sip.

"You first," she said. "You're the one lugging all that."

"Well, if you aren't thirsty, I wouldn't mind a sip." Alan sauntered by grabbing the canteen from Stephen's hand as he passed before joining Bean and Shaw on the brick steps. Water splashed on the ground with Alan's enthusiastic swig. Stephen watched as the liquid pooled for a moment before seeping in between the brickwork. Alan's lack of regard regarding the availability of clean water was yet another indication of how much the world had changed since he'd gone into the pod. "I am surprised. When you stayed behind, I thought you had some place you needed to go."

I do, so why don't you give me back what you stole? "We thought you could use some more protection. I mean, it's a lot different out here than when you…"

The corner of Alan's lips turned up. "How considerate." He took another drink before handing the canteen back to Stephen. "It has a bit of an aftertaste, doesn't it?"

"That would be the iodine," muttered Stephen.

Alan snorted. "I suppose that would explain it."

Shaw's leg started to twitch. He hopped back upright. "That's about as much of a break as I can take. You ready yet?"

Bean placed a hand on one knee and began to rise. Alan stopped her. "Why don't you run ahead and let your boss know we are coming? I can get us there from here."

Shaw paused. "Um, I'm not so sure that's a good idea."

"And why not?" Alan gestured. "We're old friends, right?"

"Hmm. You were…once," Shaw glanced at Bean and then at Stephen. His eyes tightened as his forehead wrinkled. "But who knows what kind of friends you've been keeping since then? Lots of people have changed."

Alan's face took on the look of exaggerated innocence. "Ah. I can appreciate your concern, but you have nothing to worry about. This is my son."

Stephen fought the shock from showing on his face. Had he heard Bean call him his father during the seizure, or was Alan making up a story for Shaw's benefit, and if so, why?

Shaw took a step toward Stephen. His nostrils flared as if taking in Stephen's scent. *Exactly how far had he taken the genetic modifications?* Stephen found himself wondering. Shaw grinned before slapping himself in the face. "I can't believe I didn't pick up on the resemblance before." He spun on his heel. "Right then. I'll see you at the Reef." Launching himself into a run, Shaw disappeared from view within a matter of moments.

"I hope that means something to you," Stephen commented. "Last I checked, the ocean was in the other direction." *Which is exactly the direction I should be going.*

Alan smiled. "It's been awhile, but some places have a way of sticking in your memory."

TWENTY-SIX

The road narrowed as they approached what once served as the center of the city, a brick sidewalk lining one side and a rusted chain fence on the other. Trees growing up and out made it seem more forest than a town; however, a stench worse than a field of livestock overpowered the clean smell of the woods. Bean's nose wrinkled in disgust, too. At least they knew they were almost at their destination. As there didn't appear to be any farmland nearby, the smell could only mean they were near a group of people living together.

They turned another corner, and the road they'd traveled most of the afternoon opened up. A gray building with a blue roof appeared in between the overgrown grass, more trees, and the remnants of crumbled buildings. A metal fence surrounded the building, but unlike the other fences they'd passed, this one was well tended with shouts coming from nearby.

Figures emerged from the building's entrance. Their outlines appeared human, at least from a distance, and Stephen released a breath of relief. As they neared and their features came more in focus, Alan extended a hand in greeting. Stephen noticed both had skin like tanned leather, lined with deep grooved wrinkles, though one's skin was dark while the other was light. One wore a faded blue ball cap that only seemed to enhance the crookedness of his nose. The other's hair was streaked with white but cropped close to his skull.

The ball cap man laughed. "Well, what do you know? It *is* the one and only Alan Dronigh. I guess I owe Ahman here a drink." He gestured at the hatless man by his side. The man, who Stephen assumed was Ahman, said nothing, but instead placed his hands on his hips and nodded once. Ball cap tilted his head, "You haven't changed a bit." He scratched his chin. "What I wouldn't give to have genes like yours. One of these days, you need to tell me your secret."

Alan chuckled as he caught Stephen's eye before turning his attention back to the pair. "What about you, Ahman? Aren't you happy to see me?"

Ahman grunted.

"Oh don't mind him. He hasn't been the world's best conversationalist since…" Ball cap looked at Ahman with an unspoken question in his eyes. Ahman's jaw clenched as he closed his eyes and sighed. Ball cap continued, interpreting Ahman's response as consent. "Well, not since Cal—"

Alan tapped his chin. "Ah, Cal. How old was he when I last saw you? Six? And already planning to follow his father's footsteps?"

"He *was* five." Ball cap's use of the past tense was unmistakable.

"Oh. I'm sorry to hear that. Did he get sick?"

Ahman's eyes went flat as he shook his head. Ball cap filled in the unspoken question. "No. Not the plague." Ahman's expression darkened. "Well, it wasn't." Ball cap shot an apologetic glance Ahman's way. "At least, not technically speaking." Ball cap brightened. "The team actually was barely hit by the plague at all. Probably due to all that extra conditioning Mr. D had us do." Ball cap winked, but the smile withered on his face the minute he caught Ahman's expression.

"We thought we were lucky." He chewed his lip. "Turns out others considered us a little too lucky." Ahman's fists clenched by his sides. "We didn't know…didn't realize how bad it'd gotten until a handful of folk decided that the playing field needed to be"—Ball cap looked back at the stadium behind him—"leveled."

Stephen blinked as the man's implication sank in. A kid had been murdered, and for what? The crime of surviving? It occurred to him then that the same might have happened to him if Ed and Helen hadn't gotten him out of town when they did.

"Well, we made sure those responsible aren't around to do it again. Didn't we, my friend?" Ball cap put a hand on Ahman's shoulder as the man looked away. When Ahman faced them again, his expression was like granite, as if daring them to criticize their version of justice.

"I would have done the same," said Alan, and the tension that had crept into the conversation like humidity before a summer storm dissipated. "Had it been a child of mine." He rested his hand on Stephen's shoulder.

Stephen fought the urge to shrug off Alan's hand as the corner of Ball cap's lip turned up. "Shaw mentioned when he got back that you were traveling with your boy." Stephen bit his tongue to help keep his expression from giving away any of his feelings on the subject. "He looks like his mother."

Do I? Stephen filled his lungs and counted to five before releasing the pent-up air. He tried to picture her face, but all he could think of was Helen. He glanced at Alan's hand. *He's distracted. Tackle him, grab the wand, and run.*

Alan squeezed his shoulder. His grip was tighter than Stephen expected. "Don't I know it? Sometimes I used to wonder if he was even mine."

Stephen tried to meet Bean's eyes and failed. The moment passed.

Ball cap laughed. "Well enough of this small talk for now. Let's get you all inside. Jeremy is anxious to meet you." Ahman followed him like a silent shadow as he turned, passing what appeared to be one of the stadium's entrance gates. Instead, they descended a ramp to the side of the building where another, less noticeable door awaited.

Alan leaned into Stephen and said in a low voice, "We got off easy. Darnell was one of the trainers back in the Sharks' heydays. A great assistant, but always a little chatty. A few years ago, the sun would set before he wrapped up the greetings."

As they passed under the arches, a numbing sensation spread throughout Stephen's body like a fog. He attempted to call up Finn's map for more information about their location, but nothing appeared.

"While physical modifications were acceptable, use of nanotechnology during games was deemed unsportsmanlike." Alan sniffed. "There are signal dampeners buried under the field, which are or were powered by the simple act of walking. They have a limited range and don't block everything, but the effect does take some getting used to." He rubbed his arms. "I'd say they are still operational."

Darnell chattered away as they walked. "It used to be the only people who could use this entrance were the field service crew. We sealed off the rest. Too exposed. We didn't like people coming in having the aerial advantage." The hall opened up to what once must have served as a football field. In its place was a shantytown filled with reclaimed metal structures, which appeared scattered across the ground with little sign of any true organization. Ball cap/Darnell looked over his shoulder at them. "I know what you are thinking. Why not the skyboxes? We tried that. Gets hot up there surrounded by all that glass. Only the boss or whoever draws lookout duty goes up there now. Nope, it may be very different from some of the mansions the other guys were living in before the shit hit the fan, but trust me, this is a much better option. Easier to defend, too." He turned the rest of the way so that he walked backward while gesturing toward the structures behind him. "Who needs a mansion when you are living in a fortress? Welcome to the new Reef."

Darnell led them through the structures until the group had reached a point resembling the center and stopped in front of a hut as nondescript as any of the others. He knocked on the structure's side, and a man stepped out into the sunlight.

"So, this is the person responsible for all the recent excitement," the man said as he outstretched his hand. Alan glanced at the man's hand but made no effort to accept it. The man's lips tightened into a line as he swept the hair out of his face in a smooth motion as if he had never intended to extend the arm in greeting in the first place.

Alan frowned. "I know you." It was more accusation than statement, and Stephen could sense Darnell and Ahman tense without looking at them. "You worked for Evans."

Bean tensed. The man, who Stephen assumed was Jeremy, smiled, unaffected by Alan's tone. "Well, isn't that a pleasant surprise." He chuckled at a joke, which might as well have sprouted wings for how it flew over Stephen's head. "I guess I must have done something right then to have gained *your* notice."

"Just because I left the ACI, doesn't mean I stopped paying attention." Alan rubbed the tip of his middle finger against the pad of his thumb on one hand as he spoke.

"*Left*, is it?" One of Jeremy's eyebrows rose. "I guess I heard a different version of the story."

"I suppose you would have. Your former employer was always good at telling himself what he wanted to hear."

Jeremy threw his head back with a laugh straight from his gut. "Isn't that the truth? If I could have gotten a dollar for every time I had to bite my tongue as he took credit for something." He wiped an unseen tear from his eye. "Still, I never would have guessed he'd—"

"Who would? You'd have to be some sort of psychopath to anticipate a person would do something like that."

Jeremy nodded solemnly. "Well, that's over and done with now. All we can do is move forward." He turned to address Darnell and Ahman. "Why don't you two go and take the children on the grand tour? I believe Dr. Dronigh and I have a few more things to discuss." Darnell gripped Stephen's arm as Jeremy reached under his collar and pulled out a pendant similar to the one Rotledge wore. "Such as how you intend to thank us for answering your rescue call."

Stun him. Stun them all. You might not get another chance. He made a fist. His skin remained flesh colored. Then the man, Alan, and the wand were gone, disappearing into the hut.

"Where should we start?" asked Darnell. Ahman shrugged. "Yeah, that's what I was thinking, too." Darnell led the group along a winding path through the series of huts until Stephen was no longer sure he'd be able to locate the one Alan entered.

Fan-freaking-tastic. His fingernails dug into the meat of his all-too-normal-looking palms. Sweat dripped from his forehead, though the sun was past its peak heat. *There goes another chance.* A vision of Ed's bloodstained bandage came uninvited. The stain grew, spreading until all Stephen could see was red. He was running out of time. Alan said the damper didn't block everything. If he could only get a message to Wes, maybe Wes could explain the situation to Finn in a way he'd understand. *You are supposed to be super strong.* He imagined the computer terminal. He opened his fist. Pink half circles marred his skin where his nails had been. He pushed the message with all his might.

Darnell paused and cocked his head. "You need a bathroom, kid? You don't look so good."

The fog-like sensation intensified. The logo on Darnell's ball cap blurred, and Stephen's stomach churned.

"He's hungry," said Bean. "But what else is new? He's always hungry." She pursed her lips. "We heard shouting before. Where is everyone?"

"I'm glad you asked. Let's finish the introductions," Darnell answered.

TWENTY-SEVEN

The huts backed to a great green wall of foliage. Ahman parted its leaves and entered it as one would a door. With Darnell still gripping his arm to the point that Stephen wouldn't be surprised if he lost feeling in it, Stephen followed the two through the opening.

Stephen estimated there were roughly thirty men on the other side engaged in a series of coordinated drills, like a small army, while an additional handful lingered to the side of the worn field. Darnell raised his fingers to his lips and whistled. Heads turned in unison in their direction. Stephen suppressed a shudder. Darnell and Ahman's human-looking appearance put them in the minority. Some had noses that were flattened to the point of non-existence save for a pair of nostrils in the center of their faces. It was a look, which reminded Stephen of a snake. Others had more snout-like noses. Some wore shirts highlighting wins and champion seasons long past. Most didn't bother to cover their torsos. While many chests were covered in thick hair, Stephen noticed two of the shirtless men had a gray cast to their skin ridged like a rhino's. *Probably as strong, too*, Stephen thought as he attempted to control the growing unease in the pit of his stomach. *Let's hope they have better tempers.* Stephen scanned the field to see if there was another way out of this nightmare. Instead, all he could see were more misshapen limbs, which would have looked less out of place on a jungle cat. Coming here was a mistake. They should have taken their chances with Finn, with or without the wand.

One stepped away from the rest of the group. *Rotledge. He must have run back here the second he woke up.* Bean stepped forward and raised her chin as if daring the man to come closer. *What are you doing?* Stephen wondered. *There're only two of us, and what?* He looked out at the row upon row, unkind smiles filled with fanglike teeth. *They aren't a team. They're a pack.* A dry hacking sound from behind him caught Stephen by surprise. Darnell's eyes widened. "Your girl's got some spunk. I can't think of the last time I heard Ahman laugh."

"That's laughing? He sounds more like he is dying," Bean replied. Her body remained tense, though many of the men on the field now appeared more relaxed than they had a second ago.

"I suppose you could say that about all of us." Darnell frowned. "But then again, if I were you, I might be a little more concerned about my own health right now."

Rotledge tilted his head at Darnell, who nodded ever so slightly while the others on the field turned their backs and resumed their drills.

"I believe you've met." Darnell's tone was all business.

"We may have gotten off on the wrong foot," replied Bean. If she felt at all intimidated by the situation, there was nothing in either her voice or body language to give it away. "No hard feelings?" When Rotledge didn't react right away, Bean commented to their guides, "He's not much of a people person. Is he?"

Ahman let loose another round of his hacking laugh while Rotledge's eyes burned with an unspoken fire.

"Rotledge," a voice sounded from behind them. Alan and the man from the hut stepped through the foliage wall and out onto the field. "I believe the girl was trying to apologize."

As the other man took in the scene, Rotledge's head dropped. "No hard feelings," repeated Rotledge though his eyes never left the ground.

Jeremy smiled, but the expression didn't quite reach his eyes. "Excellent." He clapped his hands. "Now we can all be friends."

"I feel so much safer now," muttered Bean to Stephen. "Don't you?"

"Now about that little matter of payment," said Jeremy, turning to Alan.

Alan patted his coat pocket. "Not here."

"Why not? Too public?" Jeremy frowned.

"It won't work."

"What about our agreement? Does it not work anymore?" Jeremy's eyes narrowed. "Is that it? Is the device so fragile it broke on the walk over here?" he sneered. "I thought your tech was supposed to be better than that."

"It will work exactly as I promised. Just not here, as in on the field. It needs a signal."

Stephen perked up. A signal meant another chance.

Jeremy raked his fingers through his hair. "Oh. Right. My apologies. We can go to the locker rooms under the stadium. The walls should block the jammers enough. There's also only one way out if we find out you're lying."

Alan's mouth tightened into a fine line. "I don't lie."

"Well then, what are we waiting for?" He looked back at the field. "Rotledge," he shouted. "Come along. This involves you."

The sounds of the beastmen grew muffled as they reached the entrance to the interior of the stadium. Stopping at the top of an incline, Jeremy picked up a pair of solar-powered lanterns, which grew in brightness as the natural light dimmed. More lanterns hung at the base of the incline on either side of a doorway opening to a room lined with cabinets. He took a seat on a bench in the center of the room. "Now about that payment."

"Right. Rotledge first?" Alan suggested. "After all, he did find us." Jeremy nodded as Alan reached his hand into his pocket and pulled out the wand with a flourish.

"You can't give that to him." Stephen's hands tightened into fists. "It's ours." He visualized lightning bolts, but instead of illuminating the room with purple light, his legs buckled, and a chill danced down his spine. *The drain.*

Way to follow the plan, Bean's voice played in his head. He didn't have to look at her to know her eyes were rolling in their sockets.

"Is that so?" Alan made a *tsking* sound. He addressed Jeremy. "As I said above, I don't lie. I don't have to steal either. Unlike some people." He closed his eyes and took a breath.

He pivoted back to Stephen. "You are mistaken. I know it is mine because not only did I help make it, I also made sure its design included an anti-theft element. Oh, the others thought I was being paranoid, but I knew someone might try to take it without appropriate authorization one day. I might not have been able to receive it right away, but an alert was sent to me the second you left the facility. The so-called *secure* facility." He opened his eyes and his expression was the definition of serenity. "At some point, I would like to hear how you were able to perform that little trick, but I believe now is not the time."

Alan addressed Rotledge, "What can I say? Kids. So dramatic." He shrugged. "Then again, Jules always did like to say that I had a flair for drama. Must run in the family."

"Jules?" Rotledge wrinkled his forehead. "I thought your wife's name was Betty."

"Ah, I was referring to my former partner, my *development* partner." Alan's smiled. "You don't remember her?" He made a tutting sound with his tongue. "She wouldn't like that at all. No, not at all." Alan glanced down at the wand in his hand and his smile deepened. "Well, I guess that means it is up to me to make sure at least a portion of her work lives on. He extended his hand so that the wand lay exposed on his open palm. Rotledge leaned in and sniffed the rod, only to pull away. Alan waved it in front of him. "Go on, take it," he urged.

Rotledge took the wand from Alan's hand as if it might still rear up and bite. He inspected it from end to end. "What's this supposed to do?"

"Oh, you'll see." Alan touched the rod with one finger. Rotledge's knuckles turned white where they touched the metal. The rod appeared to blur in Rotledge's hand as it began to vibrate. He whimpered as his eyes rolled back. Then, as quickly as it started, the rod came into crisp focus once more.

He dropped the wand as if burnt, and he fell to his knees.

Then there was laughter as the beastman regained his footing and stepped more fully into the artificial light. Rotledge was different. For one, the limp was gone and he seemed to stand straighter. His misshapen leg no longer looked quite as out of place, as if his entire body was growing inches in front of their eyes. Then Stephen noticed the age spots, which marred Rotledge's exposed skin, began to shrink. His hair darkened and appeared to thicken. Even the skin on his face seemed to tighten as wrinkles faded from view. Jeremy sat dumbly on the bench as Rotledge's laughter continued.

TWENTY-EIGHT

Stephen stumbled toward the wand. The laughter stopped. "Don't even think about it." Rotledge snarled as he scooped the wand up. "My senses haven't been this sharp in years." He smirked. "One of the mods I had done was to help me sniff out the opposing team's trick plays and you don't have half their skill." Rotledge tucked the wand into his waistband. "Go if you want, but you're not leaving with this thingy. It's ours now."

"You don't understand," said Stephen. "I need it. Lives depend on me bringing it back."

"You know? I smell something else." Rotledge took an exaggerated whiff of the air. "Something that smells a lot like bullshit."

"He's telling you the truth," Bean spoke up.

"I don't recall asking you." Rotledge barred his teeth. "Which reminds me, we never did get to finish our introductions."

"I thought we were past that." Bean squared her shoulders. "Fine. I'm sorry I tasered you."

"Tasered?" Rotledge straightened his back even further until he towered at least a foot and a half above Bean. "That was no taser, and we both know it." He took a step toward her.

"I know what you are." He took another step. "I know all about where you come from." Step. "A couple of us went there, looking for help." Step. "You people—you aren't human."

"Says the dog man." Bean's eyes narrowed. "You know *nothing* about me, old man. Nothing." She crossed her arms over her chest. "But I know *all* about you. You think you were abandoned out here? Well, guess what? So was everybody else. The difference is the rest of us didn't get paid millions to sit on a bench before. We were used to not getting everything we wanted exactly when we wanted it." She dropped clenched fists back to her side. "And guess what? I'm glad whatever happened to your friends happened. Welcome to the real world."

"Bitch."

"Has-been."

What are you doing? Stephen wanted to shout. *We're not far enough away from the signal damper.*

She met Stephen's shocked gaze with a small smile. *What I have to,* he heard her voice say in his head. Aloud she said, "or should I say, never was."

The beastman's eyes glazed over in a fiery rage.

"No," shouted Stephen, summoning what little remained of energy reserves, as he threw himself between the two as Rotledge charged.

The impact of his body colliding with Rotledge's shoulder felt much like Stephen imagined getting hit by a train might. He sagged. Rotledge grabbed Stephen by the cowl of his shirt before he could drop to the floor and pulled him back upright. Stephen's eyes watered as he sucked in air to replace what the blow had taken from his lungs only to get a whiff of Rotledge's breath. The wand hadn't been able to return all of Rotledge to a fresh state. Stephen continued to gasp as he braced his body in anticipation of what Rotledge might do next.

Stephen didn't have to wait long. Stars burst across his vision as his entire body flew back across the room, hitting a wall. The force of his impact was great enough to send one of the lanterns swaying, which caused shadows on the walls to dance like a horde of demons come to collect their souls before the device toppled to the floor. "That the best you can do? I thought you guys were supposed to know how to tackle."

Rotledge roared as he stomped over to where Stephen lay, hoisting him back up. Rotledge's fist pounded into his ribs, forcing out what little breath remained in his lungs after the initial impact. Stephen's body wanted to double over, but Rotledge's fists were relentless. Over and over they pummeled him. Stephen tried to put up a defense, but Rotledge's fists were too fast to dodge. The man was a machine of violence.

Stephen lost sight of Bean, his attention locked onto a dribble of spit, which had formed at the corner of Rotledge's mouth. It made him appear even more like a rabid dog. His reaction time slowed by the previous hits and, unable to look away, all Stephen could do was watch as Rotledge wiped the spit off his knuckle before driving that same fist into Stephen's face. He decided then there was little reason to even attempt to open his battered eye as the blows continued.

Then pain no longer registered. *I must have lost consciousness,* he thought, as he considered the shapeless darkness. The idea that he might be conscious of his non-consciousness amused Stephen. He wanted to laugh at the situation, but he no longer had any sense of the rest of his body either. It was as if he was simply a floating mind out in the emptiness of space. It occurred to him it wasn't that much different than how accessing the data stream that first time had been. *It's better,* he thought. At least this time it didn't feel like he was going to drown any minute. No, after thinking about it, Stephen concluded that getting beat up by a berserk beastman and blacking out wasn't the worst thing to have happened to him since leaving home. Not even by a little.

He tried to imagine what he must look like on the outside in the real-life world. *Probably don't want to think about that too hard.* It occurred to him that his current state might be worse than unconsciousness. He could very well be dying. Rotledge didn't strike him as the type of person who would hold back just because his opponent had tapped out. *Would that really be so bad?* Stephen couldn't decide. *What if you are already dead and this is the afterlife?* He had never been religious. None of them had. Ed was too afraid of picking the wrong one. Helen preferred to restrict her worries to the things she could control. Even so, he found himself reaching out, probing at the edges of the darkness. If there was a God out there, Stephen would like to know why he, she, or it had abandoned so many lives to their suffering.

He detected a presence nearby and directed his floating consciousness toward it, moving much like he imagined a hot air balloon would. As he approached, the presence seemed to expand like a flower blooming, with data unfurled like the flower's petals. He stretched a tendril of thought toward the petal, and the blackness surrounding him dissolved into a new setting. He was in an office, seated in a high-backed leather chair. A nearby open window let in a warm breeze scented with the smell of lilies.

A strange voice caught his attention coming from a mahogany desk. A figure leaned over. "It was a good thing you came to us when you did," a woman's voice purred.

Another female voice spoke, a voice much like Bean's, but older and with a helpless desperate quality to it. "You can help," the voice demanded. "We were told you could help."

"Please?" another voice spoke up from behind. This voice was a male one and also the voice of a person filled with fear. "We'll do anything."

"It was an accident," a third voice entered the mix. Unlike the others, which sounded somewhat distant, this voice seemed to be directly on top of him. It had the high pitch of a child, but Stephen recognized it as a younger version of Bean's. It was the same as the out-of-body experience he'd experienced during the body switch incident with Alan on the basement floor, with the same disorientation. The only thing Stephen could think of which might explain what he was experiencing was if his consciousness had somehow found its way into Bean's thoughts, too. He tried to pull away as the scene took on a sepia hue. Stephen was stuck in the memory as if he was living the moment in real time.

The speaker's face came into focus. She appeared a few years older than Helen but not by much. A few lines of age creased the corners of her lips as well as her eyes, but the majority of her skin was unmarked. Her stormy gray eyes locked on his, and he recognized the woman as Dr. Lambda. "Your name is Beatrice, right? Why don't you tell me what happened to your sister?"

The vision shifted down, and all Stephen could see were Bean's hands as they fidgeted in her lap.

Stephen's/Bean's arm felt as if it were being ripped out of its socket at the force of his/her arm being pulled to the side. The man's voice practically spat in her ear. "Tell her what she wants to know, Beatrice."

"Bean." The man's grip tightened on Stephen's/Bean's arm. Pressure formed behind his/her eyes, but the tears refused to flow.

"That stopped being cute a long time ago."

"Mr. Kunegunda, I believe you are scaring her," suggested Dr. Lambda.

"Scare? Her?" The man shoved Stephen/Bean back into the chair. "Don't you believe it for a second. The girl is a psychopath. The fire was bad enough. I mean it's chaos out there. Kids make mistakes. But when we found out she'd first put her sister in a coma…before the flames." The man's voice broke. "It was no accident."

"I know this has been hard for your entire family, but I do need to hear the story from her perspective. It might be better if you and your wife stepped outside."

"With all due respect, you don't want to do that. You saw what happened to our girl when we left them alone."

"There is a man waiting in the hall. Ask him to come in as you step outside. Don't worry," Dr. Lambda added when no one immediately reacted. "He's the one who told me about your case in the first place. Nothing is going to surprise him." Stephen could hear the sound of the couple's footsteps as they turned and hit the tiled floor behind him; however, his/Bean's gaze remained fixed on the doctor's hands as her fingers continued their restless dance on her lap.

She looked up only at the sound of the door opening and turned around long enough to see the man and the woman leaving the room without looking back once. When the door opened wide once more, another man stood in their place.

Stephen recognized this man, too. The same man had threatened them at the base of the barricade at Finn's tower. He'd been but a tiny figure before, ragged and half-defeated, but now he loomed before Bean like a terrible child-eating giant. Bean must have thought so, too. He could feel Bean press her body further into the chair as he approached the desk, seeking whatever extra protection it could offer.

"Now, shall we begin again?"

Bean's focus shifted back to Dr. Lambda. "We were just playing," Bean whimpered. "It was a game. That's all."

The woman straightened, pulling her palms together almost as if in a prayer as she rounded the desk and came over to Bean's side. "Well, we can all agree the time for games is over." The woman's voice was honey-covered steel. "Instead, it's time you told what really happened."

"We were just pretending to have magic," said Bean in the same panicked tone he'd heard during their escape from the blaze in the tavern. "Like in the stories. It was just supposed to be a game. It wasn't supposed to work."

"What wasn't supposed to work?" Stephen could feel Dr. Lambda's fingers stroke Bean's hair as if they were passing through his own locks. He could feel Bean's heart beginning to settle in her chest. As she calmed, his/her eyes caught on a picture on the desk. In the center of the photo was a man with a dark mustache giving a speech. Beside him was a stunning blonde woman whose eyes, filled with pride, were fixated on the speaker as if there was no one else in the world. Slightly behind the couple, seated to the right of the podium, was an even younger Dr. Lambda, wearing an equally crisp business suit as the one she was wearing now. A man's hand rested on her knee, but the younger Dr. Lambda's attention was as riveted onto the mustached man giving the speech. Stephen wondered if the man seated next to her had noticed and was trying to stake his claim. Feeling sorry for the man, Stephen focused on his face only to realize he recognized him, too. The man next to Dr. Lambda in the photo was the same person the beastmen referred to as boss. Jeremy.

Twenty-Nine

The photograph, desk, and even the smell of lilies faded. Then Stephen's world exploded into pain once more. He had to be back in his own body. Stephen risked opening his eye but gave up when he couldn't manage to open it by more than a crack. Alan peered down at him. "Oh good, you're still alive. For a while there, I wasn't sure."

"Rotledge," Stephen attempted to say through a bruised if not broken jaw, though the sound that came out of his mouth was unrecognizable.

Alan raised an eyebrow and looked to his side. "Hmm, perhaps it would be better if you didn't try to speak for a while." He extended his hand. When Stephen didn't take it right away, Alan harrumphed. "Would you prefer I leave you on the floor?"

This time, Stephen took his hand and tried to sit up. Every inch of his body seemed to be on fire as he looked around the room for his attacker. He found him lying on the ground by his feet. Startled, Stephen attempted to scoot away, sending another burst of pain throughout his body.

"He's dead," Alan commented drily. "A fact, I feel, I must mention is going to be somewhat awkward to explain." Stephen took another look at the man's form, only now noticing its motionlessness. The memory of Rotledge's iron fists as they pummeled him over and over again returned in full force. Each hit had been so rapid; he hadn't had time to defend himself. Had he managed to get a lucky hit in any way? Stephen stood, bracing his back against the wall as his brain sought to make sense of the situation.

Leaving him at the wall, Alan knelt over Rotledge's body and turned the body over, bringing Stephen's attention back to the dead old man. And it was clear he *was* old again. If anything, he was even older now than he had been before. Rotledge's hair was white, and large clumps lay beside him. The strands must have fallen out of his scalp as Alan turned him over. The skin of his face was sunken, and the smell of rot and decay overpowered the scent of sweat, blood, and dirt in the room. *What happened to him?*

"Hmm," Alan muttered as he inspected the body. "This reminds me of a movie I saw once. What was the name?" He tapped his finger on his chin. "Something about a crusade." Alan looked back at Stephen and shrugged. "Ah, I suppose that wouldn't mean anything to you. The movie was already considered a classic when I saw it, but it ended with the villain getting the life sucked out of him."

Between the smell and the man's appearance, Stephen was unable to ignore the sourness of his stomach any longer. He turned and vomited, sending painful spasms through his abdomen and causing his eyes to water. "How?" Stephen managed to say once the contents of his stomach emptied. Stephen blinked the tears away as he remembered he hadn't been alone in the room during the attack. "Bean," he whispered. Stephen tried looking around the room, but couldn't find her in his limited range of vision.

Alan gestured at the pile of dirt that was all that remained of Rotledge. "She sucked the life right out of him. Drained him dry." Stephen's legs went out from under him, and if Alan hadn't returned at that moment, ready to catch him, he would have fallen back to the floor. "Careful now." Alan wrapped Stephen's arm across his shoulder. "You're lucky she's gone. She might have done the same to you."

"What do you mean *she's gone*?"

"I mean, while I was over here making sure you weren't dead, too, she bolted." Alan sighed as he shifted Stephen's weight. "I must say, I think you can do better, but your love life is the least of our concerns at the moment." Alan gestured to the corner of the room where Jeremy sat propped up next to the wall with a slack-jawed grin and a vacant stare.

"What happened to him?"

"I found his happy place."

"His *what*? Why?"

"Do you see that chain around his neck? I assume they've been using those for communication." He shifted Stephen again. "Those trinkets were developed to give people who didn't have the stomach to be upgraded a means of accessing the data stream. It's a poor substitute for the real thing with one serious design flaw. Namely, it makes it possible for another person to alter the device's effect and can trap an individual in an alternative reality of their creation." Alan readjusted Stephen's arm. "How much do you weigh anyway?" He shook his head. "To answer your other question, I was forced to take advantage of the flaw when your loyal girlfriend decided to pick a fight with one of our host's favorite lackeys." Alan leaned and braced them both against a wall. "I can only imagine what would have happened if I wasn't here to take care of Jeremy after she pulled that stunt. Don't you know anything about pack behavior? Only the alpha is allowed to put a rogue one down. Anything else would be seen as a challenge." Alan scanned the room. "Do you think you can stand?"

Stephen took a nervous step forward on his own. When the floor didn't immediately rise up to meet him, he nodded.

"Good. Stay right there." Leaving Stephen where he stood, Alan returned to Rotledge's body. Grabbing him by his armpits, Alan started to pull the man toward the row of empty lockers. Stephen heard a snapping sound like a branch breaking and watched as Alan stumbled backward with a single arm still in his hands. The urge to throw up overpowered Stephen once more.

When the dry heaves stopped, Rotledge's body was gone. Alan stood, wiping off his trousers. A mound of a substance that looked like ash lay at his feet. "Well, that solves one problem," said Alan to himself as he dusted off his palms.

"Hey, boss?" a voice called from the direction of the ramp.

Alan whispered, "Don't say anything." He rubbed his throat and shouted in Jeremy's voice, "What is it?"

"We've got company."

"Well, take care of it."

"It's Wendy, boss."

Alan glanced back at Jeremy. A long trail of drool hung from his lips and chin. "We're going to have to risk it," Alan muttered. "Tell her I'll be right outside."

"What about the others? Dr. Dronigh and the kids?"

"Nothing that Rotledge can't handle. Isn't that right." Alan's face twisted. He rubbed his throat again and, in Rotledge's voice, added, "You know it."

"Okay, boss." Footsteps raced away.

Alan held a finger to his lips and cupped his ear. He nodded. "I believe it would be best if we put as much distance between us and the Reef as possible before anyone thinks to check on their leader, don't you?"

Stephen's shoulders sagged. Only then did he notice the lack of the straps' weight on them. "Where's my pack?"

Alan scanned the room. "Your friend must have taken it with her when she ran." He shrugged. Alan patted the pocket where he'd stored the wand before. His eyebrow shot up. He cocked his head as he nudged the pile of dust on the floor with his toe. He turned and looked at Stephen up and down before his lips tightened. His eyes took on a glazed over look. Seconds passed without him saying a word, then Alan blinked, and his gaze was bright and clear and furious. "Your pack isn't the only thing unaccounted for."

Stephen's stomach threatened to roll once more. *The wand.* She'd taken the wand and left him here. Would Finn still honor his promise to stand up to the Watch and rescue Ed and Helen if he wasn't the one to hand it over? Stephen feared he soon would find out.

THIRTY

Clouds the color of ash filled the sky as Stephen limped his way outside. "I can't believe she left without me."

"Who knows why women do what they do sometimes?" Alan's scowled deepened. "You do realize we wouldn't be worried about a pack of jocks with reason to kill us now if you'd told me why you had the wand in the first place."

"Right. As if you would have given it back."

Alan shrugged. "I suppose we'll never know now, will we?"

"I needed it to rescue Helen and Ed. There is a guy, Finn, who lives in a tower with an army more than capable of taking out the Watch, but first needed me to bring them the wand so the energy drain from using their abilities didn't kill them."

"Seems unnecessarily complicated. Who are Helen and Ed again?"

"The people who raised me."

"You mean the people I entrusted with your care who failed at the task so miserably. Those people? What about them?"

"Entrusted?" Stephen sputtered. "You didn't *entrust* me with anyone. You left me. A four-year-old. By myself." He stared at Alan in disbelief. "Who does that?"

"You want to have this conversation now?" Alan asked, waving his hands back toward the exit. "This is our chance to get out of here while we still can. You want to blow it by talking, be my guest, but I'd prefer to remain in one piece." He glanced at Stephen who had fallen behind. "However, I recommend you do the same. I don't think you can afford to be torn into much more."

They passed under the arches, and a tingling sensation flooded Stephen's limbs. He summoned the map and was relieved to see its information projected over his vision once more. He focused his thoughts and composed the same message to Wes as he had earlier. He visualized pressing a 'send' button. Stephen squinted at the horizon as he dragged his injured leg. It was going to be a long walk back to the train station.

"You need the wand back. So do I. Now, all I have to do is locate it." A vein in Alan's forehead throbbed. "She's done something to it. Hidden its signal from me."

"She learned about our abilities the same time I did. She wouldn't have the first idea how to do something like that. Not to mention, why would she?"

Alan stopped short. "The simplest explanation is often the correct one." The scowl vanished from his face.

"What does that even mean?" asked Stephen, shielding his eyes from the brightness of the setting sun.

Alan laughed and shook his head. "It means, she lied."

"About what?"

"About when she learned about her abilities."

"No." Stephen's brow knit. He thought about the memory of Bean's interrogation with Dr. Lambda. "Okay, maybe she'd used them in the past by accident, but it's not like she knew what she was doing back then. She couldn't. I mean, I saw her when Finn told us about everything. She had even more questions than I did."

"Did she?" Alan laughed again. "Here's a tip they used to teach young lawyers—never ask a question you don't already know the answer to. It is a way to lead a witness's testimony without being accused of actually leading the witness. If she asked a lot of questions, it could be she was attempting to keep you from asking any of your own." He slapped his leg. "Clever girl. My guess? She's been working for this Finn person for a while as a recruiter of sorts. It was all a ruse to gain your trust and get you to lower your guard. Then once you'd gotten them what they want, all there would be left to do is dispose of the loose ends."

Stephen remembered the taste of her lips during their kiss and that moment in the moonlight by the waterfront. *You can't fake a connection like that.* "No. That's not possible. She wouldn't do that to me."

"Oh, don't be upset with her. It's a technique that has been used since the dawn of time," Alan replied. The corner of his lip turned up. "I may have even performed a similar job in the past." He tapped his lip. "I wonder... But that would mean... Of course, that does explain..." His eyes twinkled with mirth at a line of thought that Stephen couldn't follow. He waved whatever it was away, returning his attention back to Stephen. "Before you ask, I didn't read your mind. The look on your face is clear enough. Well, the look on that swollen mess that currently is your face." Alan arched his neck to look out across the parking lot, where a figure stood waiting by a truck. "I suppose that must be Wendy."

Stephen's eye watered. Between the blurred vision and the fading light, he couldn't make out the woman's features, but he recognized the red armband at once. "Dr. Lambda. We need to get away." A chill settled into his bones, causing his teeth to chatter.

Alan patted him on the shoulder. "And what good would that do? She's already seen us and you can barely walk, let alone run." He muttered to himself, "Lambda. How many can there be?" His gaze took on the vacant look Stephen now associated with a person accessing the data stream. "Ah, she's a medical doctor."

"She's also in charge of the Watch."

"Is she? Isn't that convenient?"

"Maybe for you."

"It would seem our host had no intention of letting us join his little community." Alan made a *tsking* sound. "I'll need to have a talk with him about that later, but for now…" He raked his hand through his hair, and the color changed as his features shifted. Stephen's stomach turned, but there was nothing more in it to expunge. When the effect subsided, Alan wore Jeremy's face. He pushed Stephen forward.

"This is a terrible idea," whispered Stephen.

"Play along," he whispered back. Louder, he said, "Wendy, how nice to see you again."

"Cut the crap, Jeremy. You and I both know this is the last place I want to be." She looked at Stephen. "I see you caught the boy. I suppose I should thank you for not dragging this out like you normally do, but did you have to rough him up like that?"

"What can I say? He picked the wrong person to mess with."

Her lips narrowed. "I am beginning to suspect he does that a lot. What about the other one?"

"What another one?"

Dr. Lambda rolled her eyes. "I'm not in the mood for games. The girl he was traveling with. Where is she? Your associates said you'd found them both."

"She got away."

"Of course she did." Dr. Lambda closed her eyes and took a calming breath. "Well, don't just stand there. Put him in the back."

"So what's the plan now?" Stephen whispered as Alan opened the double doors in the back of the vehicle while Dr. Lambda went around to the driver's side. "We zap her and take the truck?"

Alan raised an eyebrow. "Always so quick to violence." He shook his head. "Now you are going to lay back and let the good doctor take you where she will." He pushed Stephen onto a gurney.

"Like hell, I will." Stephen tried to struggle, but his arms and legs didn't respond to his commands. "I can't move." His eyes widened as Alan tightened the straps. "What did you do to me?"

"I'm not doing anything. Your body, on the other hand, is shutting down. You need medical attention. Now you have it." Alan stepped back and slapped the truck door. "He's all yours."

Dr. Lambda glanced into the rear mirror. "You've changed. If you'd been half this cooperative before, maybe we wouldn't have gotten divorced."

"Good chat. Try not to lose him this time. I'd hate to have to clean up your mess. Again."

"Ah, and there's the Jeremy I know."

Alan slammed the truck door as Dr. Lambda cranked the engine and put it into gear. All Stephen could do is look out the window at the sky that the storms that threatened. He closed his eyes. *At least I might find out whether Ed and Helen are still okay.* Then he gave into sleep as the truck raced away.

Thirty-One

He was in a lab like the one where the wand had been stored, but different. A woman with black hair stood in one corner. Terminals and equipment, the purpose of which Stephen couldn't hazard a guess, were arranged in tidy rows.

"How did I get here?" a feminine voice asked.

The black-haired woman's lips narrowed as she moved around the equipment and positioned herself in the center of the room with her hands on her hips. "You aren't really here, Betty. It is just the virtual world. I just had to come up with a location that we both knew."

"Where is my son?" the disembodied voice asked.

"I'm not sure, but I believe he is still in the hospital."

"I can't stay here. I need to go back to him." The view of the room spun. A door blocked his path. His hand reached out to the door, then dropped to his side. The view of the room changed again, but this time the movement was slower. Then he was face to face with the black-haired woman. "Why can't I wake up?"

The other woman's pinkie tapped on her side. "I wish I knew. It's what I've been telling you to do for some time now."

The scene and the woman faded away. Stephen grumbled to himself as he attempted to fall back to sleep. It was as if a pitchfork was being driven into his skull. He shifted, seeking a more comfortable position. The pain across his temple intensified followed by another spike of pain.

He opened his eyes and was surrounded by darkness. *What a bizarre dream.* He must have fallen asleep in the barn and forgotten to bring a lantern. Helen was going to kill him if she caught him sneaking back inside. An intense desire to run took him by surprise. He sat up. He clutched the fabric under his hands as another wave crested. *Fabric.* He tightened and loosed his grip. There was fabric under his hands, not wood and straw. *Where am I?* A strong whiff of antiseptic chased the last of the disorientation of sleep away. Memories of the last few days came flooding back.

"What should we tell his parents?" a man's voice said in the hall. "They saw the truck arrive."

A wedge of light cut the darkness as a door swung open. "Tell them there is too great a risk of infection to let them see him now," said a voice Stephen recognized as Dr. Lambda's. He lay back down and pretended to be unconscious as she entered the room.

"I don't think his mother is going to like that," said the man.

"And I think I'm in charge of this facility." Dr. Lambda sighed. "More lives are at stake than just this one. They should just be grateful I need him to be stabilized first."

There was a pinch on his arm and his headache eased, while the rest of his muscles felt as if they'd been transformed into pudding. "Can't go," Stephen muttered as the drug injected into his system took hold.

"Was he awake?"

"A fever dream," said Dr. Lambda. "Nothing more. Now, I've given him something to help him rest more peacefully.

Here, cover him with this blanket. He should be out until morning."

Then Stephen could fight sleep no longer.

Sunlight filled the room when Stephen risked opening his eyes. He was relieved that this time there was only about a third as much pain as the evening before. His head flopped to its side. He had as much control over its movement as he might a wet noodle. Dr. Lambda stood by a counter on the other side of the room, writing notes.

She tilted her head, catching his movement. Closing the folder, she walked to his side and pulled out a wheeled stool. "How are we feeling today?" she asked as she sat down.

"Like I was hit by a truck." He tapped his thumb with his index finger. It was as if the digit belonged to someone else.

She pursed her lips as she folded her hands in her lap. "Well, I suppose after the state we found you in that is to be expected. The good news is, as dinged up as you may feel, you managed to avoid any serious injuries which is no small feat all things considering."

"I hear I have good genes."

She arched an eyebrow. Standing up once more, she reached over and checked a bag hanging from a metal shaft beside him. She tapped the bag and frowned before examining the cord that ran from the bag to his arm. "So we are feeling funny this morning. That's an encouraging sign, I suppose."

"Oh yeah, I'm feeling much better. In fact, I think I feel well enough that if you want to go ahead and, you know, unplug me—"

She tapped the bag a second time. Its contents gleamed in the morning light. "I believe it would be best if you rested a while longer."

"Thanks for all your help, but really, I feel fine. Well, fine enough." He touched the pin entering the veins at his wrist, relieved at the rushing sensation of blood returning to his limbs, even if it felt like a thousand needles stabbing him.

"In layman's terms, I've given you a neurologic chemical inhibitor. The same sort of drug that once was used to treat Alzheimer's disease. Unfortunately, I've found its effects to be temporary at best, but better than nothing. You may feel groggy. You may also experience loss of appetite and increased bowel movements." Her lips twisted as she caught sight of what he was doing. "Please don't do that. It is for your own safety. Do you have any idea what you looked like when I arrived?"

"Probably like I'd been through a meat grinder, but I can handle it. I'm sure you have patients who need you more."

She smiled and placed her hand on top of his. "You don't trust me much, do you?"

Stephen fought the urge to move his hand out from under hers. To pull the needle out of his arm himself. To stun her and not look back, but then he thought of Ed and Helen. The man mentioned they had seen his arrival, which not only meant they were alive but also near. He couldn't risk anything until he knew where they were.

"That's okay. I'm not quick to trust anyone nowadays either. Your parents would approve."

"They're not my parents. Not really." He cringed. What exactly was the drug she'd given him inhibiting? *Was it something like a truth serum?*

The corners of Dr. Lambda's mouth turned up, making her appear years younger. "If you mean biologically, I know. They told me. They told me quite a bit about you actually. Anything they could think of in an attempt to protect you after that getaway stunt you pulled." She winked. "Of course, they didn't know about our deal." She folded her hands in her lap. "Families are made up of so much more than biology, don't you think? Take me, for example. I've never given birth, but I've cared for a whole ward of children as if they were my own."

"Right. So now that I am medicated and all patched up, are you going to send me back to the tower? I still had a few days left. I can get you through the barricade. I know it now."

The smile left Dr. Lambda's face. "That deal is off. I wasn't aware of who you were then. I am now." She stood. "The IV should have been empty by now," she said, pointing at the clear bag that looked half-full. "Either that or you shouldn't be talking about how fine you feel." She paused. "Unless, that is, of course, you were dead." She walked over and pulled the needle out of his wrist in a single-handed motion, causing Stephen to suck in his breath at the pain. A single bead of blood welled up where the needle had been. "Your blood stopped it. You are healing yourself faster than I could with any medicine."

"That's impossible."

"Yet here we are and I have the proof." She waved the bag in front of his face. "Do you know how many people have died because of the so-called upgrade?" Her nose wrinkled at the word. "How many children? And yet, instead of doing the decent thing and going to the public about your identity, you've been hiding all this time." She began pacing around the room. "You should have told me your real name from the start. Your real last name, that is."

Stephen stared at the drop of blood. When he wiped it away, he noticed the skin beneath it appeared bruised, but there was no trace of a puncture wound. "If I can heal myself, it's news to me." He touched his face. Had the swelling gone down?

"Did you know you don't exist? That you are officially dead? Stephen Dronigh, only son of Alan and Elizabeth Dronigh. Died at age four like so many other unfortunates. At least that's what the official records say."

"I don't understand."

"I took the certificate to be a dead end, but I wasn't willing to give up," she continued. "The original virus was man-made, after all. I was certain it would have been designed with a kill-switch. I thought if I could find the right carrier, I could develop a cure for the disease and save all those children. Because that's what the upgrade is. A disease." Her knuckles turned white where they clenched the bag. "That's why it was so important I gain access to the tower." She paused her pacing and let the bag go, letting it fall to the floor with a slapping sound. "I should have tested you more completely before making that deal with you, but I thought the opportunity was too perfect to waste. I know now I made a mistake."

"So now what? We make a different deal?" He held out his wrist, exposing his arteries. "If I agree to donate some blood to test your theory, you'll let my family go?"

"If I am correct, I may need a bit more than that."

"Oh," replied Stephen, turning his wrist back over. "Well, I guess if I can heal myself, I can spare a pint or two, right? How much blood do you need?"

She approached the cot, pulling out a cloth. "I'm afraid I'm going to need all of it." She reached out with the cloth until it hovered above Stephen's face.

"I can't let you do that." A man-shaped shadow blocked the sunlight entering the room through the open door.

She dropped the cloth. Her eyes narrowed. "You aren't authorized to be here," said Dr. Lambda.

"So arrest me." Ed closed the distance between them with a single step. Grabbing the cloth from where she'd dropped it, Ed used it to cover her mouth. Dr. Lambda's eyes went wide before they rolled back in her head and her body went limp.

Ed lowered Dr. Lambda to the floor before stepping over her form, coming to a stop by Stephen's cot. He held out his hand.

"There's something about Helen and me I think you should know."

"If you are about to say something nuts like you've also been lying to me all this time about who you are and have only been taking care of me all this time because you suspected I was some sort of chosen one born with some mystic abilities or something, I really don't want to know."

Stephen watched as Ed's mouth formed a small O.

Thirty-Two

His legs were like sacks of grain—heavy and awkward to maneuver—as Stephen swung his feet off the cot and onto the floor. He wondered if he was as ready to travel as he'd claimed a second before.

"You may want to put these back on," said Ed, grabbing a pile of clothing from where they lay on the opposite side of the counter from Dr. Lambda's paperwork.

Stephen's cheeks burned when he realized he was only clothed in a sheet. "Did you kill her?"

Ed set his jaw as he threw a glance over his shoulder at the woman on the ground. "I would guess that contained some sort of knockout agent like chloroform. I expect she'll be on her feet and back to her charming self before you know it." He kicked the bag of fluid away. "I was sneaking down here to check on you. It's been two days since they brought you in. Then I was to circle back to Helen. We knew you were hurt, but were told you were being taken care of. We had no idea…" He knelt and touched Stephen's damaged face. "If she's responsible for this…" His eyes glistened.

"She wasn't." Stephen grasped Ed's arm and pulled himself upright. Together, they stepped over the unconscious Dr. Lambda. "But she was going to kill me. Said my blood contained some sort of kill-switch." His body felt surer by the second.

Ed paused in mid-stride.

"Does it? Does my blood contain a cure?" He stuck his head out the door and looked around. The hallway lay empty.

"A cure? You say that like you think you have some sort of disease."

"She thought so," replied Stephen, gesturing behind him with his thumb.

Ed's lips curved, but there was a worry in his eyes. "You see, years ago—"

"Finn told me all about it. I'm a freak."

"You're not a freak. You're my son."

"Yeah, yeah I know. And really, being found by you guys was the best, but now's not the time." Shadows appeared on the other side of double doors with frosted glass windows. Stephen moved to the side and stumbled into a vacant room on their left, pulling Ed along with him.

"No, you don't understand. You don't know the whole story." Ed chewed on his bottom lip again. "We didn't just *find* you. I might have had a part in creating you."

"What? So Alan isn't my father?" Stephen looked into the hallway. It was still empty, but the shadows remained, moving in animated discussion. He ducked back into the room.

Ed blanched. "No. He is." His eyes widened. "I would never cheat on Helen. Never."

"Then are you saying I was some sort of test tube baby?" Stephen risked another glance in the hallway. The double doors remained closed and the shadows were gone. He turned to Ed, signaling all was clear.

"No, nothing like that. You were created the usual way." Ed grimaced, and his face flushed red. "I mean, er...I was on the team that originally came up with the upgrade in the first place." His expression bunched. "It wasn't my discovery, but I was there. If it wasn't for me, your mother would never have been injected, and I'm pretty sure no one else outside of the original test group would have either." He looked away as if seeing the distant memory play out once more. "It's one of the reasons we went on the run. Well, at first, we were just trying to get someplace away from the city to wait for things to settle down, but they didn't. Instead, they got worse." He rubbed his temple. "I started thinking about what would happen when people found out. It was bad enough thinking about what would happen if people found out my part in all this, but if they found out whose son you *really* were... So, we hid and kept it a secret. Even from you. My name in that previous life was Chad." Red streaked his cheeks. "I'm sorry I was afraid. I should have trusted you. "

Stephen looked at the man whose paranoia he had always dismissed as endearing but unnecessary. He tried to imagine what it must have been like to have left their old lives to protect him.

"No. Ever since I left home, everyone I've met has been one doctor's note away from being certifiably insane. First, it was the guy who thinks he is a wizard making me go on some quest to retrieve a magic wand. Then, I met my long-lost father, who guess what? Hasn't been dead all this time, but has instead been sleeping in some underground tomb for the past fifteen years. I've spent almost a day with people who think fangs and claws are a good look, and I just found out the leader of the closest thing we have to a civilized government wants to bleed me out. Oh, and I almost forgot. The girl I thought liked me was only using me, and may or may not have killed a guy. So yeah, you were right to tell me not to trust anyone."

Ed's hand froze. "You saw your father." He dropped his arm to his side. "Is he here, too?"

Stephen's lips twisted. "Would you believe it? He's the one who tricked me into going with Dr. Lambda and then he ditched me. Again."

Ed sighed. "I'm sure he had his reasons."

"It doesn't matter." Stephen threw up his hands. "We've wasted enough time. Where's Helen?"

"She was on the sixth floor when I left her." Ed bit his lip. "It's how we knew they'd found you. It has the best views."

"And what floor are we on?"

Ed bit his lip. "The second."

Stephen stretched. While the muscles still ached, at least the pain was nothing compared to what he had experienced the evening before, and it was getting better by the minute. Even so, getting to her would not only require avoiding detection by the Watch. It required stairs. Lots of stairs.

"Do you think you will be able to make it?" asked Ed. "You could hide out in one of these rooms. I could find Helen and bring her to you."

The corridor intersected with another hallway lined with doors on either side. A sign mounted on the ceiling indicated stairs straight ahead. "I'm done hiding." Stephen crossed the tiled floor with a stride that was both straight and strong. "He's not my dad, you know. You are. Now let's go get Mom and then get out of here."

THIRTY-THREE

Stephen and Ed wove in and out of the building's corridors and stairwells, ducking behind thick doors or into empty rooms whenever they heard footsteps or voices. The layout of the hallways played tricks on them as much of the time the sounds proved to come from elsewhere. *If only there was a way to see ahead*, he thought. He considered risking another round of dash-and-duck when he remembered Alan's talk about the nanobots in materials and how he'd been able to see through the walls in the lab where they'd found the wand.

Stopping at another pair of double doors, Stephen cleared his thoughts and touched the metal plate affixed to their side labeled 'Press to Open.' His vision blurred for a moment; when it cleared, Stephen could visualize the nanobots embedded in the electric panel as if they were a thousand times their size. He projected a command, taking control of sensor clusters found in the tiny electronics, and redirected their readings into his brain. An image of the hallway on the other side materialized in his brain.

X-ray vision, ta-da. A week ago, he would have laughed at such an idea. *Two days ago you would have laughed.* He corrected himself. *Now stop distracting yourself and focus.* His vision jumped ahead. A quick scan proved that the final flight of stairs was open; however, now that he was accessing their network, the signals emitting from the surrounding nanobots were like a symphony. Each producing its own music and yet complementing those around it. He didn't want to turn them off. Stephen's consciousness jumped from one to another. With each jump, his awareness expanded further out until it was no longer restricted to the walls of the building.

A group of furry shapes bounded in and out of view at the edges of town. *The beastmen. Why are they here?* More motion caught Stephen's eye, closer to the Watch's headquarters. Another group was making their way down the main road, but coming from the opposite direction on horseback. He narrowed his focus to process additional detail. A man who looked vaguely familiar rode in the center of the group. Neither Wes nor Finn was there, but the man was surrounded by more than a dozen of the people wrapped in the color-shifting clothing from the tower, though the garb had not yet been activated. Stephen spotted Gavin, Baron, and Laura's pink hair. His focus slid off their faces as it registered another. Her expression was as much determination as it was agony. He almost hadn't recognized her without her cap. *Bean.* Her hair, no longer hidden, floated on the morning's breeze. Gone was all the dirt from her face. She was breathtaking. So breathtaking, Stephen almost forgot about why his feelings were conflicted about her.

"I'm sorry, Stephen." The sensors picked up the vibrations of her whisper.

He pulled his consciousness back to his physical body. *What was she sorry for?* He tried to grin, but his cheeks were still too swollen to allow for more than the corner of his lips to rise. She hadn't abandoned him, after all. She was making Finn keep to the terms of his original promise. She'd given them the wand, and now they were mounting a full-on assault on the hospital and everyone in it. The joy fled his face as Dr. Lambda's words came back and her reason for needing his blood. The Watch weren't the only people wandering around the halls. There were innocents and children here, too.

Helen saw them first as they flung open the doors to the dining level. "Stephen," she gasped. "Ed, he has no business being out of bed. Why in the world are you letting him walk around?" Armband clad men and women turned, locking their attention on the trio.

Ed hadn't kidded about the view. From shoulder-high to the ceiling above, the walls were made of glass, providing a panoramic view of the town below. *I get why it's called the Watchtower.* Stephen's stomach growled as he caught the scent of food wafting from a back room. "We don't have time." Stephen took a deep breath. He covered his ears as the cackle became pops, which became a high-pitched squeal as the remnants of a speaker system came online.

"Members of the Watch." Gavin's voice seemed to come from every angle. "We have someone with us who wants to say hello."

"Many of you knew my mission," a new voice boomed. "Many of you knew what I intended to do. I am here today to say that everything we are—everything we've stood for—doesn't have to be this way. We can be so much more."

Stephen's brows knit. He'd heard the voice before, but couldn't place it. The speaker nearest them sputtered and popped before going silent. *It doesn't matter. Stay focused.* Stephen scratched his head as he ran through what options they might still have. If only there wasn't so much noise, he might be able to think.

Another boom sounded. This time it came from gathering clouds outside rather than the aging speaker system. *Just great,* thought Stephen. *Another storm.*

Large drops of water began to fall from the sky, creating pings like mini-missiles as they ricocheted off the windows. A bolt of lightning streaked across the clouds. Stephen ducked out of instinct. Trying to move a bunch of sick people in an electrical storm wasn't the smartest plan. *But what other options do you have?*

A blonde man with a red armband spoke up, "You should return to your rooms. We've got this covered." The man turned his attention to another. "Go find Dr. Lambda. Tell her we have a situation."

It dawned on Stephen that the man must think of him as just another patient. The others began turning tables on their sides and taking defensive positions. Clicks and slaps rang out as guns were pulled from holsters and cartridges loaded. One of the men instructed another.

You know what they say about taking a knife to a gunfight. Stephen thought about how the Sorcerer woman, Laura, had disabled the gun with a touch at the base of the barricade. The members of the Watch were too confident. They were outclassed in the weapons department and didn't even know it. It was going to be a slaughter.

Small red text appeared over top his vision. 'Message failed to deliver.' *What message?* Stephen remembered the message he'd sent to Wes. *Idiot. Why didn't I think of it before? I'll send a message to Bean and tell her to call it off.* He sighed as he composed the message. He visualized pressing the 'send' key. He imagined a whooshing sound. *There. One problem down, which just leaves how to get home before Dr. Lambda raises the alarm.* It was somewhat surprising she hadn't already done so. He thought of the pendants Jeremy and Rotledge used to communicate over distances. *I guess she's wishing she kept a bit more technology around now.*

Rotledge. He remembered the vacant look in Jeremy's eyes after the flaw in the device had been used against him. He shuddered. *Maybe it's not such a good thing*. The beastmen would be reaching the hospital's entrance in a matter of minutes. *Why are they here?* Stephen's eyes widened. *They know you left with Dr. Lambda. They are here for revenge.* Going outside was not an option.

'Message failed to deliver.' Red blocked text filled his vision. *Was there something else blocking the outgoing signal?* He tried again. 'Message failed to deliver.' Stephen cursed. "What's the point of having superpowers if you can't use them?"

"Superpowers?" Helen asked.

"Never mind."

The Watchman shouted at them. "Once again, I strongly encourage all three of you to return to your rooms. We'll notify you when the threat has passed."

Sure you will. "I want to help out. Does anyone know where the children's ward might be?"

The Watchman crouched into their positions.

"Anyone?" He looked around. "Good talk." He closed his eyes, knelt down, and touched the floor. Connecting with the nanobots, he summoned their sensor readings once more. As he did so, he imagined he heard a woman's voice announce, *Now entering the arena.*

THIRTY-FOUR

Based on the heat signatures, Stephen suspected the majority of the Watch lived on the lower floors; however, none of the rooms contained more than one or two people, and all of them were adults.

If you were a ward for children, where would you be? He called up a map from the data stream. A block labeled Pediatric A&E caught his eye. Stephen tapped into the nanobots once more. His consciousness jumped to the area marked on the map. He hit a wall. *That's weird.* He tried again. The nanobots didn't respond to his command. It was as if there weren't any. A loud boom rang out. *Was that thunder or a gunshot?*

"What is it, honey?" asked Helen.

He made his choice. "We need to get to room 3124," said Stephen.

"What's in 3124?" asked Ed.

"I might be wrong, but it's better than standing around doing nothing up here."

The way back through the labyrinth that was the hospital complex was easier with the members of the Watch distracted and the map overlay to guide them. Sounds of shouting spurred them on their way.

They rounded the final corner. The hairs on the back of Stephen's neck rose. The nanobots still weren't responding, but the closer he got, the more convinced he was that it wasn't because they were broken, but because someone else had already taken command and was shielding themselves from view. He could well be leading his parents into disaster. "Maybe it would be better for you two to wait out here."

"We can handle whatever is on the other side of that door."

No, you can't. Not if they think you are with the Watch.

The hard line of Helen's face informed him the matter was not open for discussion.

The hinges swung without a sound, revealing a large room. Between the storm outside and the painted glass windows, the natural sunlight was dim but enough to see inside. Rows of empty beds lined either side of the room, divided by worn cloth curtains painted with balloons. Paper cutouts of animals hung from the ceiling.

He summoned the map again.

An orb of pale purple light formed behind one of the curtains.

Stephen banished the map and created his own version of the light albeit dimmer. His light flickered. "I'm one of you."

"No. You're not." The curtain slid to the side, revealing white blonde hair. "You shouldn't be here."

"Yeah, I know, but I am. You need to call the attack off. There are kids. A ward full of them, maybe not in this room, but they are around here somewhere. If things get out of control, they could die. When I couldn't get a message through to you, I thought I would find them and, I don't know, protect them somehow."

Bean's features hardened. "There is no ward."

"Yes, there is. The doctor told me so."

"And you believed her." Bean pulled the curtain closed as she crossed the room until they were separated by less than a yard.

"Well, she was planning on killing me right after telling me about it, so I'm pretty sure she was being honest." He took a step toward her. She held up a hand. Lightning danced across her palm.

"I bet she told you we were the ones with the delusions, too." Gavin's voice startled Stephen from behind. "Are you done in here? The others are waiting." He passed Stephen on his way to meet Bean, dismissing him as Bean lowered her hand and banished the spark. He squeezed her shoulders. "It was even easier than we expected. She was just lying there."

She met Stephen's stricken gaze with one of stone as Gavin pulled her toward the door. "What should we do about them?"

"Who, him? The guy you called an idiot before? You said all he wants to do is go home. After our victory today, I'm feeling generous. I say we give him what he wants."

"And his parents?"

Gavin snorted. "They can go, too. What do I care? They can't do anything."

Stephen stood outside the Watchtower under a concrete overhang. A wall of water poured on the other side, limiting his sight.

"I know you are hurting right now, honey, but you're better off. Life can get back to normal this way," said Helen.

"Normal. What is that anyway? I mean specifically, what part of my life up until now would you describe as normal?" He sighed. "You don't need to answer that." A dark shape cut through the rain. An odor of wet dog tickled Stephen's nose.

How could I forget? "Ed, remember asking me who did this to me? You might be about to find out."

Dark shadows resolved themselves into monstrous silhouettes as the beastmen approached the entrance to the Watchtower. Stephen raised his fists. Bolts of lightning matching those that crossed the sky encircled each. His legs gave out from under him, and he fell to the ground.

"Stephen, what's wrong?" Helen dropped to his side.

His teeth chattered as a frost settled into his limbs. "Too much." Stephen's body shook. "Need energy."

The beastman closest snorted and pushed Ed aside. "Looks like your boy could use a longer stay."

"If you touch him, I'll kill you."

"The boss says we're not here for him," another voice said as more legs came into Stephen's view. *Darnell.* "Consider this your lucky day."

"We're here for what's ours," said Jeremy as the other beastman parted. "Any idea where we might find your girlfriend? No? That's okay. I'm sure we can sniff her out." Stepping over Stephen, Jeremy opened the glass doors to the Watchtower.

"Must warn Bean," said Stephen. He tried to compose a message. His body's convulsions grew stronger.

"Ed, help him." Helen covered his body with her own. "He's freezing."

"I don't know what to do," said Ed.

"Do something."

"What?"

"Maybe there is a drug or something inside that can help."

"I wouldn't have the first idea. What if I choose wrong?"

"Find a doctor, then. I don't care. Just do something."

Ed raced back inside, leaving Helen and Stephen under the overhang. Stephen's eyes rolled back in their sockets.

"There, there, sweetheart. It will be okay. I'm here with you." She touched his cheek.

Adrenaline and euphoria flooded his system. Although his vision faded and thoughts became hard to pierce together, his remaining other heightened senses detected an additional source of glorious energy. It was just out of reach, on another side of a wall. It called to him, offering him a power beyond anything he'd ever experienced. All he had to do was break through the wall.

He pushed with his mind. The wall bent, but didn't break. He narrowed his focus, visualizing his intent. He honed his will until it resembled a spear and threw it, piercing the wall. The pain vanished, replaced by exhilaration. He flexed his muscles. Were it not for a weight on his chest, Stephen might float away. Nothing could stand in his way. His vision cleared. The concrete slab above him came into sharp focus. Each individual nook and pore in the material magnified. Grain-shaped packets of electronics pulsed in a net made up of millions if not billions of strings. *The nanobots.* He smiled as their vibrations took on a new frequency. They sang to him, waiting for his command.

He shoved the weight from his chest in a single movement. He was invincible, power made incarnate. He could change the world. He would bring them out of the darkness.

"What have you done?" Ed's voice broke his concentration, and the real world came crashing back.

THIRTY-FIVE

Helen lay in a crumpled pile at Stephen's feet with her hand outstretched from touching his cheek.

Ed rushed to her side and cradled her in his arms. Helen's head flopped backward. Dead eyes looked out of gaunt gray flesh, which had been aged before its time. She'd been drained of life like Rotledge, only this time there was no one else to blame. "What have you done?" Ed whispered again as he pushed a strand of hair out of her face.

"I didn't know." Stephen took a step back. The power he'd sensed on the other side of the wall. It had been Helen's life force, and in his half-dead state, her touch was all the invitation he'd needed to claim it as his own. "I never intended… I didn't mean—"

"You didn't *intend*?" Ed's shoulders slumped. "You say that like our intentions matter." Ed turned away. "You are your father's son, after all. He never stopped to worry about the consequences before acting either."

"Ed?" He reached out with arms that no longer showed evidence of cuts or bruising. "Dad?"

Ed pulled Helen's lifeless body closer to his chest. "I used to think I wanted you to call me that."

"What should I do?" The euphoria that had consumed him only moments before became bile. All this time, he'd been so afraid of what the Watch would do to his parents, he never considered himself to be the greater threat. The beating he'd taken from Rotledge was a mere scrape compared to the hurt which now consumed his soul. *And yet*, the small voice inside him whispered, *to be in command of that much power, can you really trust yourself not to try it again?* Stephen let his arm drop. He now understood why those who lived in the tower, stayed there.

"Do whatever you want. I'm done deciding for you, just don't follow me." Ed stood, gathering Helen into his arms. "I found this with your clothes." A small piece of wood fell to the ground—the handle from Wes's antenna. Then Ed turned away and walked into the rain, still carrying Helen.

Stephen picked the handle up and turned it over in his hands. Wetness that had nothing to do with the storm that raged beyond the overhang streaked down his face. *You should have thrown it away already. A piece of junk.* He cocked his hand back, ready to chuck the scrap like Bean suggested back at the train platform. *Bean.* He clung to her name like a life raft floating in the middle of a hurricane-tossed sea. The beastmen were hunting her down as they spoke. He clutched the device in his fist before shoving it back in his pocket. He couldn't protect his parents, but she still had a chance to get out of this alive, if only he could make it there in time. *No one else I care about dies today.*

Stephen summoned the map of the hospital. Gavin said the others were waiting in the operating theater so that was where he would go. He flung the doors open and re-entered the Watchtower lobby in a run, locking his hurt behind a wall in his mind before the pain could overwhelm him.

The operating theater was on the second floor, no doubt where Dr. Lambda intended to wheel his bed had she been successful with the knockout agent. Stephen climbed the stairs two at a time. The smell of wet animal was heavy in the air. The beastmen had already been this way. *Was he already too late?*

He turned at the top of the stairs and raced into the hall. One of the beastman with rhino-like skin blocked a door. Seeing Stephen approaching the man, the beastman lowered his head and charged. The impact sent Stephen flying back into the hall; however, he had anticipated the attack and had been ready. The beastman dropped to the ground as they crashed together into the wall. What Stephen hadn't anticipated was the man's crushing weight on top of him.

He twisted his hips as he wiggled his way out from under the dead weight. *So much for being Mr. Invincible.* His powers had limits, after all. It was a lesson worth remembering.

He approached the doors to the operating theater with more caution the second time. Opening them a crack, he slipped inside. The theater was constructed in a half circle with several levels of metal risers extending up the sides of the room. Orbs of purple light and barred teeth surrounded him.

Members of the Watch were positioned at the lowest levels. Dr. Lambda lay on a wheeled stretcher, restrained as Stephen had been in the back of the truck. Gavin stood in front of her alongside the familiar-looking man from earlier, while other members of the Watch knelt at the Sorcerer's feet. A beastman growled.

"Uh-uh," said Gavin, leaning over Dr. Lambda. "Jeremy, remind your people why they don't want to come any closer. I would hate to have to hurt someone you care about." Lightning danced across his fist and up his sleeve.

Jeremy held his hands out. "Stay back, boys."

"You made the right decision."

Gavin smiled. His gaze slid, meeting Stephen's. "Ah, it looks like someone else made a wise decision as well. Good to see you decided to join us, after all. Have a seat. The show is just about to begin."

Stephen's forehead wrinkled as he tried to make sense of the scene playing out before him. He scanned the crowd. Bean wasn't among those in the front rows. *Where could she be?* He looked up into the higher levels, spotting her near the topmost row. Her lips narrowed, and she gave an almost imperceptible shake of her head. He climbed the steps to her side anyway.

"You don't belong here." she whispered. "Why did you come back?"

"To save you," he whispered back. "From them. They know what you did."

"Of course you did." She snorted. "Because I've given you so many reasons to make you believe I can't take care of myself." Her face contorted into a humorless grin. "Haven't you figured it out yet?" She stared straight ahead. "How else do you think I was able to beat the drain this long? I'm a monster."

"I don't think you are a monster." He grit his teeth. "I…" The words rebelled, dying on his tongue. He didn't deserve to say them. "You are—"

She turned away. "Why did you come back, really? You did it. You rescued your parents. Why didn't you leave with them?"

"My mom is dead."

Bean's shoulders slumped. "I know."

"No, I mean my other mom died. Helen. I…" He tightened his jaw as the reality of his statement came crashing back to the forefront of his thoughts from where he'd locked it away during his ascent. "It was my fault." The image of Helen's still form as Ed carried her away threatened to undo his control. "I thought I had to come back. I-I…" He bit off his words. His heart was able to handle only so much truth. "I have no place else to go," he said instead, sealing the emotional whirlwind away once more. He couldn't afford to lose his focus now, if only for her sake.

Bean looked up with wide eyes, meeting his gaze. Her lips tightened, and her balled hand twitched where it rested in her lap. She turned her attention to the center of the room.

Gavin gestured to the man next to him. "As you were saying."

The man walked around Gavin and squatted down near one of the members of the Watch. "I know this might sound hard to believe, but it's me."

Stephen started. He remembered now where he'd seen the man before. It was the man from Bean's childhood. The same man who'd been defeated at the base of the barricade, but he was young again. The Sorcerers had used the wand on him. No band of red covered his arm. He'd joined them. *But didn't that mean he had to have abilities too, or didn't that matter?*

Movement caught Stephen's eyes as the man explained to the others about the illness Dr. Lambda diagnosed as terminal and his mission to the tower as a final act of sacrifice and service to the cause. Bean's hands were shaking where they clenched the fabric of her trousers. "He did something to you. Back when you were a kid. Did he hit you?"

"Doesn't matter now."

"It matters." He reached out to cover her hand with his.

She pulled away and turned to him with a fire in her eyes. "No. If you would start paying attention, you'd see it doesn't." She released the fabric and smoothed the creases. "We're all monsters now. What's one more in the club?"

Baron stepped forward and dropped a bag by the man's feet. Opening it, the man pulled out a gun-shaped device and a needle. He attached the needle to the device and pulled out a vial, similar to the ones Stephen had seen in the camouflaged lab. "Now, who else wants to make the right choice?"

A member of the Watch in the middle of the group wobbled as he rose. He pulled the band off his arm and raised his hand.

"So what? Everyone gets upgraded and becomes friends now?" asked Stephen. "What about the energy drain? If all the wand does is make a person young again, couldn't the upgrade still kill them?"

Bean bit her lip. "Something like that."

"But why do all of this then? I mean if Gavin wants everyone dead, why draw it out?"

"Gavin is a fan of natural selection. It's why Finn likes him."

The Watchman rubbed his arm at the site of the injection. Baron gestured for him to take a seat. The beastmen grew restless.

"You'll have your turn, too," said Gavin.

"This has gone on long enough. We aren't interested in any injections," said Jeremy. "All we want is what was stolen from us. Give us the wand, and we'll leave you to your"—he sneered—"upgrades."

"I'm sorry, but I'm afraid the only way you can have the wand back is if you join our side."

"No deal."

"Then I guess we have nothing to talk about."

"And I guess it's time we go on the offense."

Gavin's hand hovered over Dr. Lambda. "I'll do it."

Jeremy laughed. "Do whatever you want to her. She's been dead to me for years."

Chaos broke out as the beastmen launched into action. Stephen glanced to his side at an empty chair. Blonde white hair joined the melee. Bodies flew across the room. The Sorcerers had stealth, but the Sharks had strength as well as stamina.

Stephen watched as a jersey-clad giant cornered Bean. He closed the distance. She ducked under his thick crushing arms. He spun on his heel. She reached out and placed her hand on the beastman's sleeve. Light pulsed. The beastman, Shaw, laughed, pulling back the cloth. Stephen leaped down the stairs, but couldn't reach her in time as the man said, "Good thing I listened when Jeremy said we should add some shock protection to our uniforms today." His arm under his sleeve had an unnatural flatness to it like rubber. The outline of narrow cords twisted around its length. "My turn." He slammed a fist into her jaw.

Bean's head flew back at an awkward angle, and her body fell to the floor.

Stephen ran down the steps until he was by her side as the fighting continued all around. He touched her neck. A weak pulse flickered under his fingertips.

A bench crashed beside him. The cart restraining Dr. Lambda toppled over. A shot rang out. He shielded her body with his. Her pulse grew fainter. A booted foot connected to his side. Stephen grunted, but remained where he was. He thought of the knife wound in the forest and how it had disappeared by morning. Whatever was in his blood that allowed him to heal faster than a normal person, it was in her blood, too. All she needed was enough energy to speed the process along. Stephen looked at the ceiling as he tried to think. The nanobots sang to him. *Redirect the current.* Alan's off-hand remark in front of the convenience store came back to him. *That's how the Sorcerers hold the drain back. It's not just food. They feed off energy from the tower, too.*

"Move it, kid," Shaw said, kicking him again.

He focused on the tiled surface above. He closed his eyes and pictured the nanobots as he'd seen them under the concrete overhang in the front of the Watchtower. When he opened his eyes, the tiny grains of electronics responded to his command again. His consciousness expanded with every connection. The fighting surrounding them took on a surreal quality as the sensors sent readings from every angle into his brain.

The sky above the Watchtower pulsed with a violence of its own as a billion joules of energy arched from cloud to cloud. *A single bolt of lightning contains enough energy to power a sixty-watt light bulb for six months*, the data stream informed him. *That's helpful*, thought Stephen.

He returned his attention to Bean. The hair on his arm rose. Stephen pushed an errant hair out of Bean's face. The nanobots song changed. He leaned in. Time slowed as the data stream took the readings from the nanobots' sensors, such as the man's weight and the angle of anticipated impact and executed calculations on the probability of an average person's survival. The results weren't good. His instincts screamed for him to move. His heart demanded he stay. He closed his eyes and leaned forward. Redemption was never going to be an option—not for him—but she still had a chance. *You always have a choice.* Stephen pressed his lips to Bean's as lightning struck the Watchtower.

THIRTY-SIX

Jade green eyes looked up at Stephen. Bean's lips curved into a sly smile. "You better be careful, or I might start expecting fireworks on every date."

Stephen kissed her again.

"Ahem."

Stephen looked up to see Jeremy standing over them. He twirled the wand. Bean jumped into a defensive position. Stephen reached out with his mind to the nanobots, ready to channel their energy into another strike, but their signals were fried by the energy of the storm. The nanobots of the Watchtower were as dead as several of the bodies strewn about the theater floor, including Shaw whose skin was blistered and black.

"Now there's no reason to get worked up. This round is over." He gestured to the overturned bed where Gavin lay slumped. "My team won."

"What are you going to do now? Kill us, too?" asked Stephen.

The corner of Jeremy's lips inched up. "Now that wouldn't be very sportsmanlike, would it?" Bean raised her fists. Jeremy raised an eyebrow.

Stephen cocked his head. He hadn't known him long, but there was something off about Jeremy.

Jeremy's smile deepened. "When you get back, tell your leader I'm looking forward to our next match. He'll understand. He and I have a score to settle." Jeremy bent over and picked up something from the floor. He turned it over in his hands. "I believe this might be yours." He shrugged and handed it to Stephen. "I wouldn't want you to say I never did anything for you."

Then he whistled and turned away. The surviving beastmen filed out behind him, leaving Bean and Stephen surrounded by the dead.

"Don't tell me you still have that thing," said Bean. "Have you been carrying it with you this entire time?"

Stephen held the handle from Wes's antenna up. "I forgot about it." He examined the area where it had been attached to the metal rod and turned it over. A whirl a quarter of the way down its length caught his eye.

"Well, you might as well toss it now."

"Wes made me promise to keep it. I figure I'll give it back to him the next time I see him."

The smile left Bean's lips.

The urge to pinch wood at the whirl took over him. Stephen pulled on one end, and a piece broke away, exposing a tiny plate covered in copper traces. "Huh. It's not a piece of wood, after all."

"There is something you should know."

Stephen focused on the component in his hand. The copper traces were cool to the touch. He narrowed the focus of his gaze as if zooming in on his computer screen until the place where his skin touched metal was nothing more than a pixelated blur. Then he shifted his consciousness into the device.

Wes appeared dressed in an outfit similar to what their avatars wore in the game. "Mont," he began. "I've got some good news and some bad news." He waved his hand, and the rectangular window opened up. A brown-haired woman with pale waxy skin and sunken eyes looked out. "The good news is I found this memory stick in your biological mom's files. Turns out, she was a patient of Dad's. I thought you'd like to see her, even if she was unwell when she recorded her message to you."

Stephen stared at the woman in the window. He touched his face. Darnell mentioned seeing a resemblance.

"The bad news is… Well, there's really no easy way to say this. The bad news is I'm gone. As in, game over."

Stephen ripped his gaze from the woman. The drain. Wes had known he wasn't going to be making the trip back to the tower.

Wes took a step back. "Before you get weird, like blaming yourself or something idiotic like that, know that I made a choice. A choice I hope one day you never have to understand. Now sit back and listen to your mother."

Wes faded away as the window expanded, leaving only the image of his biological mother's face from the shoulders up.

His mother glanced up and to the side, as if listening to someone else before returning her attention to the camera. "Stevie, first, know that I wish I could still be there with you. If there was a way, trust that I would be. I love you so much." Her eyes welled up. "Second"—she looked back again—"there's no time." She held up a picture of a black-haired woman wearing a white-and-silver dress. Stephen recognized it as the same woman from his fever dream. "I know you must have questions. About us. About yourself. Find her." His mother reached up, tapped something unseen, and the window went black.

Wes reappeared. "My dad's notes said your mother was being treated in the end for depression and a personality disorder with acute paranoia. She claimed that her husband was into some pretty dark stuff, like mind control. She also claimed he had intentionally released a virus which he and only a select few would be immune to." Wes sighed. "The more I looked into her claims, the more I've come to the conclusion that your mom might have been onto something. Which, I'm sorry to say, would make your dad a complete psycho. It's a good thing you don't know where he is."

But you do know where he is, his mind whispered. *He's now going by the name Jeremy.*

A circle with a cartoonish image of Wes holding his thumb up appeared. "I've uploaded as much as I can of my memories into a program only you should be able to access. If you ever need a friend to talk to, I'm a keystroke away."

Stephen shook his head. "Of course you are."

"If you happen to see my dad, tell him I'm sorry, but it was the only way." He paused. "Oh, but if you see your dad, I suggest running."

The image dissolved. Stephen blinked as the real world came back into focus. Bean looked at him with concern. "What was that? Did you see something?"

Bean already thought of herself as a monster. What would she think after she learned they might have released something even worse? *No*, the small voice corrected, *what you released*.

"I need to find a woman."

Bean frowned. "Come again?" She crossed her arms over her chest.

Stephen wanted to pull her into his arms and kiss her again. Then he remembered where they were and who might still lurk nearby. "Not like that. She's got to be like fifty years old by now. Nothing for you to worry about. This file." He shook the drive. "There was a message from my mom. She said this woman would have answers. I just have to find her."

"Well, are you going to stand there, or are you going to lead the way?"

EPILOGUE

The first sound to register in her mind was the hissing sound of air escaping. Her eyelids fluttered as her mind attempted to identify its source. At first, all she could see was a black nothingness, but then as she became more aware, she noticed the otherwise complete darkness surrounding her was broken by a growing, pulsing hint of light. Her nostrils were overwhelmed by the smell of rust, dirt, and decay. The sound of metal scraping metal assaulted her ears, followed by the whirl of a dying motor.

Gradually, her consciousness woke up enough for her to more accurately process her surroundings. She was lying prone in a cylinder, the majority of her body still sealed within its frame. She had the most disconcerting feeling that her head was somehow detached from the majority of her bulk, floating separately in the darkness. Her consciousness began to expand into her body like a spider's web tying together the space between mind and limb. It was shocking and unnatural. Almost as if she was being anchored back to earth.

She attempted to shift within the capsule, biting back a scream as the muscles in her back and limbs protested the movement. She did not attempt to rise again until the sensation of pins and needles receded, indicating blood had returned to its regular circulation pattern.

After a few tender experiments beginning with a wiggle of her fingers and toes, she risked raising her arms to the rim of the capsule. Satisfied with the results, she tried pulling herself into an upright position. The effort nearly sent her reeling with exhaustion. Several more minutes elapsed before she was willing to attempt other sudden moves. She felt as if she was waking up from death and perhaps she was, depending on what a person classified as life.

As she looked out into the darkened room, the only sources of light proved to be coming from the occasional pulse of red light blinking on either side of her. It reflected off what could be shattered glass on the floor beside her tube.

She made a quick gesture. Though it was minuscule, the gesture was enough to send her swaying. The room's lights brightened, as if in response to her movement, and she was momentarily blinded. After her eyes adjusted, the increased light allowed her to better process her surroundings.

Fragments of memory began to bubble up to the surface; however, there were still gaping holes. While she could not be completely certain, she believed when she had entered this room last, it was the definition of medical cleanliness. It was for a meeting or a demonstration of some kind. Memories of the scent of lemon rind and industrial fluid danced in her mind alongside an image of several pristine white tanks. The tanks had been accented by glass, arrays of organic bioluminescent panels, and highlighted with chrome trim. Everything she thought she remembered was in stark contrast to what was currently assaulting her senses.

At least a few years must have passed since she last saw the contents of this room based on the condition of the cylinders. *But how did I get here?* she wondered.

She further scanned the room. The walls had collapsed inward in piles of rubble, along with bits and pieces of ceiling. Broken beakers and other tubes were strewn about with other crushed industrial equipment. As she better focused her vision, she noticed several of the tanks showed lines of wear along with their edges, the chrome trim non-existent. Some were also heavily damaged with large dings pocketing along their lengths. A few of the tanks' lids were open, their contents were vacant, but the majority, however, were still sealed. The occupants of these were obscured behind glass blackened by dust and dirt.

The periodic red light had come from a few of the tanks' status panels, indicating that they had nearly exhausted their power supplies. A nagging voice in the back of her mind told her this should be troubling, but could not remember why. The feeling was like waking up knowing that you had just been dreaming and not being able to recall any of the details.

She called out for help. Her voice sounded more like a frog's croak than words. She waved a hand on the chance that someone might be nearby monitoring the area. After several minutes of waiting with no response, she had to accept that no help was coming.

A piece of her wasn't entirely surprised due to the sorry state of neglect surrounding her in the room and shook her head in disgust. At her core, she knew that she had once been someone of significant value. Had she been in her center of power, wherever that might be, no one would have ever dared to abandon her like this. That feeling alone told her that she was far from home.

As her sense of self-importance began to circulate within her consciousness, so did more substantial memories. Memories she was still unsure she could trust. Large gaps remained in her life story, especially those revolving around the most recent events, but she knew one thing to be true.

There was something she had to remember above all else, something critically important, a promise or a face. She groaned, fighting a wave of nauseousness. Whatever it was, it remained stubbornly out of reach. She frowned as she battled to regain control of her body. It had something to do with her legacy, but the same could be said about many of the few decisions and events of her life she could recall. The thought didn't help trigger the memory. So what could it be? She struggled to piece together her thoughts into any sensible order. *My legacy*, she thought with a tinge of pain. She had been so close to securing her place in history. She'd been so close she could practically taste it. So why couldn't she remember what it was?

She screamed in frustration. Even that sounded weak to her ears. She wanted to scream more. She had to get herself out of this room, if for no other reason than to get the blood flowing enough to remind her just what might have been. With that final thought to bluster her energy, she pulled herself the rest of the way out of her capsule. Her muscles screamed in protest, nearly sending her to the floor. She squared her shoulders and took a determined step forward, her shoes grinding the glass on the floor into sand without breaking stride.

Focused on her goal, she wasted not a second thought on the other tanks completing their power-down sequence or if there were other occupants contained within. The darkness of the adjacent ruined hallway was as vacuous as space, the silence as still as a tomb. At least for now, she would be alone with her growing memories.

Beginning with my name, she realized with a start. Her name was Juliane.

END

End of Book Two: The Watch & Wand

WE SURVIVE, WE IMPROVISE

I waited as the plane's door latch engaged. Any minute now, I thought. Sniff. *Cha-ching*. The engines whirled to life, drowning out all but the sounds generated by my seatmates—but I'd heard enough before their roar. "Newbie broke." I turned to Darla with a grin, "just when I said she would." We all broke. Darla and I only bet on when.

Darla snapped her harness together, readying herself for the flight. "You said preflight."

"Yeah, and our wheels are still on the ground." At least they were for a couple more seconds. Sure, there was a time when betting on when the newest recruit would break down into a puddle of tears would have sounded like one of the cruelest games imaginable, but I've long since witnessed far crueler. Besides, only a fraction of the green recruits managed to survive the first few days anyway, and those who did, well… they typically didn't hold a grudge. When the only people between you and certain death are those you flew in with, you tend to become a little more forgiving.

Darla rolled her eyes. "Double or nothing."

I smiled. I'd won the last three rounds in a row. Easy bet. It was also the only bet I would make against Darla. Back before, she'd once chaperoned an entire field trip of kindergarteners to the candy factory—alone—the other chaperones having succumbed to a bout of food poisoning from the school's volunteer thank you banquet the evening before. If that wasn't medal worthy enough, she'd also somehow managed to do so while simultaneously coordinating the school's fundraising carnival and spearheading the community's clean water awareness campaign.

The rumor around the barracks suggested Darla may have had something to do with the banquet too and had intentionally given the other chaperones bad food just because she wanted an extra challenge—but I knew that story was garbage. Darla couldn't ruin a dish if she'd tried.

In another life, I might have hated her, but in this one... In this one, I couldn't think of anyone else I'd rather have on my side.

"You're on" It was money in the bank. That is, it would be if banks still existed. Still, the on-going bet helped pass the time and ensured the new faces didn't blend together.

The plane's engines roared as we began speeding down the blackened earth serving as the day's temporary runway. Traditional infrastructure had become a target in the same way as the banks had. "We survive. We improvise." I repeated our unit's motto to myself as my ears adjusted to the ascent.

"I always think it is so cute you repeat that phrase each time. It always makes it sounds like we were given a choice." If it was anyone poking fun at my ritual other than my other seatmate, Christie, I might have been offended. But I owed her, in more ways than one. Decades of mastering a world of pins and 'grams had gifted her with a number of other life-saving talents. She could disguise a weapon as a tea cozy, disarm a bomb using pipe cleaners, and could trick an eye with any number of camouflages. If I'd only known the various sites would be so useful in my later years, I might have actually paid more attention to them when I had the chance.

The smile left my face, as it always did at the thought of my former life and my kids. Especially my kids. I wondered if they still remembered their mom's face or if their 'new' mom was filling in for me in that role as well. I knew it was a bitter thought. The women, whose primary civic responsibility was now populating the next generation while caring for those left behind, had about as much say in their assignment as those of us past their prime, but it hurt to think about all the same. I kissed my fingers wishing I could kiss my children instead. If Christie noticed, she was kind enough not to say anything more.

As the plane leveled off and hit cruising altitude, our sergeant's voice placed over the speakers. "Listen up ladies. I know the last several years have been hard on us all. When the enemy struck and destroyed all of our military units in one coordinated attack, we might have thrown up the white flag. But we survived. We improvised. When that same enemy released the bio-pandemic and decimated nearly eighty percent of the population, we could have surrendered. But we survived. We improvised. We may be past our childbearing years. We may be of no use in repopulating our once great nation, but we are far from useless. Some of you volunteered. Some required more… persuasion. But each and every one of you are now part of the fiercest fighting team the world has ever seen."

The sergeant's voice paused allowing her words to wash over the ranks like a wave. Even I was affected and I'd thought myself jaded to these rallies years ago.

She continued, "I am pleased to report our intelligence has located the enemy's stronghold. Our assignment is clear. It's now our turn. They may be able to improvise, but rest assured, they won't survive. Because we are the Mother-Making army."

Cheers sounded throughout the plane. Even the woman who had been crying at take-off now looked optimistic. Darla slapped my back as the sarge's words soaked in. Could this really be it? I dared to hope and wonder. Christie grinned like a maniac. If not, at least I'd go down with the best friends a woman could ask for.

"Hooah"

∞

The engines' roar seemed louder than usual in the plane's cabin, likely because the cabin was filled with only about a quarter of the passengers it originally started with. "Let's go home ladies," Darla announced in a somber voice over the speaker system as the rest of us readied ourselves for lift off. The look in her eyes as she began making her final inspection down the aisle before giving the pilot the thumbs up sign told me our latest sergeant wouldn't be looking for another challenge anytime soon.

Home. The word sat in my conscience. Could the place we were going to really be called home? For the first time, I allowed myself to think of the family I'd left behind. Not the fantasy family that had gotten me through so many terrible nights, but the real one. I forced myself to do the math. The daughter I still saw in braids and pigtails in my mind's eye would be a woman now. She might even have a child of her own. I reached for the harness as an anchor only to recall my right arm was no longer attached to the rest of my body.

Stacy, the not-so-newbie, whose first battle proved to also be our last, pulled the belt across my body, securing it into place before strapping herself into Christie's old seat. I bit my lip. *Home.* Would I ever really be able to call it that without these women by my side?

The scent of blood, dirt, and gasoline tickled my nose, causing my nostrils to quiver and eyes to water as I took a deep breath to settle my thoughts. I certainly wasn't crying.

"Double or nothing?" Stacy asked Darla as my sister-in-arms made her way to our seats.

Darla glanced in my direction and the corner of her lip turned up. "You're on." Then she caught my eyes. "We were asked to give our all Ladies," she shouted to the masses. "And that's exactly what we served. Never forget who you are. We are the Mother-Making Army." Leaning in, she lowered her voice so only I could hear. "We survive. We improvise."

I nodded as the plane began its journey to the place that might one day be called home again. We do indeed.

Hooah.

If you enjoyed this story and would like to receive more short stories, or news about upcoming publications, you can sign up for my mailing list at http://eepurl.com/c0fcSj or visit my website at www.alliepottswrites.com

ACKNOWLEDGEMENTS

A writer, by definition, is supposed to be able to express his or herself with words, and yet once again I find myself at a loss for how to say thanks to all those who were instrumental in putting this story together. The word, thanks, simply isn't big enough. I'll try anyway.

To Jason, thank you once again for keeping me focused on the end goal even on days I wanted to be anywhere but in front of a screen and for never once wavering in your support of my, our, dream.

To Sally, Jenny, Melanie, and Kathryn, thank you for listening to all book related triumphs and troubles especially when you had no idea what I was talking about.

To Ben, thank you for always being on the lookout for dragons.

To Diana, Geoff, Kristen, Shannon, Libby, Brooke, and Lora thank you for braving various early drafts. I believe we should all be eternally grateful for your insights, honesty and keen eyes.

To Sacha, you deserve your own line of thanks, but then again you already knew that. It's probably written on a sticky-note somewhere.

And to all my friends I know by face and those I know online, your continued encouragement means the world to me.

I would also like to thank readers like you. If you have enjoyed this novel, I encourage you to contact me, leave a review, or tell a friend.

About the Author

Allie Potts, born in Rochester Minnesota was moved to North Carolina at a very early age by parents eager to escape to a more forgiving climate. She has since continued to call North Carolina home, settling in Raleigh, halfway between the mountains and the sea, in 1998.

When not finding ways to squeeze in 72 hours into a 24 day or chasing after children determined to turn her hair gray before its time, Allie enjoys stories of all kinds. Her favorites, whether they are novels, film, or simply shared aloud with friends, are usually accompanied with a glass of wine or cup of coffee in hand.

A self-professed science geek and book nerd, Allie also writes at www.alliepottswrites.com.

Feeling social? You can email Allie at allie@alliepottswrites.com or follow Allie on Twitter @alliepottswrite, Facebook at https://www.facebook.com/alliepottswrites, Pinterest @alliepottswrite, or on Instagram @alliepottswrites

www.ingramcontent.com/pod-product-compliance
Lightning Source LLC
Chambersburg PA
CBHW020957120726
47905CB00009B/2739